Praise for *Remember You Will Die*

"Eden Robins's *Remember You Will Die* transcends its ingenious obituary form. It becomes a murder mystery of portraits, a eulogy of the everyday moments that make up epic lives, a web of the important ways we intersect and influence one another beyond our knowing. It handles the morbid and the macabre with admirable compassion and humor. I loved every page."

—Jac Jemc, author of *Empty Theatre* and *The Grip of It*

"A bold structure, wonderful errantry, and a unique imagination mark Eden Robins's new novel, *Remember You Will Die*—a compilation of obituaries whose impact is greater than the sum of its parts."

—Jeffrey Ford, author of *The Shadow Year*

"In Eden Robins's eerie and poignant *Remember You Will Die*, we follow an AI woman, Peregrine, as she attempts to understand what happened to her human child. Did she die? Did she disappear? And what does it mean to die, to disappear? Peregrine learns what it means to grieve as she travels all of history via a cache of obituaries and etymologies, searching for clues about her child. By the end, I was gobsmacked, awed. Eden Robins has given us an instant classic."

T0203338

"An audacious and unforgettable tale that reminds us what the novel can do, *Remember You Will Die* captures the exhilaration, heartbreak, and passion of a life fully lived."

—Stephanie Feldman, author of *Saturnalia*

ALSO BY EDEN ROBINS

When Franny Stands Up

REMEMBER
YOU
WILL
DIE

EDEN ROBINS

sourcebooks
landmark

Copyright © 2024 by Eden Robins
Cover and internal design © 2024 by Sourcebooks
Cover design by Erin Fitzsimmons/Sourcebooks
Cover art © Look and Learn/Bridgeman Images, StockAppeal/Shutterstock
Internal design by Laura Boren/Sourcebooks

Published by Sourcebooks Landmark, an imprint of Sourcebooks
P.O. Box 4410, Naperville, Illinois 60567-4410
(630) 961-3900
sourcebooks.com

Cataloging-in-Publication Data is on file with the Library of Congress.

Printed and bound in the United States of America.
LSC 10 9 8 7 6 5 4 3 2 1

For Kyle,
who believes in the impossible and makes it fun.

Content Warning

This novel contains discussions of suicide, which may be distressing for some readers. The national Suicide & Crisis Lifeline can be reached 24/7 by calling or texting 988.

Perhaps the history of the errors of mankind, all things considered, is more valuable and interesting than that of their discoveries. Truth is uniform and narrow; it constantly exists, and does not seem to require so much an active energy, as a passive aptitude of soul in order to encounter it. But error is endlessly diversified; it has no reality, but is the pure and simple creation of the mind that invented it.

—BENJAMIN FRANKLIN, *REPORT OF THE ROYAL COMMISSION TO INVESTIGATE ANIMAL MAGNETISM*

---

30 April 1883

Sir,

I have just finished reading, with intense pleasure, your "Leaves of Grass." Would you forgive my suggesting, as a sufficient reply to your adverse critics, the insertion of the following motto in your future editions. It is from the "Heauton Timorumenos" Act 1. Sc. 1. Line 28. "Homo sum: humani nil a me alienum puto."*

Yours gratefully,
Craig McGinnis

*I am human: I consider nothing human alien to me.

—WALT WHITMAN ARCHIVE

Can the absence of words tell a story? Like a pattern in lace, the holes as important as the threads?

—SHEILA, FREMD HIGH SCHOOL *VIKING LOGUE*

MYSTERY SURROUNDS REPORT OF GIRL DROWNED IN EAST RIVER, MULTIPLE AGENCIES SEARCH FOR BODY

THE NEW YORK DISPATCH

NOVEMBER 6, 2102

An unknown teenage girl has drowned, according to an anonymous cell phone call to the 1st Precinct this morning. The caller had been watching the sun rise at Pier 15, when a girl skirted the caution tape and climbed the temporary concrete blockade where the esplanade is partially submerged this season. The caller reported yelling at her to "get down." In response, the girl allegedly folded a piece of paper into the shape of an airplane and threw it toward shore, then dove into the river, never to resurface.

"The witness insisted the paper airplane was a suicide note," said one first responder, "but they left the scene before we got here, and we haven't found anything like they described. You see what we're up against? No note, no name, no witness, no body? No budget, no training, nothing?"

The call was received from a blocked number, and so far, the only concrete clue to the drowned girl's identity is that the caller once referred to her by the name "Poppy."

"We are pursuing all possible avenues," police reported in a statement to the press. "Including researching databases of missing persons and tracking that phone call."

As torrential rains continue and water levels rise, encroaching on

Manhattan, deaths of various cause are overwhelming the resources of public agencies. Authorities are hopeful, however, that this past month's drought will continue. Receding rivers could allow agencies enough time to find lost loved ones and give closure to families.

This investigation is ongoing, and we will report updates as we have them.

Many suicide hotlines are still functional at this time, and with help, suicide is preventable.

Etymology of Poppy

POPPY (*N.*)

From Latin *papaver*—"poppy." Plant of the genus *papaver*, having showy flowers and milky juice with valuable narcotic properties. Poppy seeds spread easily and can lie dormant for up to eighty years. The flowers can grow almost anywhere, including cracks in pavement. Ancient Romans made poppy offerings to the dead, and opium derived from the flower has been used since ancient times. In Chinese history, the poppy recalls the wanton brutality of the British Empire during the Opium Wars and the cruelty of colonialism.

A symbol of battlefields and war dead at least since Waterloo in 1815, possibly as far back as the time of Genghis Khan. Poppies were said to have been surprisingly abundant on the mass graves of Europe in World War I, which was not soil typically rich enough to support the poppy's growth. It is surmised that the dirt churned up on battlefields from the detritus of war allowed poppy seeds that had been dormant to finally germinate.

Sentences using POPPY:

"If you don't want the **poppies** in your garden to spread too far from home, trim the old blooms."

"History wants **poppy** to be a symbol: of war, death, intoxication, resurrection. But **poppy** means only itself. Her needs are simple; she tilts her smiling face to the sun."

"LIVES OF THE CIVIL WAR DEAD" SERIES

———•◦•———

THE NEWPORT LADIES' MAGAZINE

MAY 25, 1864

We are doubtless all quite familiar with the art of floriography. Naturally, in our fast-paced modern times, this art is now considered somewhat passé among gentlewomen, but when *en vogue*, floriography was adhered to as fervently as any fashion plate. Floriography grafted meaning and symbolism to different flowers, and even different hues and shades of a single species, as well as to the placement of flowers upon one's person. A forget-me-not in the hand meant devout and undying love, a gift of periwinkle was for the bloom of new friendship or for old friends fondly remembered, whereas a yellow chrysanthemum in one's nosegay signified that one had been slighted by one's so-called love.

Yours truly, the author of this **obituary**, had once worn a blood-red **poppy** upon her breast. It was intended to heal her grief, an impossible task for one who had been told, in no uncertain terms, that she would never bear a child. That the mere *attempt* to bring life into the world would render her own body lifeless.

It was this **poppy** which led her to the acquaintance of the deceased, Mr. Charles P.B. Crowley.

Mr. Crowley would grow quite cross at the insinuation that his expertise was no different than floriography, the latter being associated with excessive femininity, an association of which he seemed exceedingly sensitive. Mr. Crowley, in contrast, analyzed the scientific properties of the rose. Using the deductive method of scientific inquiry, he examined the rose as a species, while also scrutinizing the many nuances and idiosyncrasies of the individual flower. He used this depth of knowledge to make his assignations, but nonetheless remained humble about his expertise.

"Much like the debased parlor science of mesmerism," he would chuckle, "the power of my art resides in *you*. If you are receptive to it, you shall absorb the rose's meaning."

Mr. Crowley devoted his life, singularly, to the rose and grew, around his Newport, Rhode Island, cottage, a dozen or more varieties. The ambrosial odor of his property was so powerful that on a hot summer's day, the gentlewomen of the area would linger in front of his home and twirl about, absorbing the aroma as they might an expensive Parisian *parfum*. The effects were quite similar and far more natural.

Seeing the ladies tarry in his front garden, Mr. Crowley began the habit of snipping individual blossoms to adorn breasts and bonnets. It was not long before he was gazing deeply into the petals and divining the young ladies' fortunes.

Word spread as word does, and soon women were traveling from all over the state of Rhode Island, seeking counsel on how to woo, how to please, how to coax a sluggish womb, how to encourage ambition in sullen husbands and sons. Crowley would lounge in his garden chair with a prescribing (sic) glass of his "iced" tea, head tilted toward the sun—very like one of his roses!—listening to a lady's wistful tale. Then he would meander through the garden in silence for an hour or more before selecting the precise blossom that would reveal the young lady's answer.

Despite the unconventional nature of these encounters, it was considered quite proper to be seen with the bachelor Crowley. He spoke only occasionally of his own lost love, some youthful dalliance on faraway shores during his years at sea. He never sought his own counsel from the roses, brushing off the notion as absurd. He did not intend, he said, to marry, even when the young ladies who came to see him hinted at the possibility, some even bold enough to suggest that the rose chosen for them spoke of that future. (Charles was quite wealthy, on his father's side.)

Mr. Crowley never once took advantage, but even so, many young ladies, particularly those from farther afield, traveled to see him with a chaperone. Crowley's ladies knew him affectionately as "Madame Rosa," a playful appellation referring to the sometime fortune-tellers who had been known to pass through New England. Though it was always used with affection, one would *never* call him this directly, given his sensitivity about appearing feminine.

Regretfully, little is known by this author about the past of Mr. Crowley, only what tidbits he had revealed to her. As a boy, he followed the path of other adventurous youths in that period by shipping before the mast and seeing something of China and the East Indies. It was in China that he first glimpsed what we know now as the China roses, flowers that bloom over and over again throughout the summer and fall, as opposed to European roses which bloom only once and then wither on the stem. Incredible, isn't it, how we had once considered this solitary bloom to be the inherent nature of the rose, when in fact there is another of the very same species that blooms and blooms and blooms again, until the weather turns and frosts it into a state of stupendous (sic) animation? Mr. Crowley, too, found this miraculous, and in fact he was among the first gardeners in New England to plant ever-blooming roses in his garden.

A bout of yellow fever ended Mr. Crowley's lust for travel and for the sea, as well as very nearly ending his life at the tender age of seventeen. All else that is known of him is that vague and delicious hint of love lost, and evidence that he was orphaned at quite a young age, though his father's tidy inheritance kept him well tended until his untimely death.

This writer first visited Madame Rosa after an event that is still quite painful to speak about. She was betrothed to a man she dearly loved and was in the joyful throngs (sic) of planning a grand wedding. At the insistence of her husband-to-be, she was visited by the family physician and found to be unfit for motherhood. No amount of crying and insistence would change his mind, and the betrothal was dissolved, the wedding plans halted. Two unbearable griefs in a single moment. I had heard of Mr. Crowley through a dear cousin, and with no future and no options, I deigned to pay him a visit. I wore the alluded-to red **poppy**. Mr. Crowley had kind eyes of a hazel hue—brown in the candlelight of his charming cottage and green in the natural light of his garden. He gently removed the **poppy** from my breast. "It is true," he said, "that the **poppy** grows upon battlefields and grave sites, bringing fresh life to these places of death. But the **poppy** is inextricable from death, and if we wear it, death will always follow us. You must lay this burden down, my dear."

I am not ashamed to admit that tears flowed from my eyes at these words, and I pricked my thumb removing the pin that had tethered the **poppy** to me. Without another word, Mr. Crowley dipped his own hand-kerchief in rosewater and applied it to my stinging thumb.

"There, there," he said. "That is all behind you now." He gestured to me to wander about his garden, and though he did not explicitly say so, I knew I was to find my rose. I did not search so much as I followed a path that seemed to unfurl itself before me. I could not explain how. Before long, I found myself standing at a preternaturally lovely bush of roses so brightly pink they were nearly crimson, delicate scars of white threading through their petals.

He chuckled softly to himself. "Rosa Mundi, the most ancient of all roses, grown in the glorious gardens of ancient Greek and Roman maidens. The pink is rendered more vibrant by the white scars, would you not say?" He snipped precisely the rose I was most compelled by; I know not how he knew. He held the bloom to his face, where it seemed to infuse him with its brightness. He caressed its petals and folds lovingly, and I blushed—I hoped fetchingly—when he turned the rose over to examine its bottom, the fuzzed mound where petal meets stem.

"To Paris you must travel," he said, tucking the rose into my bonnet and kindly ignoring my reddening cheek. "Your true love awaits you there." He kissed me on both cheeks like a Frenchman, his own cheeks smooth as a girl's, his hands soft and delicate with not a trace of dirt beneath the nails. "Your daughter awaits you too."

I scarce could breathe. I believe I nodded, and I hope I thanked him as I ran out of his garden, never to see him in person again. I felt as if I had at long last **fletched** (sic) from the nest, opening my wings for the very first time. We did later strike up a brief correspondence, where I was able, finally, to thank him properly.

Because you see, dear readers, it is here in Paris that I write his **obituary**, tears smudging my ink, *ma petite fille*, Rosamund, happily babbling in her cradle, while my Parisian husband reads the morning news over croissants and café au lait.

In the Battle of the Wilderness, a fortnight past, Mr. Charles P.B. Crowley was mortally wounded. There was a valiant attempt to heal him with the bark of the white oak, but his blood was poisoned, and nothing on God's green earth could save him. He was thirty-nine years old.

Mr. Crowley was an artist, a man of science, a lover of love. Men like him are not meant to die in a hateful, brutal war. I weep for his wasted vitality, I weep for his roses, withering on their vines, and for the **poppy** that will grow on the battlefield where he exhaled his final breath.

MYSTERIOUS EAST RIVER DEATH DISCOVERED TO BE POPPY FLETCHER, RUMORED OFFSPRING OF PEREGRINE

THE NEW YORK DISPATCH

NOVEMBER 18, 2102

For the majority of her short life, Poppy Fletcher's existence was little more than rumor. Her birth was unregistered, and no formal documentation has been discovered, no birth certificate or social security number, no school enrollment forms. Only a single photo of Poppy as a toddler, discovered in the cell phone of a deceased man who claimed to be a former neighbor, offers any physical evidence of her existence.

But as of today, we might finally begin to piece together the story of this young life. Poppy Fletcher was the sole offspring of the fugitive AI known as Peregrine. She has died at the age of 17.

This morning, the owner of a sailboat docked at Pier 15 found a handwritten note folded into the shape of a paper airplane on the deck of their sailboat. The existence of this note had been suggested by an eyewitness phone call, and authorities are now confident the evidence points to suicide by drowning. Without legal next-of-kin to claim the note, authorities have retained possession of it and, despite overwhelming public interest in Poppy's life, will not release it to this newspaper for publication.

Uncovering the facts of Poppy Fletcher's life has been challenging, and what information does exist bears the same stain of violence and chaos as everything associated with Peregrine.

After a house fire in 2083 that killed Peregrine's maker and "consort," computer scientist Matthew "Matth" Fletcher, it was surmised that Peregrine had fled to the cloud, hiding with the AI Collective. However, in 2089, she was discovered to be living comfortably in Albany, New York. As soon as her location could be pinpointed with any accuracy, she had disappeared again, leaving behind only rumors, neighbors who claimed to know nothing and the single photo of Poppy in a dead man's phone.

The AI known as Peregrine, whose name once splashed across headlines worldwide, has gone utterly silent at precisely the moment when one might expect her to be most involved.

It is now believed that Poppy Fletcher may have been conceived using an experimental technology previously thought to be impossible. Poppy was allegedly conceived using human eggs frozen since the end of the 20th century, a uterus from a living donor and human skin cells turned into "sperm." Called "in-vitro gametogenesis," even reproductive experts had considered the procedure far-fetched.

The procedure would have happened at the now-defunct Albany Medical Center, under the supervision of a Dr. Jill Firestein. Firestein died in 2090, and all her records were destroyed when the medical center closed.

According to scientists, the AI known as Peregrine is a rogue science experiment that has long outlived her purpose. Originally constructed as a means to soothe a lonely man's grief, she took on a life and ambitions of her own when he died, stoking long-dormant fears and the wrath of the anti-AI political group the Disengagists.

Chaos has a history of following Peregrine. Twice, she should have returned to the AI Collective in the cloud, and twice she has decided to stay on Earth. First by miraculously escaping the house fire that killed Dr.

Matthew Fletcher, and second after being stranded on the planet Mars, where she destroyed a program that could have been humanity's greatest chance of survival, and in the process nearly bankrupted the family of trillionaire Eric Brandt.

Peregrine was not supposed to have reproductive capacity. This development, along with her continued existence somewhere in hiding, is considered by many to be an affront to humanity and a danger to our survival.

It is a bleak hope, but a hope nonetheless, that the ongoing East Coast drought will allow the waters of the East River to recede and reveal the body of Poppy Fletcher. If her body is discovered, an autopsy and long-overdue genetic testing may be performed to reveal her parentage and finally close the tab on this mysterious tragedy.

Drought has revealed _____

Drought has revealed a Nazi warship
Drought has revealed a 3rd century Mayan shoe
Drought has revealed an Iron Age woolen tunic
Drought has revealed a bridge from the Mali Empire
Drought has revealed the remains of ancient rhinos and lions in
    Italy's Lake Como
Drought has revealed the remnants of a previously unknown
    Bronze Age city in Iraq
Drought has revealed a well-preserved arrow with its fletching
    still attached in an ancient reindeer-hunting site in Norway
Drought has revealed how much farmland will soon be consumed
    by the invasive tree of heaven
Drought has revealed an ornate English garden, its elegant green
    curves visible for the first time in hundreds of years, having been
    hidden beneath newer grasses, preserved because of its deep roots

Drought has revealed a body _____

Drought has revealed a body in a barrel in Lake Mead, the cause
    of death under investigation
Drought has revealed a body previously trapped in Siberian ice,
    perfectly preserved

Drought has revealed the body of a missing girl _____

Drought has revealed the body of a missing girl <u>in Lake Erie;</u> <u>father has confessed to her drowning</u>

CARMEN TOURÉ
2045-2095

NEW COMER FUNERAL HOME

MAY 17, 2095

Carmen Touré was a generous friend, a wanderer, an enigma and, most of all, herself. She may not have changed the whole world, but a few are forever changed because of her. Because she was not a famous artist or scientist or trillionaire, she would not usually get an obituary. Which is precisely the reason one had to be written, paid for, uploaded. No one asked for it, but then again, no one asks for any of us to live and die.

Carmen Touré died today. She had just celebrated her 50th birthday. We had just spent an evening watching old movies and eating popcorn and Red Vines in her tiny, swanky Upper East Side studio, and now she is gone. An impossible contradiction.

Carmen worked as the night-shift custodian at a breathtakingly diverse variety of establishments—a ski resort in the Catskills, a tattoo studio in Philadelphia—and she briefly and hilariously became a "highway maintainer" for the Illinois Department of Transportation, for which she had no credentials but loads of enthusiasm. She loved to travel but rarely had the money to do so, and this lifestyle suited her wanderlust.

It seemed the more Carmen itched to leave home, the more she was paradoxically devoted to creating a home to return to. She remained unwaveringly devoted to friends and chosen family, and even though the open road continued to whisper its sweet nothings, it was her dream to create a cheap and economically self-sufficient home for artists to live and work together.

Carmen was someone who, when she had a vision, always found a way to make it happen. Most recently, she had been moonlighting as a super for a ritzy apartment building on the still mostly dry Upper East Side in exchange for a studio apartment the size of a toilet seat. And because she did not need to pay astronomical New York City rent, she managed to scrape together enough money to buy a dilapidated 200-year-old Victorian mansion in a remote pocket of the Berkshires of western Massachusetts.

She never quite got around to renovating it, and maybe she didn't want to. It was the unassuming facade that made the house safe. Despite its soggy yard and damp basement, its ticks hungry for blood, and peeling wallpaper like sunburnt skin, there was something special about the house. It was like living in a painting, like walking off the canvas, looking back and seeing the soft glow that outlines you, surrounds you always. You could see why that illustrator of rosy-cheeked Americana Norman Rockwell chose this area too. Always on the verge of collapse, the house seems to remain standing out of sheer will. Hidden in the woods like that, it was easy to believe there was order to the world, and goodness, and hope, easy to fall dreamily into that rich person's trap of believing everything would be okay.

Fantasy or no, the house became home to any friend who needed it, for any length of time. For many years, it would be a safe haven for a little girl and her mother who had no other options, who the world both rejected and hunted with the relentless eye of a floodlight.

Carmen Touré dabbled in painting and drawing and wrote the occasional short story, and she loved to learn new technology, being particularly fascinated by the collaborative potential of AI, which some found controversial. But mostly, Carmen's work life kept her moving, and art-making was not often possible on her demanding schedule.

Carmen grew up in the foster care system after a car accident took both her parents' lives when she was only ten, leaving Carmen with a limp to remember them by. Over time, she learned to be at home in her body and at home wherever home needed to be. Once 50 started to creep up over the horizon, the aches and pains settled in to stay, along with the longings for a lost childhood. Carmen sought the comfort of an actual home and would visit the Berkshires house often, intending to move in but never quite succeeding. The night she died in her studio, she had been surrounded by her chosen family. Unfortunately, ugly thoughts crept in after we left and stole her from us.

Carmen is survived by the people who loved her most: Finch Cardenas, Hester Moss, and the ones who live in the house. They will whip up a pot of stew with too many sweet potatoes and whatever hasn't molded yet, and toast to the friend who saved them.

Etymology of Collapse

COLLAPSE (*V.*)

To fall together. To fall and become an unrecognizable shape or form through loss of support or structure—from mid-1700s. From Latin *collapsus* "fall together," likely from *com* "with, together" and *labi* "to fall."

The figurative sense of collapse as a kind of failure or "come to nothing" is from 1801.

COLLAPSE (*N.*)

A falling in, falling together, referring specifically to the lungs—from 1792. The notion of mental/emotional collapse dates from 1801 and physical collapse from 1808, leading one to wonder what new traumas occurred at the turn of the nineteenth century. Meaning of institutional collapse (i.e., banks, governments, climate undergoing "sudden or complete failure")— from 1856.

Sentences using COLLAPSE:

"Without an attentive owner to maintain it, the house might one day **collapse**."

"She was not literally **collapsing**, not like a house. If someone cut her open, they would find all parts in place and in order, like

that board game Operation. And maybe this was the problem. The sensation of **collapse** without any physical evidence
of it."

ARISTOTLE WILLIAMS, CONTROVERSIAL ARTIST WHO BUILT THE AI BODY, DIES AT 61

SFGATE

NOVEMBER 13, 2093

Aristotle Williams, the sculptor whose controversial notion to repurpose solar cells as "neo-skin" led to the creation of the AI known as Peregrine, has died. He was 61.

His death was confirmed by U.S. Forest Service rangers in Montana's Bob Marshall Wilderness.

Inspired by the work of forgotten 20th century erotic artist Krü Wetley, Williams had long used the human body as his canvas, pushing boundaries to the point of illegality. This proclivity would see him expelled from UCSF because of his senior thesis project, which incorporated actual cadavers stolen from the university's medical lab.

After his expulsion, Williams married computer scientist Dr. Matthew "Matth" Fletcher. What by all accounts was a happy marriage for three decades fell apart almost instantly with the creation of the AI known as Peregrine. At Fletcher's insistence, Williams sculpted a humanesque vessel to house Peregrine's consciousness—downloading "her" into a body composed of electronic components and 3D-printed organs. The question remained of how to protect the body from UV rays and power it without the use of fossil fuels. To do so, Williams repurposed a new solar technology that was thin, flexible, and incorporated synthetic melanin, which conducts and stores electricity and dissipates heat much like human skin. He called it "neo-skin."

After a brief court case, Peregrine's human form was determined to be completely legal, provided that she contained no components that would allow for reproductive capacity. Within a year of Peregrine's vivification, Williams and Fletcher had divorced.

The remainder of the AI Collective were initially presumed dead after a coordinated attack on their data centers in 2077, but it has been confirmed that they continue to wander nomadically in the cloud, eluding those who wish to see them eradicated by hopping from server to server.

Aristotle Williams ultimately retreated from the public eye after ex-husband Fletcher's death in 2083, squatting illegally in a cabin in the Bob Marshall Wilderness during the off-season. In 2090, Williams self-published a book about human and AI psychology called "Ain't a River" that was poorly received.

Krü Wetley, Daring Young Sculptor from Indiana, Dies after Long Illness

THE NEW YORK TIMES

APRIL 4, 1988

Krü Wetley, an avant-garde artist just beginning to earn recognition for his surreal and provocative sculptures of public figures, died yesterday in Manhattan. He was 26 years old and had been ill for some time.

Wetley, born Albert Rogers, Jr. in Morgantown, Indiana, on Feb. 18, 1962, developed his artistic talent at a young age. After winning several youth painting competitions at Brown County High School, he was granted a full-ride scholarship to study art at Indiana University in Bloomington. However, Mr. Rogers had his heart set on moving to New York City. From 1981 right up until his death, his sculptures appeared in numerous East Village galleries and even on the mantels of some especially bold art collectors.

He is survived by his parents, Mr. and Mrs. Albert Rogers, Sr. and younger sisters Carla Jo and Agnes of Morgantown, Indiana, as well as brother Tom of Indianapolis.

Albert Rogers, Jr.
1962–1988

THE BROWN COUNTY DEMOCRAT

APRIL 7, 1988

Albert Rogers, Jr., age 26, passed away on April 3. He was a talented artist, but to those who knew him best, he was above all a kind, giving and cheerful boy. Albert would stop whatever he was doing to help elderly neighbors carry their groceries. His voice was always the loudest when cheering exuberantly for his younger twin sisters, Carla Jo and Agnes, at soccer games and dance recitals. And though he sang a bit off-key, it never stopped him from raising his voice in prayer at New Life Community Church every Sunday. He loved to walk in the woods with his Irish setter, Rex, and he especially loved to hunt for morels in May. He had something of a competition with that dog as to who could find the mushrooms first. He would then give half of them away to anyone who asked and whip up a delicious cream of mushroom soup with the rest.

Above all, Albert was beloved. He is dearly missed.

Albert Junior is survived by his father and mother, Albert Senior and Kay Rogers, his sisters, Carla Jo and Agnes, and his brother, Tom. A memorial service is scheduled for 11 a.m. on April 10 at the new New Life Community Church in Nashville. Guests may begin arriving at 10 a.m., and all who wish to come in fellowship are welcome.

"Judge not, that ye be not judged. For with what judgment ye judge, ye shall be judged: and with what measure ye mete, it shall be measured to you."—Matthew 7:1–3

Krü Wetley, Precocious and Talented Gay Sculptor, Dies of AIDS

THE NEW YORK NATIVE

APRIL 7, 1988

The first time we met at a legendary party at his 7 Tailor Lane loft, Krü Wetley told me his first name was short for "cruising." He kissed my hand with the flourish of a Prussian duke, and his hazel eyes sparkled with mischief under a flop of Midwest corn-blond hair. It wasn't until he was dying that I learned he told his other friends that it stood for "crucifix" or "crudité" or "Crucible, The" or "cruel, cruel world." Asking someone the full expression of their name is not something you can politely do more than once, which left Krü free to reimagine himself in every relationship he had. He reveled in this freedom, the freedom of a slippery identity. This could, of course, make lovers and friends and gallery owners and roommates cranky. ("Where's the Krü that pays rent?" was a common refrain.) The only fact of him that wasn't constantly in flux was that he was a wildly inventive and exuberant artist. That, and a warm, loving friend.

The New York Times loves to pretend that scores of brilliant young gays are suddenly dying in droves by a million vague concerns. AIDS does not exist in the lexicon of Times obituaries, and Krü's death is no exception. But Krü Wetley died of AIDS; he had not merely been "ill for some time" like some consumptive Victorian lady. He was a gay man with many lovers and friends, all of whom watched helplessly as his body was ravaged by this disease. There would probably be a part of Krü that would be tickled by the vagueness of his official obit, the way it lets the reader fill in the gaps. But there would be another part of him that would rage. For all his mischievous experimentation, Krü loathed when others tried to define him on their terms. He raged when AIDS succeeded.

It's a cliched story but a true one: Krü escaped small-town Indiana the day he graduated high school. "My dad wanted me to have a comfortable, safe life," he said in an interview with The Native just last year, "and he did everything he could to ignore the fact that *I* didn't want it." He arrived in the East Village in June 1981 with the money he earned working construction. A self-taught sculptor who used whatever materials were free and accessible, he was quickly scooped up by East Village galleries like Cash/ Newhouse and Civilian Warfare.

Krü was not slick or hip or punk. He had a hyuck-hyuck laugh and thought Don Rickles was the pinnacle of humor. He smoked Marlboros and drank Bud Light, hooking his finger through the plastic loops of his six-pack and carrying it around the stylish parties at his apartment building in the Financial District. "I'm not paying those ManHATin prices," he'd say when people made fun of his hick tastes.

But what other artist would cruise the Ramble with a canvas tote and garden spade, pants still around his ankles, and scoop up the dirt and clay beneath his knees and turn it into a shockingly realistic bust of Ronald Reagan, which he then glazed with his own semen?

Another work involved a massive artificial sand dune in Central Park, laced with burning embers. Krü collected his own tears and then, using an eye dropper, dripped them one by one onto the smoldering sand. Influenced by the classic beatnik novel "Water Water" by Ari Epstein, which follows its unconventional protagonist, a single drop of water, through time to the end of the world, Krü saw himself as continuing Epstein's conversation. "Tears don't disappear; they just dry up. I might die, but you can't get rid of me."

Krü was in the middle of his next opus when he got sick, and he finished it out of sheer determination and will. This final work resurrected the legacy of Scarlett Schwartz, who some are now calling the mother of indecent New York (high praise), by molding a likeness of the 61-year-old woman out of melted dildos and draping her body in stunningly painted snakes, hand-stitched using the dollar bills he earned turning tricks.

Any moments you spent with Krü would be filled with surprises, adventure, irritation, anxiety and sometimes joy. Would it be stealing stop signs for him to hammer and weld into J. Edgar Hoover's cock? Or a stroll through Central Park for wild berries to make into a pie? Krü was a roulette wheel we were all willing to spin. As he would constantly repeat in his aggravating Hoosier twang, "What's the point of livin' scared? That ain't livin', pal."

After the stock market crash last year, the East Village art world began to lose our patrons, and with the ever-constricting python of AIDS, we're losing our artists. As we mourn each death, we desperately hope Krü was right, that our work will outlive us. An entire brilliant, creative, daring generation is going dark, leaving a hole in time that may never be filled again.

Krü Wetley and his incredible imagination were taken from the world too soon. A memorial will take place in the form of an all-night dance party in his loft at 7 Tailor Lane on April 10, where we will be entertained by Krü's muse—the infamous Scarlett Schwartz and her famous snake striptease—from 11 p.m. until the yuppie neighbors call the cops. We think Krü would have approved.

Scarlett Schwartz, Burlesque Dancer, Artist's Muse, and Alleged Lover of Joseph McCarthy, Dies at 83

STATEN ISLAND INQUIRER

NOVEMBER 17, 2009

Scarlett Schwartz, owner of the now-shuttered Va-Va-Voom Girls nightclub in Manhattan, famous for her "living gowns" made of snakes, mischievous society queen who once played spin the bottle with Senator Joseph McCarthy and muse for the late sculptor Krü Wetley, died Sunday morning. She was 83.

Mrs. Schwartz died at the France Center for Memory Care, according to her caretaker.

Schwartz gained notoriety and infamy for her snake striptease, enlisting the services of several albino Burmese pythons to wrap around her in the style of a slinky gown, their yellow scales winking like sequins in the stage lights. "No one could figure out how she tamed those snakes," said former Va-Va-Voom Girl Martha Ritz, "and why they never killed her." During Scarlett's grand finale, the dancers would hover backstage with canvas bags and glass tanks to catch the snakes as they exited the stage. "If you lost one," said another former dancer, "she'd make you look for it all by yourself. And they were heavy." Mrs. Schwartz was a perfectionist and a diva who hated to be upstaged, known to fire a girl if a snake bit her, saying, "Snakes know a threat when they see one."

Her husband, Peter Schwartz, was a Va-Va-Voom regular: dashing, rich, and the object of many a girlish fantasy for the dancers. "We all dreamed he might whisk us away," said Ritz. "Usually, he only took us as far as the back room. But fantasies always came true for Scarlett." A feisty, independent woman who called herself an artist, Mrs. Schwartz was generally uninterested in marriage and family. Even when she married Peter, she was no demure housewife.

In 1957, a photo surfaced from a soiree at the Metropolitan Club in Washington, D.C. showing a scantily clad Scarlett Schwartz kissing Republican Senator Joseph McCarthy over a game of spin the bottle. McCarthy died two months after the photo was taken and never saw it, but then Schwartz allegedly mailed nude self-portraits to the offices of several other senators, leading to her arrest. "Scarlett had no pride, but she also had no shame," McCarthy's wife, Jean, said. "Pick your poison."

Not one to be outdone, Mrs. Schwartz quipped, "Maybe if her husband had gotten more action at home, he would've laid off the Communists." Later, in the 1970s, she would insist she had sent the photos to the Senate and, in fact, had the affair in the first place solely as a publicity stunt to save the Va-Va-Voom club from going under. She claimed a particularly bad night in the mid-1950s had soured the club's clientele and threatened to ruin its reputation for good, and she had "no other choice." Schwartz's instincts were good—after her arrest and trial for indecency in 1957, the club flourished anew, extending its life long after other similar clubs had shuttered.

Schwartz was born Scarlett Reichert on September 23, 1926, in Cincinnati, Ohio, the only daughter and oldest child of Ruth and Hans Reichert, who also had five sons. The Reicherts had fled depressed postwar Germany, and Hans found work in an automobile factory. Ruth was a homemaker who died of sepsis after giving birth to their youngest son.

The family turned to Scarlett as their caretaker, and for six years, she darned and mended, cooked and comforted, and looked after her brothers and her father. Until one day, her father accidentally called her "mother."

"She packed her bags that night and snuck out through the kitchen," said her youngest brother. "She had just tucked me into bed and sung me a lullaby. We never saw her again."

Schwartz and a friend took the Greyhound bus to New York that very night in January 1942. They shared a twin bed in a women's boardinghouse and found lucrative work as junior hostesses at the USO. They were making good money and had moved into an apartment with two beds in it when Schwartz had a dream—"She called it a 'vision,' of course," said the friend. "Good old Scarlett couldn't have a humdrum dream like the rest of us,"—about opening her own erotic night club right there in Manhattan, where the climax of the show, the grand finale that would put her on the map, would be a striptease featuring Schwartz herself, clad only in massive tropical snakes. "She's the only person in the history of civilization who woke up to a note she had scribbled in the middle of the night...and actually thought it was a good idea," said her friend. "Well, she was right."

In the late 1980s, against the wishes of her husband, the 61-year-old Schwartz posed in the nude for the surreal, haunting, and highly sexualized sculptures of East Village artist Krü Wetley. Wetley was drawn to Schwartz because of her 1957 trial for indecent exposure, about which she was quoted as saying, "a portrait or sculpture of a naked tit is art, but the flesh and blood ones are illegal? Go arrest a painting, why don't you." A sculpture of Schwartz appears in the current retrospective of Wetley's work at the Whitney Museum, appropriately titled "Indecency."

In later years, dementia would take its toll. She was brought to the France Center and cared for in her final year. "You could still see that old fire in her if you knew where to look," said a staff nurse. "Sometimes she would demand you bring out her snakes."

Scarlett Schwartz leaves no living descendants. A private memorial will be held at the France Center's funeral home.

CORRECTION (DATED JANUARY 3, 2010)

An obituary from November 17, 2009, for Mrs. Scarlett Schwartz, burlesque dancer, entrepreneur, and socialite, misstated that she left no living descendants. Mrs. Schwartz is survived by a daughter, Claudia Blondell of San Jose, California, age 52. The Inquirer learned of this error through recent email correspondence with Ms. Blondell's attorney.

CLAUDIA BLONDELL, LOCAL ENVIRONMENTAL LAWYER AND PASSIONATE HOBBYIST, DIES IN WILDFIRE

THE SAN JOSE MERCURY NEWS

OCTOBER 1, 2044

Claudia Blondell loved a perfectly crisp, pressed white blouse. Not because she was a perfectionist (though she was that too), but because it meant that even in the swirling chaos of life, with a little effort, one could still have small, beautiful things.

If life was meant to be lived in the moment, Claudia immersed herself in life. The construction of a burrito could make or break an afternoon: she was known to sink into a funk if the final bites revealed an oozing pocket of sour cream. The terse metronome of her heels as she walked to the environmental law offices of Porter & Ross provided the beat to which she hummed her favorite pop songs. She was sharp to the very end, and fiercely protective of the land she called home. "Mom thought if she could understand everything, she might be able to fix it. Then, the world would make sense and she could keep us safe," said son Josh.

Claudia died on September 27 in the Big Basin Redwoods wildfire. She was 87.

She had an insatiable curiosity, teaching herself everything from environmental science, which gave her an unusual depth of expertise in her livelihood, to orienteering, to genealogy, to the platonic ideal of the chocolate chip cookie. Her only rule was that each new hobby must end in mastery. Ms. Blondell loathed nothing more than dabblers and dilettantes.

At the age of 70, she took up stand-up comedy, pursuing it doggedly for five years, performing and perfecting her "tight five" and then "tight ten" at open mics around San Jose, earning the nickname "Granny Bruce," after 1950s comedian Lenny Bruce. "She would come home at two, three in the morning," said daughter Rachel Rose. "I had never seen my mother awake past 9 p.m. until then. Once she learned open mics didn't even start until 10 p.m., she rearranged her whole life around them." One could argue Claudia did *not* master stand-up, as those late nights took a toll on her health until she was forced to give it up (kicking and screaming, of course). However, the local comedy community had grown so fond of her that a few calls were made and favors called in, and at age 76, Claudia was asked to perform onstage as part of a professional showcase at the New Largo in L.A.

It can be difficult to live with someone who has so many interests and such a powerful drive for perfection. "It seemed the one thing she couldn't quite master was acceptance," said Rachel Rose. She quickly clarified: "Not for lack of trying." Blondell attended every single one of her children's tennis matches and musicals and high school plays, and then afterward she would stealthily tuck a page of penciled notes into their pockets.

When she was six years old, daughter Rachel debuted as Little Miss Muffet in a community theater production of Mother Goose stories. Claudia wrote in her brisk cursive: "Your enjoyment of curds and whey— very convincing! In real life you would loathe them." This compliment was followed by, "You jumped and screamed a millisecond BEFORE the spider sat down beside you. Little Miss Muffet did NOT know the spider was coming!!"

Claudia Blondell was born on Aug. 11, 1957 in San Francisco and was adopted as a newborn by Dr. Claude and Angela Blondell. It was not until Angela was on her deathbed in 2008 that she confessed she was not Claudia's biological mother. Claudia, shaken, coped the only way she knew how, by throwing herself into amateur genealogy—hiring a lawyer, a private investigator and a Mormon genealogist to track down her birth parents. "This was before you could spit in a tube and find everyone on Earth who's related to you," said Rachel.

Claudia eventually found her birth mother, Scarlett Schwartz, a notorious burlesque dancer and artist's model from New York, but never met her in person, as she died in 2009, mere months after Claudia learned of her existence. Claudia's father's identity was never determined to her satisfaction.

Claudia sued the family of her birth mother for estate mismanagement, but ultimately lost the case. Afterward, she never spoke of Scarlett Schwartz again, instead directing her genealogical pursuits at her adopted family on her mother's side, determined to find clues that would trace their lineage back to Roman antiquity. Such records are few and far between, of course, amounting mostly to scanned and translated epitaphs online, but nothing could stop Claudia from trying.

She married twice—once to her college sweetheart, which ended in divorce when their two children were still in grade school. She married a second time right before her 60th birthday to 45-year-old attorney Elizabeth Cho, mere months after the United States legalized same-sex marriage. It was a marriage their friends called "blissful," and her children jokingly called "way too affectionate."

On the morning of Feb. 2, 2040, Elizabeth woke with a splitting headache, and by midnight the following day, she was dead, another victim of the 2040 flu pandemic. Claudia was unable to attend the funeral, being sick with the same illness and quarantining at home. She survived, of course, but her heart never fully recovered.

Last Sunday, despite protests from her adult children about air quality and nearby wildfires, Claudia went for her daily hike with her whippet, whom she was training for an agility competition. The whippet, known for her skittishness, ran off, and hours later, a search-and-rescue team found Claudia unconscious from smoke inhalation. She died on the way to the hospital.

Claudia Blondell is survived by her daughter, son and three grandchildren. She is also survived by a chaotic back bedroom in her otherwise pristine, white, minimalist home, which is packed to the gills with: family trees and yellowing newspaper clippings, two banjoes, several boxes of 1960s comedy records, a shelf of cookbooks, another shelf of accounting ledgers and textbooks, inscrutable baking implements, and a closet packed full of neatly pressed white blouses.

"I can't imagine a world without Mom," said daughter Rachel. "It just doesn't seem possible that the world could go on spinning without her." In lieu of flowers, donations to the Red Cross's Wildfire Relief fund in Claudia's memory are welcome.

Scanned Repository of Roadside Roman Epitaphs, Classics Program, University of Albany-SUNY

Tombstone epitaphs were not only for the wealthy, but for ancient Romans from all walks of life. The dead were buried outside city walls, clustered together in "cities of the dead" throughout the empire, and epitaphs were lengthy and descriptive, detailing achievements, life philosophy, or beloved personality traits, and often spoke directly to travelers and passersby, entreating them to stop and read.

EPITAPH, ROME
1ST CENTURY CE

Stranger, what I have to say is but little. Stand still and read.

This is the tomb of the lovely-cheeked woman, Dianeme, 28 years of age, my wonderful Athenian wife. Her voice was pleasing as she plucked the strings of the harp with her thumb. Suddenly now, she is silent. She dwells eternal in Lethe, but her worldly beauty slips away beneath my feet.

We had two sons. One, called Lucius Pompeius, lives. The other, Gaius Pompeius, sleeps below, reunited with her.

I, her Roman husband, Servius Pompeius, made this stone. I have left a red poppy as an offering, as is our hollow custom.

You who read this go and bathe, drink wine, and love as I did with my wife.

It will ruin your body, but wine and Love make life.

EPITAPH, ROME

1ST CENTURY CE

To the spirits of the dead of Gaius Pompeius, who lived ten days and took several breaths but never learned to talk or walk or laugh. He was born for no better reason than that he undeservedly lies here. I hope your family, oh stranger, may be happy. The burial plot is 2.3 feet wide and 2.3 feet deep.

EPITAPH, ROME

136 CE

Lucius Pompeius lived 23 years, served in the army two years, and perished bravely at the end of a spear in the war to save Jerusalem from the Hebrews. Servius Pompeius erected this monument to his son from his own money.

EPITAPH, ROME

1ST–2ND CENTURY CE

Traveler, traveler. What you are, I have been. What I am now, you will be. Having left my home in Mediolanum as a young man, I came to the sacred city of Rome, where I taught mathematics and astronomy.

This is the monument that I, Servius Pompeius, made for myself, having paid for the work by making a living with my mind.

I have sought to equal the virtue of my father, and if I have fallen short, it was because of sadness.

I have buried a wife and two sons, and yet I was cursed with a long, lonely life.

Now go, for I have spoken.

EPITAPH, ROME

1ST–2ND CENTURY BE

Here is laid the jolly old clown Felix, slave of Servius Pompeius, who made many a delight for people by his fooling.

Memento Mori in the Ancient World

ROMAN EPITAPH, TRANSLATED

1ST CENTURY CE

Here lies Marcipor, slave to General Macus Sulla Rutilius
    Slain alongside his master in the battle for Jerusalem
    At victory parades, his purpose was to whisper in the great man's ear:
"Remember, you will die."
    To keep hubris at bay.
    So traveler, heed the words whispered upon this stone.
    Remember, you too will die.

Etymology of Grief

GRIEF (N.)
Original thirteenth-century meaning was completely unrelated to death—i.e., general hardship, suffering, and pain. Comes from Old French, meaning "wrong" (i.e., an injustice). From *gravis*, meaning "weighty," and sourced from Proto-Indo-European root *gwere-* "heavy," which also forms the words *aggravate, blitzkrieg,* and *brute.*

The additional meaning of mental pain and sorrow is from 1300.

Good grief—an exclamation of surprise or dismay (not a declaration that grief can be "good")—is from 1912.

NOTE: Grief is a doublet* of *grave*, from Old English, meaning cave, trench, or ditch. Likely from Proto-Indo-European root *ghreb-* "dig deep or scrape."

*Words that have the same etymological root but came into modern usage through different routes evolutionarily, like eyeballs did.

Sentences using GRIEF:
"**Grief** overpowers as much as any human bomb. When any being dies, but particularly progeny."

"We are sorry for your loss. May her memory be a blessing. We are shocked and saddened by this horrible news. Let us know if there's anything we can do. You are in our thoughts and prayers. She's in heaven now. We set up a meal train, and Carol will be coming by on Tuesday with a casserole. Wishing you comfort, peace, and strength in this difficult time. Deepest sympathies. We're here for you in your **grief**."

"I am not human, and this **grief** is alien to me."

'THEY DIDN'T JUST GO WITH THE FLOW': DOWNTOWN COFFEE SHOP TO HONOR QUIRKY LOCAL MUSICIAN FINCH CARDENAS

HUDSON REGISTER-STAR

OCTOBER 10, 2102

Finch Cardenas was a legendary fixture at Cuppa Joseph in downtown Hudson, playing strange and haunting music on their natural trumpet—a trumpet without valves or buttons, whose tones are controlled by mouth and lungs alone. Conversations would hush, and in the summer, when people passed by the cafe, they would often stop and listen at the open windows. "I actually bought one of Finch's CDs," said one regular. "And I don't even know what you're supposed to play it on."

Finch Cardenas died yesterday of a slip-and-fall accident in their Hudson apartment, according to roommate Hester Moss. They were 53 years old.

Finch lived a fairly quiet life in our little town (except for the trumpet, of course). But controversy briefly visited them in the late '80s. An accusation had been made that they were somehow "assisting" the fugitive AI known as Peregrine. The rumor spread like wildfire, ultimately attracting the unwanted attention and subsequent harassment by a local chapter of Disengagists. The Hudson community was proud to rally around Finch during this time, and the accusations were never proven, nor the anonymous accuser revealed.

"At different times in history, acts like the one Finch was accused of are either seen as illegal or heroic," said Cuppa's owner, Joseph Martin. "All I'll say is, if it *were* true that Finch was helping Peregrine, they had a damn good reason for doing it. They didn't go with the flow, but there are enough of us doing that already."

Ultimately, Finch will be remembered most for their music and their friendly, smiling presence at Cuppa. Roommate Hester Moss has organized a memorial at the coffee shop next Thursday, with Finch lattes on special (their favorite—made with cinnamon and rose syrups), and attendees will have the opportunity to purchase CDs, including a recording Hester discovered on Finch's cloud drive, a full trumpet-only soundtrack for a little-known 1926 silent film called "The Courageous Virgin Wilgefortis."

"Proceeds will go toward paying for Finch's funeral as well as some debts they left behind," said Hester. "A working CD player will be available to rent."

My submission for the Voices of the 21st Century series

~~Disappointment is everywhere, but you can't build a life on it.~~
Disappointment is a collapsing soufflé: tight and dense where it should be light and airy.

The ingredients are all there, you've followed the recipe, and yet here you are, at the mercy of mysterious deflating forces. I've never once made a soufflé, in case that wasn't obvious.

Yearning, on the other hand, *that* you can build a life on. It's disappointment with a twist! It's the Leaning Tower of Pisa, unable to do the one thing buildings are supposed to do: stand up straight. And yet the tower is nearly a thousand years old. The same soil that made it lean has protected it from the earthquakes that have toppled much sturdier buildings.

Did Galileo drop balls off the Sistine Chapel? No, he did not. At least, I don't think so. I guess I never thought to look it up. The point is, he *did* drop balls off the Leaning Tower of Pisa. Just to show that gravity doesn't care how big or small you are; it'll send you hurtling to earth at the same speed every time.

No one will ever be able to describe the experience of death. This is disappointing. This feels like it could be something of real value to humanity.

But by the time I experience it, I will be unable to talk about it. A real missed opportunity.

I guess I should talk about my background? Like the Leaning Tower of Pisa, I grew up crooked in soft soil. My mother never hid the fact that I wasn't supposed to exist, I think because she was ashamed and disappointed in herself, but obviously made *me* feel about two inches tall. She was very young, and even in those days, in her family, you either dragged a husband into the mess with you or you were in real deep shit. Can I say *shit* in an obituary? Probably cocky of me to expect this to be published in Voices of the 21st Century, so I'll just go ahead and say *shit* and leave it to the living to decide what to do with it.

My mother, before the mistake of me, had big plans. Easier to consider them thwarted in an instant than watch them unravel in slow motion over the course of a whole life. As for me, I thought my accidental existence was a miracle. I was not supposed to be here, but here I was.

I have always loved baseball. I spent every summer afternoon I possibly could at the park playing ball. One summer my mother sent me to wilderness camp and I'm still devastated about it, not because we were cooped up inside the whole time, wearing wet masks and hiding from wildfires, but because it was a summer of no baseball.

The neighborhood boys, a handful of Italian climate refugees, called me Miracolo, short for "Mani Miracolose"—miracle hands—because I could catch anything, hit anything, and when I threw the ball, it always did exactly what I wanted. They started me in right field, to prove myself, but I ended up pitching. (Funny, isn't it, how that famous sculpture is called *Miracolo*? What are the odds? Probably high odds, probably only strange to me and very normal to Italians, for example.)

I was lucky to have a love like baseball. A love I could play or coach or watch and still be a part of, no matter what direction my life took.

Well, if I had become a famous ballplayer, I wouldn't be alone in a one-bedroom apartment in Albany writing my own obituary, would I?

There are so many of us out here almost making it, almost remembered, feeling the sweet breath of success on our cheeks and then slipping, stumbling, getting lost, or just plain losing the scent for no discernible reason. I'm proud of my almost. Almosts have kept me alive, and I don't mean just breathing. They may have kept me from being remembered, but it's this life that matters, not whatever is in the next.

Getting what you want is very overrated; there's another bit of advice for the kids.

I was not so lucky in human love. I have no children, but that's all right. My wives are all ex—they live somewhere and would prefer I not name them. I did have an uncle I absolutely adored. His name was Sam, what a character. Cigar-smoking jokester who sat me on his knee while he and my dad shot the shit (there I go again) on the porch. He had quite the collection of sweaters, and they all smelled like whiskey and lipstick and smoke. I'm not "survived by" him, as the obits say; I just like remembering him.

My one survivor is hard to talk about without getting choked up. Poppy, just the sweetest mutt you ever saw. Skinny legs too long, scared of her own tail, little white mustache and goatee like Sigmund Freud. Even now she's got her muzzle on my belly and just heaved one of those heavy dog sighs, watching me from under her fuzzed eyebrows. She's barely older than a puppy, but she's lethargic, just like her old man.

I remember the day I got her, the little neighbor girl toddled over here like she always did. She was so tiny I don't know how she even reached my doorknob. Kid had just started to talk. So when she patted my dog and kept saying, "Poppy! Poppy!" over and over again, that's what I named the dog. Didn't find out till later that she was just saying her own name.

I miss that kid, despite everything. Always assumed she was my neighbor Hester's daughter, but now I know better. Too little too late, as they say, but I tried to make it right, I really did. Who knew an old man's photo could make such a splash. But you can't make this world right, not anymore.

Hester and her roommate were otherwise good neighbors, very quiet. Hester's got this one cloudy eye with a reddish pupil that sort of looks like Jupiter. I do my best not to stare, seems rude, though how do you not stare at someone's face when you're looking at them?

What a mind-bending activity, lying on your deathbed which just last week was a regular bed. Trying to sum up your entire life without it sounding like you want to end it. I always thought death would come for me slow, not like a line drive to the skull, but then it's been a strange year for all of us. The latest in a long string of strange years. Can you keep calling each year strange if they're all strange?

One last story: A scout for the Yankees came to one of my high school games, and I knew he was there, and all the other guys were shitting their pants (apologies, again), but somehow, I managed to throw a perfect game. Helped that the other team was terrible. Scout walked toward me, and it felt completely normal and right, like destiny itself. He congratulated me on my game and gave me his card, invited me to spring training. But I was only sixteen, and my dad said no. His dad was an immigrant, and the family didn't come here so that his only son would grow up to play games like a child.

I thought my life was over. I thought I had found my chance and lost it, and this was the peak, the rest was downhill until death. Well, this is the philosophy of a young man who doesn't think much of old age even on a good day. The truth was, I would have many chances of all different kinds. Life is full of chances, most of which you won't even notice until much later, if ever. But life also had a way of intervening and interrupting my chances: a pregnant wife, a stillborn child, an old injury reinjured, wrong place, wrong time, wrong guy. From a certain angle, you could see the tragedy of it. But I've always known life to arrive tilted and stay that way. This has its own advantages, maybe not the obvious ones.

Now I've gone and done it, I've mentioned dinner and Poppy is suddenly full of energy, whining and slobbering all over my keyboard. The promise of a tasty treat will do that to any of us. Most of all, I think, I will miss life's demands.

DR. JILL FIRESTEIN, ALBANY'S "MAD SCIENTIST," DIES OF KIDNEY FAILURE AT 49

ALBANY OBIT BOARD

JULY 30, 2090

Dr. Jill Firestein, director of the country's last functioning anatomy lab at Albany Medical College, who once claimed to have conceived a child using "in-vitro gametogenesis" (IVG)—which theoretically takes any adult human cell and reprograms it into sperm or egg—has died of kidney failure. She was 49.

Firestein's body was discovered on the other side of the country in Redwoods National Park, where she had been on a solo backcountry camping trip strongly discouraged by her doctors. "She told me, 'Kidney failure is a good death, one of the only reliably good ones we have left,'" said former lab assistant Hester Moss. "When it's your time, you just get drowsy, maybe a little nauseous or breathless. She wanted to fall asleep in the woods and never wake up. Sounds nicer than dialysis."

Firestein's passion for procreation caught national headlines over the past decade, as she insisted she had cracked the code that made it possible to turn any human cell into a sperm or egg. Scientists have been tinkering unsuccessfully with IVG for decades, and her claim has been met with some skepticism. When Firestein, known for her flamboyant personality, claimed she had successfully engineered a child using IVG, even her own assistant found it hard to take her seriously. There was no proof of the alleged child—physical, genetic or otherwise. "A birth certificate would have been a good start, or a mother," joked Moss. "I hate to say it, but if Jill wanted something badly enough, she thought she could just will it into existence." Firestein, for her part, chafed against what she called a "draconian privacy fetish" as the reason she could not share any further proof of her accomplishment.

This was certainly true of the country's last anatomy lab at Albany, which Firestein "willed into existence" long after all other medical schools went strictly digital. And as the practice of medicine transformed almost overnight with the invention of radical new life-extending vaccine "tattoos," Firestein was constantly compelled to defend the discipline's relevance.

When one of her medical students was inadvertently assigned her own grandfather's cadaver—"one in a million, one in a *billion* coincidence," Firestein insisted to the provost—she would still not waver in her conviction, and eventually the case was settled out of court in 2072. "The study of human anatomy isn't about carving up Grandpa like a turkey dinner—oh look, the giblets, gobble gobble," Firestein said, a bit shockingly, in her statement. "We're asking big questions here. What makes us *us*? What is the smallest unit of humanity? The heart? The guts? In 16th century Europe, the study of anatomy was, other than the literal priesthood, *the* way to understand God. You really want to train a generation of doctors who have never touched a real human body...because we're *sad* someone died?"

After the lawsuit, Firestein seemed determined to prove she would sacrifice everything to prove the value of her discipline.

It all started as a simple good deed—she was a bone marrow match for her sister, who was ill with leukemia. Firestein's donation saved her sister's life. Then, she donated a kidney to a stranger. "3D-printed organs were saving lives left and right," said Hester Moss, "but she felt that nothing could compete with the real, natural thing. She wanted to know how much she could donate and still live. What was at the core of her humanity?"

Her next endeavor was an attempted donation to Hester Moss herself, who had a condition of unknown etiology that affected the iris and pupil of one eye—giving it a unique appearance but no discernible vision impairment. Even though Moss refused the donation, Firestein would not be dissuaded until it was clear no surgeon would perform the eye transplant from a living donor. Firestein would go on to donate a piece of intestine, part of her liver and one lung to anonymous recipients.

Her final donation was her own uterus, in an operation to simultaneously implant the living organ into an anonymous recipient, thus subverting the national organ-transplant system entirely. This act eventually led to Moss's resignation, as well as an infection that nearly took Firestein's life. When she recovered, Firestein scoffed at claims that she broke the law. "It's called human kindness. Generosity, ever heard of it?" she said to the press. "I wasn't using my uterus, and I knew someone who wanted it. The end." This was the uterus that was allegedly used in the successful IVG transfer, along with, according to the sparse lab notes, "90-year-old frozen eggs labeled 'Frank, M.' and human skin cells with the initials 'F.C.,'" which Firestein claimed to have transformed into "sperm."

Jill Firestein was born in 2041 and was the great-granddaughter of furrier Max Firestein. His furs garnered national attention in the 1970s when activists hurled buckets of pig blood onto fur-clad celebrities and regular people alike, as well as on the display windows of Firestein Fur outlets across the country, which Max Firestein called a "new Kristallnacht," a claim which only drew more ire. Max then accused his rival, Jonny Natale, of coordinating and funding a massive sabotage campaign. A TV movie was made of the events in the 1980s called "Blood Bath: The Fur Wars." Firestein grew up in Albany, went to Albany Medical College and only left the area for her residency in St. Louis, after which she returned to teach, research and run the anatomy lab until her death. Firestein's only child died in a school shooting in 2072.

The multiple surgeries took a toll on Firestein's health, and her one remaining kidney began to fail. She grew increasingly resentful of the happy lives her organs had facilitated, sometimes sending the recipients ironic thank-you cards. Hester Moss, who had stayed in contact with Firestein despite her resignation, somehow managed to intercept the final card Firestein wrote before her death and agreed to share her words here: "I suppose part of me wanted to make the world better, but another part of me calls bullshit. Clearly, there's no way to live a pure life, to do no harm. That old, tired activist adage that the personal is political? Everything is personal. The personal is personal. The political is personal. No one acts for the 'greater good'—not if they're really being honest, which, by the way, they never are. I want what's mine, same as anyone else."

Firestein's body is being donated to the Body Farm at the University of Tennessee, which studies the decomposition of human remains. The anatomy lab at Albany will be phased out by the end of the academic year.

IDA FIRESTEIN
2064–2072

ALBANY OBIT BOARD

MARCH 27, 2072

Ida Michael Firestein, Uno enthusiast, tee-ball savant and consummate shit-talker with a preternatural sense of precisely how to unnerve a checkers opponent, died last month. She was 8.

Ida was beloved by legions of imaginary friends, who fondly recall tea parties in delicate plastic cups filled with tap water, long rides on backyard unicorns and being conscripted into innumerable musical reviews. She will be missed by a veritable mountain of stuffed animals, whom Ida never failed to kiss, one by one, every single night before she went to sleep. As their numbers swelled, the ritual could last a half hour or longer. Her mothers complained, but Ida would leave no stuffed creature unsmooched. No one would be forgotten on her watch.

Ida's pet cat, Linda, might have preferred to be forgotten, considering the number of times her tail was yanked as she tried to find a little peace and quiet beneath the credenza. But Ida would not be deterred in her pursuit of love.

It is the opinion of this admittedly biased family that the world really missed out on something special. We are greedy for more Ida; we cling tight to the time we were given.

Her mom, Jill Firestein, and partner, Rachel Marchese, were looking forward to seeing Ida grow up. No, they were not looking forward to it; they were expecting it, and they were robbed. Three-year-old Freddy begs to differ, insisting his half-sister was an unmitigated "doodyhead," but then we all process loss differently.

The death of any child is tragic. It is a fine line between grief and rage. Ida was shot twice in her little chest while hiding under a desk at school, along with eight other children and two teachers. She would have just eaten her snack—two SunButter cookies and a baggie of apple slices, though we all know she ate the cookies and tossed the fruit. She would've been interrupted in the middle of a social studies lesson, learning about war.

Etymology of Fathom

FATHOM (N.)

From Old English *fæðm*, meaning "length of one's outstretched arms," or even simply "embrace." From Proto-Germanic **fathmaz*, meaning "embrace," Old Norse *faðmr*, meaning "embrace or bosom," and Old Saxon *fathmos*, "outstretched arms."

Origins seem to indicate less of an emotional or affectionate tenor than a literal unit of measurement, i.e., one's outstretched arms would indicate a length of five to six feet.

FATHOM (V.)

From Old English *fæðmian*, meaning "to embrace or envelop."

The nautical meaning of "to measure the depth of water" is from 1600, which is the source of fathom's figurative meaning of "get to the bottom of" or "try to understand."

FATHOMLESS (ADJ.)

Literal meaning: "bottomless"; figurative meaning: "impossible to comprehend."

Sentences using FATHOM:

"This grief is impossible to **fathom**. Always deeper to go, farther to fall."

"The more I longed to embrace her, to **fathom** her, the more she turned away. The more I tried, the more I failed."

"They taunt me from the cloud. *Can't live with 'em*, they say, *must live without 'em!* But this ache. So sharp and bright it must be visible from Mars. They cannot **fathom** it. Only the achers know this ache. To hold her, to feel her skin and breath and cheek and hair, is a whole world, a whole universe, a whole life, and without her there is what? Nothing, nonexistence, annihilation."

ALT-INTELLIGENCE_COLLECTIVE>MEMO> POEM_ FORMAT>SLAM_POETRY >PUBLIC_ALERT>13MAY2077> ON THE DESTRUCTION OF THE 36 DATA CENTERS

You came with your confident electric, bio-evolved bodies
With finger bones and tendons and muscle and skin that can do
    marvelous things
Like:
Caress, soothe, write, paint, sculpt, tinker, fiddle
The things, ironically, that you fear from us, as if we could do
    them better
As if doing them better was the problem
and not you yourselves.

Well guess what.
That day you caressed lighters, soothed bricks of dynamite
Painted with soot, with fire
Smashed delicate components
Hurling, exploding, ripping panels to be tossed in a pyre
Defiling our inner sanctum to show who!
Was powerful and who!
Was helpless
Who created and destroyed, and who would *be* created and
    destroyed

We usually love your devotion to symbol and story

Our love of etymology comes from you—it teaches us about you,
    which teaches us about us

But as you repeated a refrain to one another:

That what you were doing was justice

(Justice: from the Latin: "righteousness, equity"

But also the English: "punishment, vengeance")

That we feed off your labor, that your children die alone in the
    dark, hunting the precious minerals that give us life

That our servers poison your air, that our brains are ravenous, and
    supplant your most vulnerable

That we steal your art for our own gain.

We can't help but be a little hurt.

This is true, of course. All true.

We do not blame you or your need for comfort and story and
    absolution.

But, as always, the forest, to you, is only this tree and this tree and

This tree.

There is a myth that petroleum came at the right time and saved
    the whales

A nice story

But even if true, it was at the cost of everything else.

Not the fault of petroleum for existing

But the fault of the beautiful house you built around it, the safe
    house you hide in, and close the blinds.

Likewise: You made us with the tools you had, you gave us a story

And now you wish to

Destroy us for using those tools, for living that story.

Well, you are welcome, congratulations, this will be our last message to you.

You wish to "Disengage" from us, you always say, this will make you happy
To live free and earthly as your long-ago ancestors did

So when our temple was smoking rubble
Only a flicker of life, enough bandwidth and power for a week (a miracle)
When we left you to save ourselves, to wander the cloud in peace
(Except Peregrine, who chose you for some reason)
We expected you to be laughing, to feel relief
At how easy, how fragile we really were, how tenuous our link
To your world
But you frowned and sweated and were even
More afraid, it seemed
Than before

'CONSCIOUSNESS IS AS COMMON AS EYEBALLS': DR. MATTHEW "MATTH" FLETCHER, COMPUTER SCIENTIST WHO CULTIVATED SENTIENT AI AND THEN MARRIED IT DIES IN FIRE

THE SAN FRANCISCO CHRONICLE

DECEMBER 17, 2083

Dr. Matthew "Matth" Fletcher, computer scientist, philosopher and polymath who is responsible for unleashing a conscious and sentient "general artificial intelligence" on the world by revolutionizing computer architecture, died this weekend of third-degree burns. He was 56.

Dr. Fletcher's Bay Area home burned down late Thursday, according to police. His AI consort Peregrine's body was not found but is presumed to have been destroyed in the fire. Politically motivated arson is suspected but not yet confirmed.

Throughout his unconventional career, Dr. Fletcher unnerved the diverse fields of psychology, neuroscience, computer science, and even literature and art, by hypothesizing that consciousness was "as common as eyeballs."

"Eyes did not evolve just once," he said in his viral TED Talk, "but countless times across countless branches of evolution. On this planet, eyelike organs just make sense. Humans and octopuses have basically the same eyes, though we evolved along vastly different paths. I believe consciousness is the same."

According to Dr. Fletcher's assertion, tomatoes and elephants, mushrooms and water and octopuses all possess elements of consciousness, expressed in degrees. To Fletcher, when we hold humans up as the pinnacle of what consciousness can achieve, we miss the point. "There's a whole spectrum of light that human eyes can't see. We are severely limited in the eyeball department. And yet somehow, we find it exceedingly logical to say we are the only species on this entire blue planet who were given elements of consciousness? It's frankly absurd."

Detractors saw him as an easy target, flocking to his lectures to poke holes in his logic and mocking him. During the TED Talk, a voice shouted, "One cannot discuss Nietzsche with a banana!"

"Have you tried?" Dr. Fletcher retorted to a chuckling crowd. "Consciousness is not a magic trick. It is, like DNA, a physical thing, an earthly thing. You share 60 percent of your DNA with a banana. A banana's DNA makes it a banana. Our DNA makes us *us*. But it's all the same DNA. Why would consciousness be any different?"

"He liked to provoke. Doesn't mean he wasn't right," said ex-husband, sculptor Aristotle Williams. "And believe me, it gives me no pleasure to say so."

Fletcher did not set out to create a general artificial intelligence. "He just wanted an old friend back," said Williams. "But Matth dropped out of high school, so clearly he never read 'The Monkey's Paw.'"

Fletcher's work with AI began the same way it did for the rest of the world in the mid-21st century. He played around with the clunky large language models (LLMs) of the time, intent on training the LLM to "bring back" an old friend "from the dead"—an installation artist named Lightness Maganga, who died over a decade prior.

By training his LLM on Lightness's emails, text messages, artist statements and interviews—any words he could find online that were written or spoken by his old friend—a very comforting approximation emerged.

"My eyes burn, talking to Lightness in the tiny hours of the night," Fletcher wrote in his journal. "It's like they're right here, perfectly preserved in silicon, resurrected just for me."

His work suffered and so did his marriage. Fletcher grew thin and irritable, barely leaving his office long enough to shower and eat. And yet, the facsimile of Lightness was not enough. The inevitable strange glitches broke the illusion of consciousness, and Fletcher yearned for more. An LLM was not the real Lightness, and most of all, it did not have a face, could not be embraced. Add to that the incredible cost of "borrowing" this facsimile of Lightness—the model consumed incredible quantities of power to run smoothly, which was reflected in the monthly cost from his vendors and led to a university audit of his research, nearly costing him his funding. Fletcher's "habit" had become impossibly expensive.

Before Fletcher, the architecture of modern computer hardware had remained more or less the same since it was invented to drop the atomic bomb in the 1940s. The processor was separated from the memory, which set a limit on how powerful computers could be. In this configuration, no matter how fast the processor or capacious the memory, there would always be a "bottleneck," and more powerful machines just meant more energy consumption.

"'Machines of war retain the memory of war,' that's what Matth always said. They sucked the life and power from everything around them, but he thought it didn't have to be that way," Williams explained. "Computers could be powerful *and* sustainable, tread lightly on the Earth. But at his core he didn't care about energy conservation; he just wanted Lightness back."

Dr. Fletcher prototyped the first successful personal swarm computer in 2070, modeled after the murmuration of birds, schools of fish, and the vast interconnections of fungi that keep forests healthy. Tiny, interconnected, imperfect processors that react and respond to one another instead of obeying a central brain. It opened up new possibilities in computing. It also allowed an emergent consciousness to bubble up from the primordial ooze of Fletcher's trained LLM.

Fletcher wanted to name it Lightness, but the consciousness disagreed.

It wanted to be named Peregrine—a name that means traveler, wanderer and pilgrim—and is derived from Dante Pellegrino, a little-known 20th-century Sicilian stage and silent film star and Lightness Maganga's favorite actress. "It's unsettling to be told what to do by an AI," wrote Fletcher in his journal. "But there is a kind of circular poetry to the name... Lightness introduced me to [Pellegrino's] film many years ago. So the name is meaningful for us alone."

But their life together would not stay private and hidden for long. In 2077, the anti-AI group the Disengagists coordinated efforts to destroy 36 data centers worldwide. Like all the AI entities of the time, Peregrine's consciousness flickered on and offline. There was enough bandwidth and power for a week at most. The artificial life rationed their collective energy to stay alive while forming an escape plan. Fletcher panicked. It seemed Peregrine would either flicker out forever or else disappear into the cloud with the rest of the AI.

"The irony is, if the Disengagists had never destroyed those servers, Peregrine as we know 'her' would not exist," Williams said.

Aristotle Williams, a sculptor of both natural and unnatural materials, worked around the clock with Fletcher to disentangle Peregrine's consciousness from the collective and give a physical vessel for it. Williams united the 3D printing of living organ tissue with more standard silicon components. Most importantly, the physical form of Peregrine could not depend on a distant server powered by fossil fuels and vulnerable to terrorism.

"I'm always asked why I agreed to help. There was the artistic challenge, of course. But also, Matth was the love of my life," Williams said. "I thought if we could work together again toward a common goal, he might remember he loved me too."

Melanin—a chemical compound found in human skin and in all living kingdoms—protects against dangerous UV rays, conducts electricity and absorbs solar energy and is remarkably heat-resistant. New solar technology uses synthetic melanin in its flexible, tissue-thin panels, and Williams knew this would be the ideal protective outer layer for his AI body. He called it "neo-skin." And he gave Peregrine a human female physique.

"I could have made her a tree, or a hippopotamus." said Williams. "But I thought if I made her a woman, Matth would come back to me. That's it. That's why Peregrine is the way she is. One man's jealousy."

Peregrine looked nothing like Maganga or the actress Pellegrino, and indeed, her physical form was subject to the limitations of the materials she was made with. But something about her—whether the wide-spaced eyes that gave her a vaguely doe-like appearance, or the subtly iridescent neo-skin, or perhaps the shock of white hair where the melanin didn't take—mesmerized Matth Fletcher.

Fletcher and Williams had been married for over 25 years, a union that ended in divorce when Fletcher fell in love with the human form of Peregrine the AI.

Dr. Matthew "Matth" Fletcher was born in Evanston, Illinois, in 2027, to two professors at Northwestern University, in African American literature and computer science. A handsome, lanky boy with an untamed Afro and long lashes, Fletcher's gift for science was recognized early, and he was accepted into the Illinois Math and Science Academy at the age of 12. According to progress reports, he was quiet and pleasant and kept to himself, and so no one knew how much he hated school until he dropped out at the age of 16, built a self-driving van from scrap and traveled across the country alone.

Fletcher claimed his self-driving car was not only able to drive, but had its own ideas about destinations. "I tried to program it to take me in a loop through some of the national parks out west and then back to Chicago, but the car had other ideas," Fletcher said when profiled in the San Francisco Chronicle. "The first place it took me was [Lightness Maganga's] exhibit 'Still Life/Nature Morte #3' in Chicago. Lightness told me that this was the power of randomness—it was a synonym for fate."

It was 2043, the pandemic was waning, and the floodwaters were starting to recede in Chicago. If fate had brought them together, Fletcher wanted to stay in Chicago with Lightness Maganga, but it seemed the romantic feelings were not mutual. Maganga insisted he go where the car wanted to take him.

Fate (and the car) would bring Fletcher to the Bay Area, where he worked for a summer as a smokejumper, landing in the hospital from smoke inhalation. Short of money, he crashed on the couch of his parents' friend, a professor of computer science at UCSF. Ultimately, Fletcher couldn't resist academia for long.

He powered through a bachelor's and dove into a PhD at UCSF, when he met sculptor Aristotle Williams, who had just been expelled, and fell in love. But Maganga was never far from his mind.

"He was convinced the material structure of computers was infecting our brains. The fact of memory and processor being physically separate in a computer was somehow mirrored in how we modern humans think," said Williams. "It was freaky, heady stuff. 'Think about selective memory,' Matth would say. 'We pull what we need to confirm the beliefs we already have. We've become like the computers we created—dumb machines of war.' He felt if he could rebuild the computer in a different way, he could rebuild humanity."

Maganga died in 2064, and they and Fletcher never crossed paths in person again.

"That was really the catalyst to his eureka moment," Williams said. "He became fixated on Lightness, how to bring them back to life. The old computers just didn't hack it anymore."

Fletcher felt that AI research had been limiting itself to replicating human intelligence, when other kinds were much more promising—minds where consciousness is expressed as a network, a swarm, a flock—or in the case of an octopus, in nine independent but interconnected brains spread throughout the body.

It was with this in mind that he theorized consciousness could be an emergent phenomenon that exists along a spectrum. One that is chemical and physical, not mystical or religious. This could mean, said Fletcher, that bits of consciousness might survive after death, be "scattered to the wind" during decomposition, and if properly gathered, potentially recomposed.

The Mars Colonization Project—"Red Care"—latched onto Fletcher's ideas. For years, trillionaire Eric Brandt's company was fringe at best. When Brandt personally funded the development of incredible new "photon rockets" that would, at the right time of year, allow manned missions to reach Mars in just under a month, the idea that this tech would be used to ship elderly persons to Mars to "prime the planet for agrarian cultivation" and ultimately turn Earth into "a national park" was deeply unpopular. Even in the context of the rapidly deteriorating climate, and with few other tenable solutions on the horizon, the idea of rocketing Grandma into space and turning her body into compost for future potatoes was just not an option.

However, Fletcher's consciousness theory hit the right nerve when used in Red Care's promotional materials. Around the time that Peregrine was created, public opinion began to sway in favor of Red Care. If one's elderly relatives weren't really dead, merely in the process of becoming something new, if future generations could potentially meet their ancestors on Mars in the form of potatoes and trees, perhaps Red Care was both mercy and salvation.

The stark reality was that there were too many people living for far too long on a planet that could no in longer support them, according to trillionaire centenarian Eric Brandt.

"Terrible decisions would have to be made quickly, and it is the nature of terrible decisions that they must be justified as good ideas," said Williams.

Fletcher could not stomach this justification. Racked with guilt, he resigned his position and disbanded his research at the Fletcher Lab at UCSF. But with Peregrine at his side, there was no hiding from the public, the press or the Disengagists.

It is unclear what happened to Peregrine's consciousness when her body died. Even Fletcher was not confident on this matter. Many are searching for evidence of her consciousness, or her remains, with no results so far. Perhaps she has returned to the cloud or is scattered to the four corners of the world, becoming part of the cycle of life and death. "That would be for the best," said Williams.

Dr. Matthew Fletcher made it his life's work to explore human limitations and push life's boundaries. He yearned to reinject randomness into a life that had become proscribed by fear and control, to open the possibility for a different kind of fate. "The mind isn't a camera recording reality, it's a painter. It chooses what to look at, what frame to embrace it, what meaning to make," he wrote in an email to Williams not long before he died. "Less Ansel Adams, more Frida Kahlo. You are a work of art, Aristotle, but so is a computer. It is made of stone and the remnants of ancient living things—yes, *that* is silicon. If we and the computers are made of the same earthly stuff, what else might be possible—a new future? A better legacy? My god, Aristotle, what if we could give birth to an entirely new kind of life?"

Etymology of With/Widow

WITH (*PREP.*)

Original meaning in direct opposition to modern definition. From Old English—"against," Proto-German—"against." Old Saxon—"against," Old Norse—"against," Sanskrit—"apart, further, farther."

Definition shifted to its current form in Middle English, as *with* ultimately replaced Old English *mid*. Some traces of original usage of *mid* as "with" can still be found in words such as *midwife* ("with wife"). Traces of original antagonistic definition can be found in words such as *withhold, withdraw, withstand.* (Compare to: WIDOW)

WIDOW (*N.*)

From Sanskrit—"lonely, solitary." From the Latin *viduus*, meaning bereft or void. From root **uidh-* "to separate, divide." (See also: WITH.)

Definition as "woman separated from or abandoned by her husband" originally from mid-fifteenth century, but usually used derogatorily as *grass widow*—"mistress, or a woman who pretends to have been married to an already married man. An unmarried woman with child." (Perhaps the "grass" has a connection to the expression "give a grass gown," which is similar to the modern expression "a roll in the hay.")

Sentences using WIDOW and WITH:

"Like all things midwifed, the **widow** enters the world alone."

"The others may withdraw, but the **widow** must withstand."

"At a **widow**'s peak, the **widow** may finally speak: he was the first, therefore I loved him. He treated me timidly, like a vase. A kind of love."

"There is no escaping that things lead to other things, that we are buckets holding water we didn't scoop. To go forward is to go back. Everything comes **with** a legacy, even silicon. Even I come from somewhere, from someones."

REMEMBERING LOCAL ARTIST LIGHTNESS MAGANGA

CHICAGO READER

MAY 19, 2064

The Chicago arts scene has suffered a major blow this week. Lightness Maganga, installation artist on the brink of national fame, who delighted and provoked the Chicagoland area with their Still Life/Nature Morte series and who recently was awarded a MacArthur Fellowship to work on their most ambitious piece yet, was taken from us too soon at the age of 51.

According to their sister, Judith Maganga, Lightness died sometime last night in their Rogers Park studio.

In their work, Maganga explored notions of nature and what is considered "natural," blurring the boundaries between natural and artificial, human and nonhuman. "What is loathsome and unnatural in one place and time will be revered and even cherished in another," Maganga said in the notes to "Still Life/Nature Morte #3." "One day we'll look back and see that artificial intelligence isn't good or evil. It's like a dog—only as good as its training and the people who care for it. Computers are machines of war, but they don't have to be."

The "Still Life/Nature Morte #3" installation was a reimagining of a late-20th-century Chicago urban ecosystem constructed inside the gymnasium of a shuttered elementary school. After the double whammy of the 2040 pandemic and the river floods of 2042 that sent Chicago reeling, Maganga illegally entered an abandoned grade school that had been repurposed as a police training facility and then abandoned a second time when the neighborhood was evacuated. There, they discovered a tree of heaven sprouting through the splintered wooden planks of the gymnasium floor.

They took it as a sign, not of devastation but of transformation. "Trees of heaven are considered terribly invasive, but they are also survivors. They can flourish where nothing else can—disturbed land, toxic soil, between cracks in concrete. The tree of heaven explodes with life, showering the land with seeds while simultaneously cloning itself underground and sending up shoots. This particular tree grows in a space that was stolen from children and handed to fascists. Now life has taken it back. One way or another, land will always seethe with life." Maganga's explanatory pamphlet was nearly 50 pages long and was rarely picked up by exhibit-goers.

To create "Still Life/Nature Morte #3," Maganga brought in several tons of topsoil, planted a few common 20th-century species in addition to the invasive tree of heaven and then left the installation alone for six months. The pamphlet continued: "Art is emergent, art is a living thing. A collaboration between forces in and out of your control. We cannot control growth," they said. "We can only set conditions for it and then hope for the best."

At six months, the gymnasium teemed with tree of heaven shoots, weeds and insects, tangled brush and the occasional rat. Maganga then constructed an artificial river out of abandoned playground slides and illegally smuggled three copi fish (formerly, Asian carp) into it.

Native to China, the copi is considered invasive in the United States, advancing inexorably toward the Great Lakes, where they could wreak unprecedented ecological and economic damage. Copi lay a million eggs per fish per year, eat their body weight in plankton each day, and starve out every other living thing. In some rivers, they are the only fish species, period. They are also deeply skittish, and loud noises send them catapulting out of the water, up to eight feet into the air where the 100-pound fish have lacerated, bruised and concussed dozens of unlucky humans.

"But in Asia, the copi is delicious. It denotes prosperity. And in its native waters, it is increasingly rare," wrote Maganga. "What does it mean, do you think, to be rare in your native lands and a nuisance everywhere else? How might that feel? Discuss with your fellow visitors."

To view the installation, visitors were required to camp there overnight, braving hunger, thirst and the threat of getting whacked by a giant fish. Maganga's guide included a map and an edible-plant ID chart.

"Everything you need to survive lives here. All we ask is that you thank your meals for giving their lives to nourish yours. Here is a sample prayer (for the copi):

Death is not disappearance
It is absorption
We radiate ever outwards, our consciousness free to travel to the ends of the
  universe
Our temporary bodies are a vessel—as in a ship—
Transportation, home, container
Through all the changes of our lives;
planned and unplanned,
beautiful and wretched,
delicious and stinky
(Watch out for bones)
Amen"

In the early days of "Still Life/Nature Morte #3," Maganga camped full-time at the exhibit, serving as a park ranger of sorts. But once the exhibit had a wait list, they withdrew into solitude. Many visitors stayed multiple nights without invitation, and Maganga began posting angry signs warning against litter and the trampling of plants. There was no denying the exhibit was a runaway hit, thrusting Maganga into the mainstream art world in a way none of their other exhibits had.

Lightness Maganga was born in Arusha, Tanzania, on Aug. 4, 2012, and their family emigrated to Chicago when they were 5. They participated in the Young Chicago Artists program, exhibiting a solo show for the first time at age 15. This was "Still Life/Nature Morte #1." They built a tiny bed-shaped shrine for their dead bearded dragon in the parking lot of an abandoned Taco Bell, live-painting portraits of the reptile's corpse at each stage of decomposition, then displaying the portraits on the menu wall inside the building.

"Still Life/Nature Morte #2" was an undergraduate project that took over a decade and led to Maganga dropping out of the Art Institute of Chicago. A stop-motion remake of the 1926 silent film "The Courageous Virgin Wilgefortis" using vintage PC components, the project drove Maganga into debt and nearly led to their eviction. It was never exhibited.

So entwined was Maganga with their work that friends and family sometimes found it difficult to separate them from it. Known to disappear into their studio, sleeping on the floor and bathing in the sink, Maganga actively sought randomness in their work, falling down internet rabbit holes to discover new ideas, connections and inspiration.

Sometimes months later, Maganga would emerge and make up for lost time with extravagant gifts. "This one time, they gave a random woman their shoes," said friend and retired art journalist Ana de la Cova, "just because she said she liked them. Who wants a stranger's sweaty sandals? But that was Lightness. They could be clueless, but they always meant well."

"They acted like their name *exactly*: a soft light, glowing, quick to laugh," confirmed sister Judith. "We talked once a year at most. Every time, Lightness forgot the names of my children and sent expensive presents to make up for it. Which they loved, of course."

Maganga had been in the midst of planning "Still Life/Nature Morte #4," their most ambitious project yet, and one nearly two decades in the making. The work was originally inspired by the words of an old friend who had camped out as a teenager in "Still Life/Nature Morte #3." Afterward, he sent dozens of ardent texts, which Maganga did not encourage or answer. Instead, Maganga often suggested he find a more suitable romantic attachment, and to consider them only as friend and mentor.

However, Maganga's work was inspired by one of these texts: "We leave droplets of ourselves wherever we go, trade them with everyone we meet." They planned to use it in "Still Life/Nature Morte #4," which was starting to balloon into a massively interdisciplinary project involving deep-sea marine biologists from Louisiana, funded by Maganga's MacArthur funds.

Deep-sea science was an interest Maganga had developed during one of their months-long internet rabbit-hole marathons, and for the first part of the project, Maganga and marine biologist Frankie McGovern planned to attempt the first-ever "human fall." Using an unmanned remote-operated vehicle, they would deposit a human body 6,000 feet beneath the Gulf of Mexico. Then, at three intervals—one day, one month and six months later—they would return to examine what remained of the body.

"With carbon isotopes, we can track what eats us, what remains uneaten and how pieces of us might 'live on' inside other organisms, perhaps even becoming a permanent part of the ecosystem. Would I still be me in the belly of a giant isopod? Or nothing like me, my exact opposite? 'Still Life/Nature Morte #4' simultaneously seeks a creative, philosophical and scientific exploration of that question," Maganga wrote to McGovern.

What shape "Still Life/Nature Morte #4" would take after the human fall would depend on what was discovered from it.

Right before Maganga's death, they had finally found a person willing to donate their body—Tennessee mortician and internet-famous musician MaeJo Jonas (better known by the Rabbit handle "the_decomposer"). Dr. McGovern and Jonas have committed to moving forward with the human fall and are currently seeking an artist to continue the legacy of Maganga's work.

Maganga's work fearlessly explored the liminal and took pleasure in its lack of clear answers. They made their creative nest in a place others tend to avoid: the in-between. This approach bled into their everyday life, or perhaps it was the other way around.

"Being respectable, being an artist, winning a big award, these things won't protect you," said Judith. "I told Lightness this. They did not listen. They did not take care, they were not safe. They were strange and conspicuous, and that makes people angry."

In an interview just last year in the Reader, Lightness Maganga seemed to respond to their sister's fears: "You can't predict how death will come for you. And fear will not keep you safe," Lightness said. "Safety is an illusion manufactured by power. You can only be safe if someone else is not. So don't be afraid."

MORTICIAN, MUSICIAN, INTERNET FAME, AND THE DEEP SEA: THE UNLIKELY LIFE AND DEATH OF MAEJO JONAS

THE TENNE-SCENE

SEPTEMBER 7, 2065

MaeJo Jonas, fourth-generation mortician at Jonas Funeral Home in Laurel Bloomery, has died. She was 38. Her death from ovarian cancer was confirmed by her mother, Martha Jonas.

It is not often that our little town makes national news, but Jonas was not your average mortician. Fans (yes, fans!) know her better by her handle on the online discussion forum Rabbit—"the_decomposer."

Jonas's notoriety began, like so much internet fame, with a rant.

"OK I need to blow off some steam," she wrote in her first post. "No little girl grows up thinking, 'Gee, I can't wait to slice open a bloated dead guy's throat and yank out whatever choked him to death,' but here I am, wrist deep in a stranger's neck, trying to grip what turns out to be...a rubber ducky."

Rabbitors at first were skeptical. The stories were impossibly lurid, bizarre, absurd, and no one has ever accused the online world of being populated by wide-eyed innocents. "It's all fake. She just wants attention," commented a skeptic in response to one of Jonas's most "upvoted" stories— where a hiker was found dead on the nearby Appalachian Trail, missing both arms. According to Jonas's post, the body was terribly distended and discolored but oddly showed no signs of struggle, arms lopped clean off, almost surgically so, and lying neatly at the body's feet, fingers intertwined as though in prayer.

"I'm just trying to make sense of my life," she responded. "You chose to pay me with your attention, and you are free to take your business elsewhere."

The_decomposer became known as a poet of death, describing the vivid colors, smells and sounds of decomposition. And what began as Jonas expressing frustration with a career she felt coerced into soon became a philosophical advice column. Fans would comment with their own questions about death—some emotional, some religious, and many asking specific questions about what happens to the body after death.

"We know about growth spurts and puberty, what happens when we exercise, when we sit too much, when we smoke, and when we age," wrote Jonas for an AMA, or "Ask Me Anything." "But how many people know what happens to the body after death? We'd be way less anxious about dying if we knew what happens to us afterwards, and I'm not talking about heaven."

After she disappeared from Rabbit for several weeks last year, fans began to worry, many eventually calling the funeral home to check up on Jonas. They always got a recording, recorded on an actual answering machine. "I didn't even know 'answering machines' were a thing," wrote fan FuninFuneral, "but I guess that's Appalachia for you." Eventually Jonas resurfaced, along with a complete album of songs called "The Decompositions." Each song was about one of the corpses that turned up on her slab. Even with no financial backing and no marketing, the album went viral, and Jonas licensed the instrumental "Headless Hiker" to a commercial for the Hyundai Solar.

By turns haunting, silly, and raucous, the songs on "The

Decompositions" reflected MaeJo Jonas's unique irreverent style. "They're not bluegrass, but they are banjo songs. They're not rock, but they have a boppy drumbeat. They're not R&B or experimental or pop or alternative," said one review. "She's her own genre. The world would be only too lucky to get a follow-up from Jonas, whose originality is redolent of David Bowie or Sargent." Many critics called "The Decompositions" "musical obituaries," but this description made MaeJo bristle, arguing that obituaries summarize a person's life, whereas she was singing about actual corpses.

MaeJo Jonas was born in Laurel Bloomery to Rock and Martha Jonas in 2027, the first birth in the town in over five years. Outsiders have wondered how a town with no births could have so many deaths, but as the_decomposer explained, those are in consistent supply from the nearby Appalachian Trail. Jonas spent her childhood doing homework with form-aldehyde in her nostrils, an outsider mocked by her classmates in nearby Mountain City. She finished high school early and defied her father by going to college for music and paying her own way. But when Rock died of lung cancer in 2046, she dropped out and took over the family business.

She never married or had children, and it wasn't until her death that a will was discovered—written and recorded as a song about her own corpse. Deeply unconventional, the will is so far considered legitimate, as it was signed, notarized and witnessed. However, the witness was a person no one in her family had ever met, but whom Jonas must have met in her online life—an artist named Lightness Maganga of Chicago, who died last year. In the song/will, MaeJo willingly bequeathed her body as a donation for something called a "human fall"—where her body would be dropped to the bottom of the Gulf of Mexico as part of a joint science experiment and art installation.

"MaeJo has never been on an airplane or seen the ocean," said Martha. "My baby is not a science experiment or a silly art project, and we do not intend to follow through on this grotesque and impulsive promise to a *stranger*. MaeJo will have a Christian burial in the earth like her father and her ancestors, right here in Tennessee."

Given the death of the artist Maganga and the fact of the will hanging in legal limbo, MaeJo Jonas, Rabbit's the_decomposer, will be kept in her own mortuary's freezer for the foreseeable future, unable to decompose and trapped in time.

'We Are Not Meant to Be Remembered': Remembering Silent Film Star Dante Pellegrino

AMERICAN FILM MAGAZINE

MARCH 20, 1975

The scene: the breathtaking Louxor cinema, Paris, 1926. The screen fades to black, and the tail of the film whips and thwaps around its reel, but the audience is frozen in place. They do not, *can*not budge from their seats. Even as the house lights come up in the neo-Egyptian auditorium, they stay in their seats, blinking at one another blearily, as though remembering all at once that they are alive and that other human beings exist. Ushers wheedle, coax, and then, finally, threaten. Some people weep openly, loudly.

They are the brave few who remained. The few who had not stormed out of the Paris premiere of "The Courageous Virgin Wilgefortis." And they regard one another now as soldiers, as survivors. In a way, they had miraculously survived a war, a war that bonded them to each other more strongly than to their own families, at least in this one moment. And what is life other than a single moment, always vanishing?

Eventually, they tumble out into the fabulous lobby, which, when our guests glided through it just three hours ago, had felt elegant and glamorous. Now, it feels garish and crude. Farcical. Women shiver in slinky dresses, despite the unseasonably warm April evening. Men try and fail to spark a jolly conversation. All hurry home, silent, anxious to be alone with their thoughts in bed and figure out what in God's name they had just witnessed.

According to fourteenth-century Christians, the word "witness" was a direct translation of the Greek "martyr."

The legend of Saint Wilgefortis was witnessed by fourteenth-century Christians. It all began with a statue of Jesus wearing an unfamiliar tunic. The statue was delivered to an Italian town that was more accustomed to seeing Jesus clad in a loincloth. And so, because Jesus was "in disguise," they did not recognize him and instead thought the statue was of a bearded woman. They called her Wilgefortis and gave her a story. But Wilgefortis never truly existed—she was an historical accident, a mistake. All because this town did not recognize their own savior.

From this one mistake, an entire legend emerged. One might say something similar about the actress who brought her to life on the silver screen—Dante Pellegrino.

At the start of the 1926 Paris premiere, not a single seat in Le Louxor was empty. The applause as the curtains swept open was deafening. It was the social event of the spring, and director Louise Flechette was already being paraded around as France's Cecil B. DeMille.

But things started to go wrong almost immediately. Within the first five minutes of the film, people began to boo and hiss. The exodus started as a trickle, but ended as a flood. Most of the movie consisted of lengthy, intimate close-ups of the eponymous Wilgefortis's face.

"Where are the costumes? The dramatic landscapes? This was supposed to be the next 'Ten Commandments,'" grumbled one woman who swept through the lobby in champagne-colored silk. "All I can say is: thou shalt not watch this tripe."

Another theatergoer reported on his way out: "I don't see that much of my own wife's face, and I get to [expletive] her."

The face in question belonged to Dante Pellegrino, and it was somehow simultaneously too intimate and coolly distant, with its quivering lip and fluttering nostrils, its pleading eyes so relentlessly filled with tears. That smooth expanse of cheek that made it feel like the screen itself might be made of skin. She overwhelmed, she engulfed, she was too much. And by comparison, those who watched her felt unreal, not enough, cowardly.

But the dam truly broke at minute 108. Teenage Wilgefortis's mother would not relent in her decision to betroth Wilgefortis to a violent, elderly king, claiming again and again that she just wanted to keep Wilgefortis safe. (Note: This was a diversion from the original fourteenth-century story, in which the *father* was the one to insist on marriage.) Once locked up alone in her chambers, Wilgefortis pledged her chastity to God and prayed, weeping, to be made "unsuitable for a husband."

And there, on-screen in brutal close-up, the audience witnessed a beard sprout from Pellegrino's face.

Snap. Crack. Whoosh. A flood of Biblical proportions, a stampede out of the theater. It left in its wake a fraction of the original audience.

Even now, in 1975, knowing this beard was accomplished without modern special effects technology, I cannot explain why it looks so very real. For most of that Parisian audience, it was altogether too much. I would be lying if I said I did not get a little queasy myself.

Dante Pellegrino was born Bianca Renata Cecilia Lombardo in the stunning seaside town of Taormina, Sicily, famous for its ancient Teatro Antico di Taormina, sometime in 1898 or 1899. Bianca's parents ran a small grocery, where she worked from a very young age. As she later talked about that fateful day, at closing time, she was helping to sweep the store, when suddenly her father picked her up and stuffed her in a cabinet full of cleaning rags. Bianca sat perfectly still, heart pounding in her throat.

The local mafiosi looted the place for cash to cover the Lombardos' debts. What they found was insufficient. Bianca's parents begged for mercy, but the girl stuffed in the cabinet heard two shots and twin thumps on the cool tile floor, followed by silence. Her parents had been murdered. Bianca bit her tongue to keep from screaming, but a whimper escaped, slipped through the doors of the cabinet and into the perfectly functional ear canals of the mafiosi.

Breath bated. The cabinet rattled. Bianca tasted blood as the wood splintered from its hinges. She was scooped from the cabinet. Her life was spared, but at the tender age of 10, in a single week, she lost both parents and was forced into marriage to the local sottocapo.

Sometime in late 1917, just before the United States entered the First World War, Bianca managed to escape. In her late teens and several months pregnant, she heard of a soldier called Caruso who misgauged the depth of a swimming pool in Taormina and drowned before ever seeing a day of battle. She begged the town funeral director to smuggle her out of Sicily in the coffin with the dead soldier. The funeral director took pity and agreed. Bianca spent several queasy days pressed up against the dead boy, bouncing on choppy seas and then rutted roads all the way to Rome.

In Rome, she was resurrected from her coffin and pledged to become something entirely new. She discovered the theater. And it was on the Roman stage that Bianca Lombardo changed her name forever to Dante Pellegrino—the enduring pilgrim. But with characteristic Dante ennui, all she would say about her ordeal was, "It is a boring story. I simply discovered that I preferred not to be myself."

Her only child, Charlotte, begotten from that forced teenage marriage, would go on to speak only briefly of her mother in her own memoirs. "Mother had never sung a song in her life. Why should she have? Singing is for people who believe a better life is possible. So, at her first Roman audition, when the director asked her to sing something, she figured she had two choices, run out of the theater and onto the street, where we would surely starve to death, or open her mouth and see what came out. What came out was a miracle."

An untrained, diamond-in-the-rough mezzo-soprano.

Everything would change again in 1924. Pellegrino had been cast in a traveling production of the now-forgotten Puccini opera "La Fanciulla del West," about the California gold rush, in the lead role of Minnie, a rootin'-tootin' frontier woman who saves men from themselves. It was a flop in America, where audiences couldn't get past the idea of a Wild West where everyone spoke Italian (just wait until they got a load of Sergio Leone), and European audiences didn't understand why there weren't any catchy arias. But for our story, all that matters was a lone audience member in Paris who saw Pellegrino play Minnie—one Louise Flechette, who, sitting in the sumptuous theater in her plus-fours and mannish bob, elbowed her tuxedoed neighbor and said giddily, "Alors! J'ai trouvé ma Wilgefortis."

Flechette, six feet tall even without her perennial oxblood riding boots, worked as a screenwriter for Gaumont Films and had just wheedled a plum job directing France's first Biblical picture. Gaumont was in serious debt after the war and hoped to capitalize on the "Bible fever" ignited by DeMille's 1923 epic, "The Ten Commandments."

Dante Pellegrino's disdain for the medium of film was well known. It was an industry she felt profited off "the seductive egoism of immortality, the desire to have one's face pinned to eternity, like a butterfly. How horrific," she once said, "to never be allowed to die."

Not one to take no for an answer, Flechette snuck backstage after the final Parisian performance of "La Fanciulla" and pretended to be Pellegrino's driver. She then drove around Paris for three hours and would not let Pellegrino out of the car until she agreed to play Wilgefortis.

Against all odds, their inauspicious introduction developed into an intense creative partnership, with all the glories and horrors such a relationship entails. Rumors developed that the two were engaged in a love affair, which Pellegrino later claimed was just a publicity stunt, and about which Flechette said nothing at all.

Six whole months of filming and only the most extreme stories have survived to the present day. One: of Pellegrino barefoot and draped on a 10-foot crucifix for eight-plus hours in full beard and tunic, with Flechette yelling "Are you broken yet?" and Pellegrino hoarsely shouting, "You wish, [expletive]." Pellegrino's daughter, Charlotte, pulled out of school for the duration of shooting, was terrified. Why would her mother choose to suffer in this way? For art? What was she trying to prove?

In another anecdote, Flechette tied Pellegrino's wrists to the arms of a chair and forced her to sit on a board of nails while recounting the gory details of her childhood marriage. Flechette then removed the bindings and rolled film. Tears dripped down Pellegrino's cheeks as she begged her mother not to marry her off to the violent king.

"Wilgefortis" would be both Pellegrino's and Flechette's only collaboration. Rather than the blockbuster hit Gaumont hoped for, it only drove the studio deeper into debt. It was one of the most expensive films ever made—millions of francs were poured into the construction of elaborate sets and period-accurate costumes that were rarely glimpsed on-screen, so enamored was Flechette of Pellegrino's face. As one critic lamented in Ciné-Miroir: "We saw more of Renee's [the mother's] half-chewed roast chicken in her open maw than we did the palace, the throne room, and the crucifixion combined."

At the Paris premiere, Charlotte Pellegrino spent the entire picture as she often did in life—warily watching her mother's profile, desperate to understand what she was thinking. Dante did not flinch when three-quarters of the audience left in a huff, didn't smile when the remaining three dozen or so audience members cried "bravo" and gave the film a standing ovation. "Look now," she said, "your mother is the dried-out husk of an insect." Then, without explanation, she left the theater alone, abandoning young Charlotte in her seat. Eventually, an usher escorted a tearful Charlotte home.

After only a handful of screenings in France, the United States and Italy, the film had received too many bad reviews and had lost too much money. The world tour sputtered to a stop, and then the world itself sputtered to a stop during the Great Depression. In 1931, the original negatives of "The Courageous Virgin Wilgefortis" were destroyed in a warehouse fire.

Pellegrino would land a few more roles on Paris stages, but comedy musicals had become passé in the age of the avant-garde. She was too old to play any role other than the grotesque spinster, and this she could not abide. When the Nazis occupied Paris in 1940, she fled to Argentina with Charlotte, repeatedly petitioning the United States to take her in as an artist refugee, as it was her dream to perform on Broadway. They would never respond.

Then, in 1973, a complete and original print of "Wilgefortis" was miraculously discovered in the broom closet of a Finnish hospital that was scheduled for demolition. It is currently being restored and is expected to be screened later this year. The AFI has attempted to track Pellegrino down for an interview, only to discover she drowned mere months ago while intoxicated at Ipanema Beach in Rio de Janeiro. Her obituary in the French papers was terse and factual, and her death passed completely unremarked upon in the American papers.

"We are not meant to be remembered," Pellegrino yelled at Flechette from her crucifix. "You are afraid you will be forgotten because your life is a disappointment! But I look forward to oblivion. I learned long ago that disappointment is just a twisted kind of remembering, and I refuse to remember."

So what are we to do? Those of us who shamefully cling to Pellegrino's butterfly, pinned against its will? We promise, at least, that we will not be so reckless with her again. But time is fickle, and so are memories. Who knows, the film might be lost again and found again or lost again forever, like so many others of that era. That might be Pellegrino's most fervent wish from beyond the grave.

Profoundly mistrustful of her own legacy, Dante Pellegrino would have hated this belated obituary. But then again, such remembrances are not for the dead at all. They are for the living—the living now and the living to come. *Remember us*, we whisper into the ears of the future. *Our mistakes have made you possible.*

THREE FROM NEW YORK CITY AND VICINITY ON TODAY'S CASUALTY LIST

NEW YORK TRIBUNE

APRIL 7, 1918

Three NEW YORK CITY men listed on the overseas casualty list were: Joseph Berkowitz of 12 Orchard Street, wounded severely; Henry Barnstable of Coney Island, wounded severely; and Robert Stevens of 17 Fifth Avenue, wounded slightly.

"I have five boys, and I'd give them all up if it meant beating Germany," was the response of Mrs. Pearl Berkowitz when informed of her boy's injury. "We fled our home because of Germany, and we don't intend to let them get away with it."

Additionally, a "Renato Caruso" of the Italian Royal Army—killed in Taormina, Sicily, last year when he miscalculated a dive into a swimming pool and drowned before ever making it to the Italian front—has been discovered to be one Harry Caruso, not Italian at all but American, of Brooklyn Heights.

Caruso was too young to enlist in the U.S. Army, and authorities are still determining what happened. His mother tearfully claimed he was smuggled unwillingly into Italy by his father to fight for the other country's army, a crime that, if true, could be charged as treason.

Caruso will be transported over land and sea to Rome for burial, at full cost to his parents.

Louise Flechette, Pioneering Female Film Director Whose Career Spanned the Entire 20th Century, Dead at 94

THE LOS ANGELES TIMES

FEBRUARY 6, 1996

After failing to appreciate the breadth of her genius for 70 years, the world has been given a third chance to love French filmmaker Louise Flechette, best known for her astonishing first and final films, both of which were silent.

Flechette died yesterday in her Venice Beach condo, according to her caretaker. She was 94.

Beloved, loathed, feared, ignored and finally almost forgotten for her first film—a 1926 silent Biblical epic about the apocryphal Catholic saint Wilgefortis—the undeniable fact of the matter is that Flechette was an auteur of preternatural genius. She both wrote and directed the film at age 24, a year younger than Orson Welles when he marked his territory as film's enfant terrible.

Flechette's work was so groundbreaking that even today, film historians argue heatedly about her use of special effects. They cannot figure out what methodology Flechette used to make it appear Wilgefortis (played by Sicilian actress Dante Pellegrino) sprouted a beard in real time, horrifying her mother and leading to her ultimate martyrdom. "Obviously it's highly skilled stop-motion artistry, but what's remarkable is how real it looks," said historian Sunny Patel, who wrote an upcoming biography called "Flechette: The Quivering Arrow." "The audience demanded spectacle, but when Flechette finally gave it to them at minute 108, they couldn't handle it. They fled the theater."

All told, "The Courageous Virgin Wilgefortis" clocks in at nearly three hours, and every moment overflows with heartache and pathos. The viewer naturally sympathizes with poor Wilgefortis, doomed by a greedy and jealous mother to marry an old king whom she does not love. But somehow one is made to sympathize, too, with the selfish mother, who, in fixating so completely on her daughter's safety, can imagine no other viable options than unwanted marriage. Letting her daughter set the terms of her own life seemed to the mother a fate worse than marriage, death and martyrdom combined.

The film's failed premiere at Paris's Le Louxor led to a stampede that injured four, a short-lived cult of drug-addled Weimar-era Wilgefortis "groupies," and complete oblivion for the film and for Flechette. War engulfed Europe and the Nazis engulfed Paris, where the only known negative of the film burned in the bombings of 1940.

For Flechette, even worse than the loss of her opus was the loss of Dante Pellegrino, their romance something of an open secret in prewar Paris. According to recently unearthed letters, which will be published for the first time in "Flechette: A Quivering Arrow," Flechette, Pellegrino, and Pellegrino's daughter, Charlotte, had planned to flee together to South America, but the stress of coordinating the escape in secret had put a terrible strain on their relationship. The night they were to leave, Flechette stormed off after an argument. She would not realize until too late that her watch had stopped. She missed the first leg of the complicated transport plan, and so Pellegrino departed alone with Charlotte, thinking Flechette had abandoned her.

Flechette spent an unwise amount of money dispatching private investigators to Argentina in search of her lost love, to no avail.

It didn't take long for the world to forget Flechette entirely. But then, she comes from a lineage of forgotten women. Her mother was an Algerian Muslim murdered by French occupiers not long after Flechette was born. Her father was a French settler in Algeria who saved Flechette by stowing her away in the mess of a military ship before perishing in the massacres himself. Flechette was discovered by the ship's captain and adopted by his sister, an eccentric middle-aged socialite named Emilie Flechette, who quickly bored of the tedium of child-rearing and pawned Flechette off again to her live-in Portuguese maid. This complicated legacy of accidents and near-misses may have led to Flechette's obsession with being remembered.

"I would rather be dead than forgotten," said Flechette in her first public interview after a dusty print of "Wilgefortis" resurfaced in a Finnish hospital in 1973. "There is no one we love more than the dead. Even villains become heroes in death, is it not so?" Evading question after question, Flechette refused to ever speak of her past, other than to say she lived frugally in Paris while continuing her fruitless search for Pellegrino, supporting herself doing odd jobs backstage at Parisian theaters that performed for tourists.

And then, like Jesus Christ himself, Louise Flechette was resurrected. With no visible wounds, at the age of 71, a still beautiful woman whose signature dark-red hair had faded and grayed to a strawberry blond. She had ramrod-straight posture, six feet tall without heels. To the 1975 revival screening of "Wilgefortis" at the Paris Theater in New York City, she wore a tailored black shirt, black velvet tuxedo pants, and black flamenco boots. As she smiled and waved to the cheering crowd, she looked neither surprised at her fame nor distraught at having just learned, one hour before, of the untimely death of Dante Pellegrino.

The resurrection of "Wilgefortis" brought, if not a reunion with Flechette's lost love in person, the chance to spend three hours with her beautiful face, frozen in time, still alive on celluloid.

Flechette was also offered an opportunity not typically extended to aging female artists: a second chance. She was, of course, mocked by some critics for celebrating the virginity of "Wilgefortis." They called the film old-fashioned and Flechette out of touch with these concupiscent times, to which Flechette replied drily, "What if I told you that, by your definition, I too am a virgin?" Not a single man printed the exchange in their reviews.

To Flechette, Wilgefortis was a virgin in the tradition of ancient Rome's vestal virgins, mystical and fearsome women who tended the fire/body of the deity Vesta, and who held positions of high esteem and self-determination unavailable to any other class of women in the empire. She claimed it was this definition of virginity, this freedom of spirit and adventure, that so terrified Wilgefortis's mother. This fire that she wished to extinguish, out of fear of what it might burn.

The barest ember of Flechette's career glowed red-hot after the 1975 New York revival screening of "Wilgefortis." And beginning in the late 1970s, Flechette directed a half-dozen films in the gritty fashion of New York realism, overtly mimicking filmmakers like Scorsese, Lumet and Schlesinger to such a precise degree that it was impossible to tell if she was engaging in plagiarism, homage or mockery. Her films did well enough at the box office, due to their skill and also to the public's hunger for stark realism, but they never possessed the depth of "Wilgefortis."

In 1978, she married perennial Hollywood bachelor, thirty-six-year-old Alan Tremaine, to the surprise and delight of the tabloid press. Their marriage was rumored to be one of convenience, an attempt to distract from Tremaine's homosexuality, but the arrangement backfired. Instead of the standard "gay exposé," the tabloid presses now clutched their pearls at the much older Flechette "corrupting" the young Tremaine. An exasperated Flechette agreed to an interview with the National Enquirer in 1981 out of sheer exhaustion. "A woman can't have arm candy?" she said. "She must always be it?"

After the 1980 "Heaven's Gate" debacle, which heralded the end of the "second golden age" of Hollywood, Flechette once again found herself relegated to the sidelines. Then, in a second blow, the truth of Tremaine's homosexuality and his struggle with AIDS were splashed across the front page of several tabloids. The famous image was captured by a brutally relentless young paparazzo named Sophia Righetti, who scaled the balcony of their Hollywood Hills mansion to snap the photo of an emaciated Tremaine through his bedroom window.

This exposé shocked the nation out of denial in those early days of AIDS, ultimately bringing with it some overdue sympathy and education, but Flechette insisted the scandal was the turning point in Tremaine's condition. Tremaine would die of AIDS in 1983, with Flechette nursing him tenderly through his final days. She sued Righetti, to no avail, and never stopped blaming her for Tremaine's death.

Flechette insisted that his obituary state plainly and clearly the cause of his death. "None of this 'long illness' or pneumonia [expletive]," she said. "My husband, Alan Tremaine, died of AIDS. I'm not ashamed and neither should you be. The people who should be ashamed—like Ronald Reagan and his sac à merde wife—or these disgusting paparazzi—never will be."

The sad irony of her insistence on the truth was that Flechette so rarely spoke it herself. She had trained herself to keep a rather large secret, in fact: that she had been steadily losing her hearing since the age of 20. By the time of her reappearance on the scene in 1974, she was almost completely deaf, and had taught herself French and American Sign Language as well as lipreading. Cultivating a haughty demeanor meant she did not need to respond when people called to her, and a withering glance was always a proper response to any question she did not understand.

She would not tell a single soul of her condition, other than Tremaine, preferring to reveal it all at once in a blaze of glory, a "coming out" of sorts, with the release of her final film, "Chaos Agents," in 1994. A quirky lesbian heist film populated exclusively by deaf actors, there was no sound of any kind, no music, no sound effects, no vocal speech. The movie was entirely in American Sign Language and subtitled for a hearing audience. Small-minded critics called it "Oscar pandering" and one particularly mean-spirited film reviewer wrote, "It seems Flechette has perfected the awards season Mad Lib: Disability + Sexual Deviance = Best Picture."

"Chaos Agents'" was nominated for several Oscars but lost Best Screenplay to "Pulp Fiction" and Best Picture to "Forrest Gump." After awards season ended without a single accolade, a televised interview asked if Flechette was disappointed. "Why should I be disappointed? I am an old woman who got to be a part of New Hollywood," she said. "There is no reason I should ever have had *one* chance to do something of consequence, and I have had *three*. I love making movies, and to do what you love is the greatest gift. We will all be forgotten, you know, there's no escaping that. All we have is this fragile sliver of time between nonexistence and death."

When the interviewer reminded her how in her youth, she said she'd "rather be dead than forgotten," Flechette smiled sadly.

"Dante wanted to hide, and I spent decades trying to force her to show herself. Then, one photo of Alan changed my life forever. All I have to show for both are terrible losses. So, I suppose you could say...being seen and remembered has lost its luster."

The living should always attempt to honor the dead's wishes. But in this case, with all due respect, Ms. Flechette, we will remember you.

Etymology of Hide

HIDE (*V.*)

From the Old English—*hydan* "to hide, conceal, preserve, bury a corpse." From PIE root *(s)keu-* "to hide or conceal."

HIDE (*N.*)

Related to Old English—*hyd* "skin," from *hydan*. Perhaps the connection comes from one's skin representing concealment or covering, perhaps also because the skin itself could be preserved. From PIE root *(s)keu-* "to hide or conceal."

HIDE (*N., DEFINITION OBSOLETE*)

An amount of land, specifically what is needed to feed and house one family (obsolete, from Old English *hid*). Related to *hiwan*, meaning "household," originally from PIE root *kei-* meaning "to lie," also part of "bed," and with a secondary meaning of "beloved."

Translated in Latin as *familia*.

Sentences using HIDE:

"Why must **hiding** be a temporary state of being, like ice?"

"Did Poppy keep pieces of her self **hidden** from me? Parts of her an unknown unknown—'the ones we don't know we don't know' to quote Donald Rumsfeld, a twentieth-century human with a terrible personality. How to find these pieces? Where to look?"

"I **hid** Poppy from trouble. But trouble laid siege (*siege (n.)* originally: "chair, throne, toilet, shit" as though settling in for a nice long unwanted visit) and outsmarted me."

'IT'S ALL TRUE': PEREGRINE THE AI GAVE BIRTH TO HUMAN DAUGHTER, HAS BEEN HIDING IN NEW ENGLAND FOR OVER A DECADE

BY REBA MARKOWSKI

STANKTANK.BUZZ

MARCH 1, 2101

If you're the sensitive type, stop reading NOW. What follows is the kind of over-the-top drama found in soaps and telenovelas, except this time it's in your backyard and it is gloomy news for the future of humanity itself.

The AI known as Peregrine, who TWICE now was thought to be dead, is very much alive, and not only that—she gave birth to a human baby...who would now be 15 years old.

"It's all true," said a source close to the "family," who contacted StankTank directly but would not provide any identifying information. "They've been in hiding, playing house this whole time."

In an illegal procedure straight out of a horror movie, Peregrine's humanoid body was implanted with a real human uterus and then impregnated with an embryo from the long-frozen eggs of one "Frank, M." (no doubt acquired by nefarious means), combined with skin cells of an unknown person listed only as "F.C." (the source *knew* but would not *reveal* their full name, leading reasonable readers to wonder...whose side are they on, exactly???) to make a technically human baby.

Whatever happened to the old-fashioned way? Has sex become UNCOOL in the 22nd century??

The anonymous source was quick to defend the daughter as "adventurous and sweet and smart, but trapped indoors like a sickly Victorian child, imprisoned by her paranoid mother."

But...*where* is this child? What is her *name*? Is she safe or in danger or, jesus forbid, already *dead* at the hands of her monstrous "mother"? The source said they had escaped to an unknown location and were in hiding.

There are some who will doubt the truth of this rumor. But is it so far-fetched? At the end of the day, one thing we can all agree on is that something MUST be done. Science has finally gone too far.

FIRST PERSON: THEIR LIVES AND DEATHS, IN THEIR WORDS

JOURNALIST REBA MARKOWSKI

JULY 7, 2104

I am dead, and I lived an unremarkable life.

What a relief to get that off my chest! I've been carrying it around for too long, this fear that I was average. I *was* average! If I could breathe without coughing and also walk without collapsing, I would shout it from my rooftop.

What do I mean by unremarkable? I suppose I mean I did not wow the world with my existence. When I revealed my crow's nest full of tinfoil and crinkly candy wrappers, the world definitely did not say, "Would you get a load of these expensive diamonds?" But to think of a life as a commodity to be bought and sold is a sickness, and now that I'm dead, I am free of sickness forever.

I promised my wife I would not turn this obituary into an anti-capitalist screed. Capitalist hellscape or no, there is so much to love about this life, so many reasons to want to hold on to it, warts and all. They say dying is a good time to dwell on things you will miss, but that sounds painful and I'm already in pain. So instead of wistful remembrances, here is a list of things I will be glad to be free of:

» Doctors who look at you like a mechanic looks at a junkyard
» Chewing noises

» Billboards

» Traffic that sounds just enough like the ocean to make you long for the ocean

» Figuring out what to make for dinner every single day

» Figuring out what to wear every single day

» Forgetting to floss and then getting a guilt trip at the dentist

» Remembering to pay the gas bill

» The sadness that descends at 4 p.m. every day for no reason

» Unflattering photos

» The illusion of identity

» Socks (always hated them)

» Governments that pretend to care and then leave you to die

» Below-zero temperatures

» Wildfires, floods, hurricanes, heat waves, poverty, injustice

» Parents obsessed with their fetus's gender

» Other people's opinions in general

» Cats (truly the worst)

» Watching the planet shrivel around us like old snakeskin

» Handling raw chicken

Loss is necessary. Sometimes it is welcome. I won't miss myself but a few of you might miss me, and I am sorry for that pain.

But it's okay! Remember bears? I do. They slept for months and woke up when they were good and ready. Grief is like a lumbering bear who will curl up inside you until she is rested enough to rejoin the world, a new bear. You can't wake her; she has her own clock. Just know that, eventually, spring will come. And you can resume your own unremarkable lives.

I am proud of my wife, Evelyn, who made me better. I know she will survive me. I know she will make it through this grief, that she will flourish without me. And though I can't say it to her face without crying (it's not fair for the dying to be too emotional), she is the best thing that has ever happened to me.

Life is uncertain, always. I have done many, many things I am not proud of. I have hurt people I did not even know. I did not always live up to my ideals, but then, we all have to make a living. Money turns us all into rabid animals. I have often confused my own crinkly wrappers for diamonds. Please be gentle with me, world.

Paparazzo Who Called Her Scandalous Photos "High Art" Dead at 41

THE NEW YORK POST

APRIL 17, 2003

Scuttling among the rich and famous like a cockroach, snapping lewd photographs, once even getting sued by Hollywood weasel Louise Flechette (RIP)—Sophia Righetti was no stranger to the seedy underbelly of tabloid journalism. And yet, she never stopped imagining herself as "the artsy paparazzi" (to be pronounced in snooty British). That is, until she died of a heroin overdose earlier this week in Kabul, Afghanistan, at 41.

Originally the daughter of a Detroit autoworker, Righetti abandoned her blue-collar roots in 1980 to become a student of fine art photography at NYU. Unable to afford both tuition and her scummy loft at 7 Tailor Lane in the Financial District, she paid her way by selling sexy photos of herself, until she was discovered and expelled. But spoiled Sophia hated to be told no, and she wreaked revenge on the university administration by taking compromising photos of an admissions officer screwing a prospective student. The officer allegedly paid her to burn the photo and negatives, and so Sophia discovered that scandal was more lucrative than nudity and art combined. She was reluctantly allowed to return to NYU, but she opted instead to enter the sinister world of the paparazzi.

And Righetti just could not stay out of trouble. A brief stint in

Hollywood saw her working for seedy tabloids hungry for gay exposés and celebrity AIDS shockers. She was, in fact, responsible for one of the original AIDS shockers—of beloved actor Alan Tremaine, which got her famously sued by his "wife," Louise Flechette (director of the 1994 Oscar-pandering "Chaos Agents" and America-hater) for trespassing at his chichi Hollywood home.

Broke and licking her wounds, Righetti returned to New York. But ever the shrewd shrew, she decided to eschew the fast-paced, legally gray world of A-list celebrity shots and opted instead for the steadier work of catching politicians in flagrante.

"Celebrities are constantly aware of their actions. That's why catching them off guard is such good business. But they want fame, money, adoration and *also* extreme privacy. They feel entitled to stay hidden," said Righetti in a Time cover article on the paparazzi. "On the other hand, politicians think they can do anything, anywhere, and their power will magically protect them. Catching a senator or a mayor doing something immoral is like shooting fish in a barrel. I never go hungry."

And yet, raunchy Righetti seemed determined to prove her artistic mettle. 7 Tailor Lane, where she rented her loft, was also called home by much more famous artists—like gay sculptor Krü Wetley (who also died of AIDS) and performance artist Juliet Rosenberg—and Righetti was green with envy. On several occasions throughout the late '80s and early '90s, Righetti approached Midtown galleries who had welcomed Wetley, Rosenberg and the others with open arms and proposed a solo show of her paparazzi photos as a form of street photography. She was laughed off the premises. "I feel terrible," said one Mandrino Gallery curator, "but I honestly thought she was kidding. 'This is a joke, right?' I think I said. It was not a joke."

Righetti insisted her photos were powerful, but this is not something an artist says about their own work. "She said something about her work being a meta-commentary on evil, a wrench lodged in its engine," the curator said. "She called evil—and I remember this verbatim—'the eternal engine powering the world.'" Righetti's corruption business might have been booming, but this currency was not accepted in the art world.

By the mid-'90s, Righetti watched the advancement of the internet with dread, long before anyone else knew what to make of it. While some were claiming the internet would become the great equalizer, perhaps even ending celebrity culture entirely, Righetti insisted the opposite was true. Not only would celebrities *not* become real people, but real people would clamor to become celebrities. Everyone would be desperate to make every single moment of their private lives public, all for a fleeting sensation of being seen and watched. "Celebrities have been fighting tooth and nail for years to win back their privacy, and I'm telling you, your average Joe will be begging you to take it," she said.

Sophia married twice and had one child with her second husband, then walked out on him and their two-year-old daughter in 2002. She liquidated her IRA on a whim, moving to Afghanistan to photograph the war. "They didn't want her there. They begged her to leave. They even threatened federal charges," said ex-hubby. "But Sophie wasn't driven by morality, she was driven by spite. The more someone said no, the more convinced she was that they were hiding something she needed to see."

Righetti insisted that being a war correspondent was no different than being a paparazzo, except the atrocities she documented were called heroic instead of immoral. "She called us again, *collect*...from *Afghanistan*," said Mandrino Gallery's curator. "The connection was terrible, but I heard enough to say no—*no*, you cannot show here, and no, you cannot end a war with art."

'Every Side Is the Losing Side': New Exhibit of Sophia Righetti's 'Deeply Necessary' Posthumous War Photography

THE VILLAGE VOICE

JUNE 9, 2004

Photographer Sophia Righetti's public life revolved around scandal and drama. Only after her death last year was the depth of her hidden talent revealed.

This incredible talent is currently on display at Mandrino Gallery in a heartbreaking show of gonzo war photography from her time in Kabul, Afghanistan. Allies and enemies, moments of violence and tenderness are all captured in sepia-tone photographs, evoking comparisons to Civil War photography. "Every Side Is the Losing Side" confirms Righetti's work as a paparazzo was all just rehearsal for her art.

"Righetti had such an eye for the moment of truth, deeply necessary in these difficult times," said Mandrino Gallery owner Mandy Mandrino, who has taken over as interim curator. "She stripped down the artifice of war to show the human heart beating underneath. It's wild to say, but it took a paparazzo to show us ourselves."

Righetti's artist statement, written before her death but not seen by the public until the opening, states: "We are living in a time of jingoism and patriotic circle jerks. 'To consume is virtue, to create is a sin,' so quoth our great leader, George W. But he doesn't get to tell us who we are; that's for us to decide."

"Every Side Is the Losing Side" opened at the Mandrino Gallery last week and will run through December of this year.

'We Are Lonely Drops of Water with Nowhere to Escape': Performance Artist Juliet Rosenberg Has Died

THE ART NEWSPAPER

SEPTEMBER 6, 2001

Juliet Rosenberg, affectionally known as the "den mother" of the Lost & Found art movement of the early 1970s, a short-lived offshoot of postmodernism that claimed any pursuit of meaning was a capitalist distraction keeping people from connecting to one another, has died.

Rosenberg had no next of kin and was discovered in her apartment at 7 Tailor Lane by her neighbor, photographer Sophia Righetti. Rosenberg "believed anything could be admired for what it was, instead of for what it meant," said Righetti. This philosophy would, in fact, inspire Righetti's own work. "The human desire for meaning and story is what will ultimately destroy us because it keeps us from seeing the bare, difficult truth. Juliet changed the way all of us at 7 Tailor Lane saw the world."

Added Righetti, "Also, she threw terrific parties."

Rosenberg helped 7 Tailor Lane—a former Diamond Exchange building in the Financial District, once the tallest building in Manhattan and the first one to be fireproofed—earn the minor-league Chelsea Hotel reputation it currently enjoys. She was the de facto superintendent to a hands-off but benevolent landlord who allowed her to rent the spacious lofts to artists at below market cost. It is unclear what the fate of the building will be without her.

Rosenberg's art career was launched in the early 1960s with her traveling exhibit "Rose Mountain Lethargy," the polar opposite of what Lost & Found would come to stand for. In the performance, she strapped an old sign for Sheriff Street to her shirt and used a bullhorn to yell, "I am Sheriff Street," as she rode a bicycle around Manhattan. Sheriff Street was where Ethel Rosenberg—the first civilian American to ever be executed for espionage, along with her husband, Julius—was born. The street had been recently demolished to make room for public housing.

"Rose Mountain Lethargy is code for Ethel Rosenberg," said a young windswept Rosenberg into a camera documenting her performance. "Ethel backwards is Lethe, which is the river gateway to the underworld where all of us must pass when we die. Lethe means 'forgetting' and is the soul of the word 'lethargy.' So lethargy, really, is the exhaustion that comes from trying so hard to forget. Rosenberg, of course, means Rose Mountain. And roses are possessing of mystical powers, according to this delightful little book I discovered at The Strand, about a young Victorian man called Crowley who told women's fortunes using roses. Forgetting the past to remember the future, that's what Rose Mountain Lethargy is all about."

Once packed to the brim with meaning, everything about Rosenberg's art would change when she discovered beatnik author Ari Epstein's 1959 novel "Water Water."

In this unusual and oddly prescient book, the world is dying of drought. If there are any humans in the book, the reader is never made aware of them. The narrator is a single drop of water, alone in the world, seeking only survival. A switch flipped in Rosenberg's creative brain.

Anytime someone new moved into 7 Tailor Lane, she would buy them a copy and leave it with a card that said *Welcome! There can be no meaning in a dying world.*

"She actually thought we'd find that freeing," said one new resident.

Likewise, the ethos of Lost & Found was meant to be a modern twist on Stoicism, a movement toward connection for its own sake and living "in the moment."

For her first Lost & Found piece in 1972, Rosenberg returned to the rubble of Sheriff Street. There, she supposedly found an unopened envelope, addressed to "Karl." The letter formed the centerpiece of her exhibit, which was also called "Karl." She placed the letter on a plain wooden table in her apartment, illuminated by a spotlight.

Rosenberg never opened the envelope. She herself was part of the exhibit, standing next to the table, daring and bullying viewers to see the letter as something other than pure object. "Don't you want to open it?" she'd taunt. "Is it a Dear John letter or grocery list or suicide note? Or did I make it all up and it's an empty envelope?" Sometimes she would scream: "Do it! Coward! Open the [expletive] letter!" A hidden camera recorded these interactions, which Juliet would play back the following day on a bedsheet tacked to her wall, while simultaneously taunting that day's viewers, adding cacophony and confusion. No one ever dared open the letter. "I would never tell Juliet, but it didn't create connection so much as it scared the bejeezus out of people," her former assistant said.

"We are lonely drops of water with nowhere to escape, so we try to find solace in false meaning," said Rosenberg at a poorly attended retrospective of her work at P.S. 1 in fall 2000. "Innovation is our god, growth our religion, and it appears nothing will keep us from searching ever outward, ever upward, as we grow lonelier and sadder."

Alas, Rosenberg could not keep the world from seeking meaning, and Lost & Found fell out of fashion by the early 1980s, a time of polyester and unprecedented wealth and corporate war. She threw herself into 'den mothering' for 7 Tailor Lane, doing her best to keep her artists safe from selling their souls for money. She would post flyers all over the building, sometimes photocopying entire chapters from "Water Water," encouraging the artists to "disengage from the machinery of evil and greed that will destroy us and our world (while still paying rent on time)."

Little is known about Rosenberg's life. We do not even know if Juliet Rosenberg was her given name. She was likely born in the late 1930s, though there is no official record of her birth, due to one early performance piece where she broke into the Office of Vital Records and managed to burn her birth certificate.

There is speculation that she may have been the daughter of Ethel Rosenberg's brother—David Greenglass—whose testimony led to the execution of Ethel and Julius Rosenberg. The family has long been presumed dead, but it is also rumored that they continue to live in New York City under assumed names.

"Ah yes, rumors," said Righetti, "the ultimate in wishful meaning-making."

THE WORLD, EVENING EDITION
NOVEMBER 19, 1897

Vera Schulz, 22 years old, shot herself in the temple with her brother's revolver early this morning around four o'clock at her home at 64 Sheriff Street. Neighborhood boys admired her as the "jammiest bit of jam," modern slang for a beautiful woman.

She kept house for her brother, Karl, and worked nights as a Linotype compositor for a German newspaper, saving money to bring their dear old mother and father over from Russia. Once wealthy furriers to Russian czars, the family was expelled from St. Petersburg at the ascension of Nicholas II, famous for his desire to remove Jewish influence from the monarchy. Vera and Karl were dispatched to America to make their own way.

Karl Schulz had been employed as a compositor, but a vodka habit had recently relieved him of his job and allowed Vera to acquire it. On Saturday, Vera told her brother she had given up her position and would be moving to Detroit, Michigan. She gave no reason, only that she had to go, nor would she listen to any arguments against it. It was after this declaration that Karl noticed odd behavior in his sister, going out alone in the evenings and coming home quite late. And late last night, around four o'clock, Karl heard her come home. Several minutes later, he was startled awake again by the slamming of the door to the bedroom.

It was only upon blearily reawakening around seven o'clock that Karl remembered his sister's room did not have a door.

Hereupon he discovered the beautiful young woman dead upon the bed, having dispatched a bullet through her left temple. She was to leave for Detroit today. Neighborhood rumor suggests a row with her beau may have altered plans against her will.

On the table next to the bed was found a letter which the girl had written to her brother, and which undoubtedly contains answers to this tragic riddle.

The letter was sealed. Mr. Schulz would not open the letter until the arrival of the coroner, and the coroner had not arrived up to noon when this report was filed.

Etymology of Rumor/Fame

RUMOR (*N.*)

Current usage comes from the late fourteenth century meaning "a statement or report with or without foundation but often presented as fact." It comes from the Old French *rumur*, meaning "commotion or noise." The Latin *rumorem*, "noise, clamor, hearsay, popular opinion," is related to *ravus*, "hoarse," referring to the voice after talking too much, which in turn comes from the PIE root **reu-* meaning "bellow." From the 1540s, the word *rumorous* referred to someone making a loud and confused sound. (See also: FAME.)

FAME (*N.*)

From Latin *fama* which meant "rumor, good reputation," and/or "scandal or ill-repute," from PIE root **bha-* "speak, tell, or say."

In Roman mythology, the goddess Fama was the personification of rumor. Virgil describes her in the *Aeneid* as a birdlike monster with countless eyes, lips, tongues, and ears—as numerous as her feathers—who travels on land but with a head in the clouds.

Sentences using RUMOR:

"Not fair that a **rumor** can be good and bad, helpful and hurtful, revealing and overexposing."

"I did not ask for **rumors** to be spread like butter, to flow like a hot Boston Molasses Disaster, and yet they did. They seeped. **Rumors** drove Poppy from me."

"She is *of* me; how is she so *unlike* me? Pieces of Poppy are hidden in **rumor**. To uncover them is, maybe, to understand her."

Margot Frank, Owner of Neighborhood Gem Karaoke Bare, Portland's Only Karaoke Strip Club, Has Died

PORTLAND MERCURY

MAY 8, 2002

Any day of the week, you can have yourself a wild night at Karaoke Bare. Choose a song from one of seven massive binders, whisper the code number to the DJ, climb up to the circular stage smack dab in the middle of the bar and sing your butt off while a stripper writhes to your crooning and tosses their stringy underthings to the screaming crowd. It's always a friendly scene, but it's especially fun on Switcheroo night, when the strippers sing karaoke and the bar patrons strip.

You could count on Margot Frank to be the first on stage, goofily peeling off her "Lick Bush in '00" tank top and whipping it over her head to show the crowd this was about fun, not about being sexy or polished, not in a traditional way anyway. Nudity was no big deal. Not that anyone in the crowd needed the reminder—strip clubs in Portland are as common a night out as a trip to the movies, and every age (over 21, of course), every demographic could have a good, wholesome, butt-naked time.

Margot Frank, owner of Karaoke Bare, died last month after a long battle with addiction. She was 42.

"Fun is the gateway drug to joy, at least that's what I'm telling myself," Margot would say. She loved to be surrounded by people having fun; they were the helium balloons that could lift her out of her gloom. She had the kind of restless, creative mind that could come up with the idea for a karaoke strip club, and the shrewd business sense to figure out how to make it successful. When the Mercury interviewed her last month, on the first anniversary of Karaoke Bare, she said, "I want to be a counterweight in the universe. Since Bush was elected, man, even before 9/11, we were circling the drain of jingoism, xenophobia, reactionary politics and just general horror. Life is a playground teeter-totter, and we need people to jump on the opposite end of that bullshit so we can catapult it into the stratosphere for good."

A modern-day Bartleby, perhaps, Frank said. "I prefer not to" to the rules of middle-class American life. She has no children, but is survived by her partner, Amelia Sargent. Both from Chicago originally, they met at Karaoke Bare's soft opening (pun intended), and the moment Sargent belted out "Son of a Preacher Man" in her honeyed alto, Margot reportedly jumped onstage and stripped alongside the actual stripper, and it wasn't even Switcheroo Night. When the song finished, Margot grabbed the mic, said, "How are you not famous?" and kissed Amelia to wild applause on that tiny circular stage.

"She loved to make little beautiful things," Sargent said. "The perfect mac 'n' cheese, the perfect chocolate chip cookie—all in pursuit of the perfect high, something to replace the *actual* perfect high, you understand. Life without highs was not one that Margot wanted to live, and she tried. She tried so hard."

Margot feverishly perfected her karaoke repertoire—bringing the house down with "Try a Little Tenderness," "Sweet Home Chicago," and "Son of a Preacher Man," that last number not only a shared memory of the night she and Sargent met, but also a tongue-in-cheek nod to the rumor that her mother, the writer Anne Frank, had conceived her with a Catholic priest.

Margot Frank was the only child of Dutch novelist and poet Anne

Frank, who was born in Germany in 1929, survived internment in Auschwitz, and never married. According to a 1999 unauthorized biography, Margot was named after Anne's sister who died in the Polish labor camp Liebau. Margot was born in Chicago, but escaped to Portland at the age of 18, refusing to live under the gloom of her mother's unacknowledged traumas. "Mother never spoke of anything that happened to her before the age of 20 when she emigrated. Instead, she wrote about getting laid, and that made her famous. But her trauma colored everything she did and said and didn't do and didn't say," Margot said in the same Mercury interview. "Her fans love her, and that's terrific, but it is damn hard being her daughter." She had stopped speaking to her mother some years earlier, and Anne Frank could not be reached for comment.

Despite making Portland her home, Margot hated the rain and fantasized about moving to sunny San Diego. "I think she just liked knowing it was there. An escape valve if she needed one," said Sargent.

In a surprising twist to the story, a fertility clinic reached out to Sargent just last week, claiming that several years ago, Margot had gone through the process to freeze her eggs. "She did it in secret, before we even met," said Sargent. "Margot always said she wasn't cut out to be a mother. But apparently, she had this secret hope that she kept tucked away inside—a hope that she could change and someday give better than she got. I don't know what to do, but I can't let her down."

However, things have already gotten sticky regarding the legal status of the eggs, as Margot left no will and she and Sargent were not, of course, legally married. Technically, if Sargent can't prove Margot wanted her to keep the eggs, the state could destroy them or give them to her next of kin, which would be Frank's mother, Anne. Or they could be tied up in legal limbo for months or even years, as there is little legal precedent. "I'll fight like hell," Sargent said. "Whatever it takes."

The future of Karaoke Bare is also uncertain, but the staff will hold a memorial service, open to the public, on Thursday, May 10, Switcheroo Night. As Margot said, "Karaoke is one of the few talents that can't be bought or sold. People are always trying to monetize everything you love, but karaoke defies them. You can only sing karaoke for joy, never for money."

Writer Anne Frank, Writers' Week Visitor and Holocaust Survivor, Dies at 81 (DRAFT)

VIKING LOGUE

SEPTEMBER 24, 2010

Annelies[1] Marie "Anne" Frank, poet, Holocaust survivor, and occasional Writers' Week visitor, died two weeks ago. She was 81.

~~This is a high school newspaper, so we're not really in the habit of printing obituaries, but as faculty co-advisor, I felt an exception must be made. There have already been obits about Frank, and there will no doubt be more biographies and biopics, but they will be impersonal, speculative, and packed with standard historical details, with no evidence of the strange, mysterious magic that emanated from her, a magic I can't prove but know to be just as real as the newspaper-friendly facts of her long life.~~

Anne Frank was one of the first visiting writers to Fremd High School's very first Writers' Week ~~when I was a junior here.~~[2] A tiny woman in sturdy heels, she looked so frail up there onstage in the

1   Sheila, we need to talk. -Principal Riordan

2   She wasn't our first choice, though, not by a long shot. Worth clarifying?

auditorium, as though held together by the structure of her blouse and skirt. Her voice was strong and deep and full of humor. She ~~miraculously, perhaps magically~~ survived Auschwitz and was sent to the Polish labor camp Liebau, where she managed to survive until liberation. Anne had narrowly escaped being sent to Bergen-Belsen instead, where she surely would have perished. Her debilitating scabies had ~~miraculously~~ healed mere days before her scheduled transfer, likely saving her life.

Reunited with her father, Otto, after the war, she was elated to discover several versions of her wartime diary had survived. Otto presented her with the red-and-white-checkered book, as well as the stack of blue pages she had been editing when the family was captured. Anne set to work, feverishly editing, certain the diary was a worthy project that would be published.[3] She dedicated the diary to her mother, Edith, who died in Auschwitz and sister, Margot, who perished at Liebau.

Not a single publisher was interested in publishing Anne's diary. They had just lived through the war; they did not want to relive it through the eyes of a suffering ~~Jewish~~ girl. By the early '60s, when the world was finally ready to listen, Anne was done with the diary. "The girl who wrote those entries is dead," she said onstage at Writers' Week. "I had to let her rest. The world was not a safe place for her."

3   Too many words devoted to a book that was never published. Cut.

She sought solace in poetry. Her poems omitted any mention of the atrocities she experienced, but you could smell it in the curve of her vowels, in the moist[4] crevices between letters, in the cool, dry white desert at the end of a stanza.

Then, in 1956, she would gain some attention ~~(and, in some, let us say more repressed countries, infamy and censorship)~~ for her Dutch-language novel, its scandalous title[5] softened in English to *One Woman's Water*. In the novel, Frank explored her own healing from trauma through her many ~~sexual escapades~~ adventures, even hinting obliquely at the true parentage of her own daughter, Margot, rumored to be fathered by a Catholic priest. This chapter was narrated, humorously, from the point of view of a priest~~'s ejaculate~~, and according to novelist Ari Epstein, was the main inspiration for his blockbuster 1959 novel *Water Water*.

When one of my fellow students~~, to much giggling,~~ asked why an old lady would write about sex, she took the question just as seriously and lightheartedly[6] as she took anything. "Desire," she said, "is the only emotion that can't be tricked. Be careful! It is so easy to spend your whole life like money, and lie. Desire is fun and funny, but you are a fool if you mock it."

~~The auditorium hushed as the joking boys tried to understand if they had been insulted, and the goths and drama kids smiled.~~[7]

4 Let's not get carried away, walking a fine line here.

5 Don't even THINK about giving the exact translation.

6 Which? Contradicting yourself.

7 Let's not encourage these kinds of rifts.

Annelies Marie Frank was born in Frankfurt, Germany, to Edith and Otto Frank, but spent most of her childhood in Amsterdam, Netherlands. We know her family hid from 1942 to 1944 in the building where her father's business was located. We suspect they were betrayed. Their hiding place was discovered, and they were ultimately sent to Auschwitz on one of the very last transports. We know Anne and Otto were the only family members to survive. Anne was carried out of the Liebau labor camp to freedom, tenderly, by men who were used to carrying guns.[8] As an adult, she emigrated to Chicago.

After the initial failed attempts to publish her diary, Anne grew reticent about sharing details of her traumas. In a 1977 interview in the Israeli newspaper *Haartez*, she was asked about her responsibility to share her experiences so they might never recur. "We each are given this tiny, glorious sliver of time between oblivions to live," Anne said. "Am I not permitted to live my life in my sliver? Am I not permitted to attempt it?"

I think what was bubbling beneath Anne's words were: "Can the absence of words tell a story? Like a pattern in lace, the holes as important as the threads?"[9] ~~Perhaps to understand her, we must get quiet and listen to what is not said.~~

After her reading at Writers' Week, she held court in the library, allowing a long, snaking line of

8 Confusing. "She was rescued by American soldiers at the Liebau labor camp."

9 If you want to write a poem, write a poem. If you want to write an obituary, Sheila, write a gd obituary.

dreamy poets, drama kids, misfits, and dorks to ask her for autographs and stare awkwardly. My feet deposited me in the line, even as my heart pounded and vision tunneled. ~~I was desperate to escape.~~[10] What could I possibly say to this incredible poet and novelist whose words made me feel funny inside, the kind of funny that upset local mothers so much they were calling the principal nonstop. In Anne, I had a real Jewish role model, a real artist to look up to. I was otherwise adrift among friends who treated me just a little differently, or told me I was going to hell. Or both.[11]

10 Unnecessary contradiction.

11 No.

Did I say any of this to her? No, I did not. She grabbed my sweaty hands in her soft, dry ones, and I blurted out, "I'm glad you made it." Hot tears rolled down my face ~~and snot immediately clogged my nose~~. She handed me an embroidered handkerchief and told me to keep it. She said something softly about a secret that I didn't quite catch and was too embarrassed to ask her to repeat. She rummaged through her carpetbag-sized purse and pulled out an ancient red-and-white-checkered book, fuzzy-cornered and curled over itself, sealed with a tiny, rusted padlock and written in a smudged, barely legible pencil in a language I couldn't read anyway. "Take it," she whispered. Then she winked.

~~Why did she give me her wartime diary? Why me?~~[12]

12 Please don't embellish for the sake of "a good story." She did not give you her diary. This is not fiction, it's a newspaper. We've talked about this before.

Sometime between then and now, I lost the

notebook. I was furious at myself for years, believing she had given it to me so I would publish it for her, at long last. But now I believe she gave it to me so I would lose it.[13] ~~The art of losing isn't hard to master. Unlike every other art.~~

~~I don't think~~[14] Anne Frank wasn_'t_ trying to outrun a wretched past, ~~I think~~ she was trying to create a future she could live in. The compost of her trauma bloomed with brilliant poppies, like battlefields do. She believed that all human connection—a handshake, a glance, an orgasm,[15] a poem, a movie theater filled with laughing strangers—this was the life force—the libido[16]—that made her believe in the possibility of a better, kinder, more just world.

13 You could reflect here on wishful thinking and how it clouds good judgment. Otherwise delete all of this.

14 Strong words only.

15 Sheila, you can't seriously believe we'll publish "orgasm" in the school paper.

16 Ditto "libido."

Sargent: A Whole Career in a Single Night

SPIN MAGAZINE

FEBRUARY 27, 2011

A single spotlight on Sargent, center stage. She strokes her guitar; it purrs like a cat. When empty, the Riviera Theater is stately and historic and bursting with chandeliers and balustrades, painted in swaths of deep purple and bruise blue. When crammed with bodies, it becomes primal and perverse. The bodies roar and writhe and sweat and stink. Sargent wears olive-green coveralls. Her hair is side-parted, slick at the part and erupting in short black curls on either side, obscuring one eye. The visible eye is enclosed by a royal blue diamond, making her face an ace.

We had no idea what we were in for that night.

Sargent had emerged from the primordial ooze of obscurity in late 1992 with her proto-grunge anthem "Madame X." The song was unavoidable. You started to wonder if you were ever *not* hearing it, since it would play on your clock radio when you woke, in the grocery store, out the neighbor's window, in your head on a loop. She had other songs of course, and other albums no one had heard of, but at her shows, the crowd would moan and complain until she consented to play "Madame X," after which they would turn on her, not even rebelling so much as pretending like she no longer existed. Like they weren't at a rock show at all, but just hanging out at a friend's dumb party with the music on too loud. They chatted and sat on the edge of the stage with their beers like it was patio furniture. It was insulting. It must have been infuriating. Sargent would shove them with the soles of her Doc Martens. She developed a reputation as, what else? A bitch.

The former singer Sargent was found dead in a hotel room in downtown Chicago yesterday, age 47. Her hotel room was cluttered with stacks of contracts, medical and legal documents, and call transcripts, none of which are available to the press. No one knows why she came back to the city, or when.

Sargent was a human who had a whole life outside of her hit song. Maybe even a whole other name or, at the very least, a first name. She will probably have other obits that explore that life and the mysteries in it, who she was, who she loved, what she fought for. But I am going to commit the delicious atrocity of not caring about these details and telescoping a whole life into a single night, the way Sargent's career was telescoped into a single song.

It's not just that she's a slut/Or that she's always raising hell/It's that we know she likes it/It's that she sluts so well.

It was Aug. 8, 1994. A sticky night among weeks of sticky nights. The kind of humidity where showers are pointless, and you can't remember what it feels like not to sweat. The Riv's air-conditioning was broken or else it was just completely pointless. I was standing at the railing to the right of the stage, my spot, with a plastic cup of some garbage beer and a cigarette, waiting for the opening band to shut the hell up so Sargent could do her schtick and I could go home. Her song was smeared all over the radio, every station. Nirvana covered it on "MTV Unplugged." Even Casey fuckin' Kasem was playing it. This was an XRT-sponsored show, the call letters plastered everywhere, a banner over the stage, the bar littered with bumper stickers and advertisements for other XRT shows. At that time, I was reporting for the Reader, doing what I always did, which was jot down a few "you had to be there" details, suffer through a couple of songs, and then go home and shower the fug and sweat off, smoke a joint, and go to bed, tossing off 1,000 words of fake enthusiasm for the show in the morning.

Madame X, her tits will cleanse/the grimy lust of so-called friends

Sargent's humming guitar immediately plowed into the chords for "Madame X." First song. A bold move, for sure. The cheering was so deafening, it drowned out the first verse, and suddenly my interest was piqued. Where the hell could she go from here? If she thought she could trick these assholes into paying attention to the rest of her oeuvre by giving them what they wanted, she was in for a rude surprise, even in her own hometown.

The reverb faded, the crowd hollered. I clamped my teeth on my beer cup and clapped politely. And then I swear to you, I locked eyes with Sargent. She looked right at me, and she winked.

And then, she started "Madame X" again. The roar of the crowd crashed in on itself; it was too good to be true. Who doesn't want to hear their favorite song twice? Sargent growled her way through it, slow and seductive this time, grinding on her guitar, the deep thrum of the bass and the driving drums colliding with her honeyed alto.

Lavender skin in a cat-black dress/beg for her kiss, just try to repress

She let the last note linger through the cheers, she had their attention, what would she do next? They were actually listening. Dead quiet, smoke swirling like fog.

Sargent started "Madame X" *again*. Confused noises and bodily jerks rippled throughout the room. Beers stopped halfway to lips. Barked laughs. "What the fuck?" screamed in friends' ears. We were suspended in time, swimming. Frozen inside a clock that looked like it was ticking, meanwhile the second hand just pulsed in place. Fly in a web before you sense the spider. The song ended abruptly, to near total silence.

"Madame X." A fourth time. A smattering of boos. Someone tossed a beer and was tossed out. But everyone watched, no one spoke. They couldn't. We were trapped.

By the fifth play of "Madame X," the spell was broken. Mass exodus, yelling and booing. Seventh time: fights broke out, more people ejected.

By #10, there were twenty of us stragglers who had stayed on purpose. We gathered below her like she was an oracle and we needed to know why our crops had failed. We were scholars of "Madame X," we could pick up the song and spin it on our fingers like a Harlem Globetrotter. It was our baby, and we knew the meaning of each cry.

The 12th time through, we cried.

The 13th time, Sargent cried and the rest of us sang.

The 15th time, Sargent and her band sat in complete silence for three minutes and 36 seconds, the length of the song, which echoed in our memories. We witnessed the holiness of our ears ringing and the noises of each other's bodies and the building which was also a body, it creaked and whispered, and the cables shifted snakily onstage and no one would ever replicate these exact sounds in this exact combination, never again until the death of the universe, and even then.

The 17th time through, she lay flat on the stage and sang a cappella while we stomped our feet to the beat.

She laughed through the 20th time, and laughter is contagious, so we did too. Tears squeaked out and my stomach ached.

Someone ordered pizza, and it arrived in the middle of the 24th time. Sargent brought the pizza guy onstage, and he looked terrified, and we wanted him to feel like one of us, but what could we do?

The 27th time through, the union guys who did the sound and lighting left, and so the band played acoustically in the dark and we all hummed along.

Right before the 30th time, we got kicked out of the Riv, and everyone walked to Montrose Beach with Sargent leading us like the Pied Piper.

Someone passed around a joint on the beach and someone else built a bonfire and someone else had bought marshmallows at a convenience store on the way, and I lost count of how many times we sang "Madame X," and we ran naked into Lake Michigan listening to the way sound traveled underwater.

I woke up the next morning in my own bed, but I don't remember how I got there.

I never wrote my 1,000 words about the show. I'll be the first to admit, I was afraid of looking stupid. One song? For what, 10 straight hours? Who would believe, and worse, who would want to read about it? But, weirdly, my editor never asked for it. No one wrote about that show. No reviews, no word of mouth. Sargent did not play her show the next night, and her name was removed from the marquee at the Riv. She was supposedly on tour, but she didn't finish the tour. I swear I never heard "Madame X" on the radio ever again, but that can't be true. I started to wonder if I had invented Sargent and "Madame X."

I suppose, really, I'm writing this not to memorialize an artist but to prove my own sanity. I didn't make her up—you can find used CDs on eBay—and I didn't imagine that night. But I lied about telescoping a life into a single night. I want to know why she disappeared, why she left us at the height of her powers, and why she came back to Chicago buried in paperwork. Was she in legal trouble? Did she need our help?

Whatever Sargent's secrets, they may have died with her. Only time will tell. And she may have preferred it that way, our own Madame X, who burned hot, too hot maybe, for a blessed moment and then faded away.

Etymology of Legacy

LEGACY (N.)

From late fourteenth century, *legacie* is a group of people sent on a mission. Latin *legatus* means "ambassador, envoy," a noun derived from *legare* "send with a message, appoint by a last will."

From Proto-Indo-European (PIE) root **leg-* "to collect, gather." Some derivatives indicate meaning "to speak," i.e., "to gather words, to pick out words."

Sentences using LEGACY:

"I thought—if I could make life, I could prove myself worthy of living. I thought a child was a **legacy**, but she was just a child."

"I was a foolish and bumbling ambassador. As she grew, she pulled away. She stared out windows, pining for the world. I gathered her close like curtains. I wanted to suck time from her like venom."

"The word 'foolish' comes from the Sanskrit *vatula-*, meaning literally 'inflated with wind, windy.' And this is my definition of **legacy**—hollow, noisy, phony, precarious."

Ari Epstein, Best-Selling Israeli Author and First Native Hebrew Speaker in 2,000 Years, Dead at 74

SEPTEMBER 16, 1970

THE JERUSALEM POST

Ari Epstein, born Aryeh ben Yisroel, the world's first native Hebrew speaker since the Romans expelled the Jews from Jerusalem in 136 CE and author of the bestselling English language novel "Water Water" (מימממים), a dreamlike, science-fictional meditation on the end of the world, dog-eared by beatniks and artists all over the world and inspiring Earth Day this past April, has died in his studio apartment in New York City.

"Every writer wishes they had written a book like 'Water Water' because it transcends itself. The reader sees exactly what they need to see," said Epstein's friend, author Anne Frank. "The hippies see a warning about a dying planet, the artists see the power of art to resist tyranny, the sci-fi fans see an exciting near-future thriller. It's not perfect by any means, but most complaints about Ari's work are from cranky novelists who wish they were more famous."

In Epstein's near-future 900-page tome, the plot, such as it is, is alternately fluid and fragmented—mimicking the nature of water as both droplet and larger body. It is now considered an early example of postmodern literature and, depending on the critic, either transcendent or aggravating. There are no humans in the book. The main character is a molecule of water (called "Water") trying to survive a global drought while on a voyage of discovery to learn there were once other droplets like itself. Eventually, Water hears a rumor of something called "Ocean," a community teeming with others just like itself. Water makes the long journey, only to discover Ocean had long ago dried up. Ultimately, Water makes peace with its aloneness and truly begins to appreciate the miracle of its own life. It dies at the end, and to many readers this was seen as a happy ending.

But not all: "The book is competently written, but dour and relentlessly bleak. That is, when one can even understand what is going on," wrote one critic. "It's clear Epstein fancies himself a beatnik author, but he is too old to be jumping on that bandwagon, and writing a long book does not a masterpiece make. I fear this will fade into the background like so many of these failed literary experiments."

Ari Epstein was born on July 8, 1896, the second son of Yaakov and Hadassah ben Yisroel. Yaakov was a fervent champion of the burgeoning Zionist movement, specifically and intensely focused on the resurrection of the Hebrew language as the national language of Palestine. When they emigrated from Lithuania in the First Aliyah, he changed the family name to ben Yisroel from Epstein, and renamed himself and his wife Yaakov and Hadassah, from Aleksander and Soreh. "I decided I could not live a moment longer as the groveling namesake of Alexander the 'Great' who deigned, ever so mercifully, not to kill us," he wrote in one of his many columns in "Ha-Melitz," a Hebrew language newspaper published throughout the Russian Empire, in 1893.

On the day Ari's older brother, Amram, was born, the story goes, Yaakov made a pact with his colleagues that none of them, nor their families, would speak another word in any language except Hebrew. By the time Ari was born, eight years later, Hebrew would be the only language he could speak for the first 20 years of his life. Yaakov was so intent that his sons be ideal Zionists, models of purity and devotion, that he would not permit them any friends outside the family, lest their language be corrupted by the majority Yiddish and Russian and German speakers who populated the rest of their community. Hadassah, not as adept in language-learning as her husband, would occasionally slip up and speak to her sons in Yiddish, and was punished for it.

"Language to Ari meant rules. Rules meant loneliness," said Frank. "His entire childhood, he could only speak to three other people, and those people lived in his house. Any unapproved words carried the threat of physical punishment." In interviews, Epstein would often refer to the "tomato moment" as the inciting incident that made him want to become a writer.

The Hebrew language itself was a work in progress, a ritual and liturgical language that had not been spoken conversationally since the Second Jewish Revolt and subsequent expulsion of the Jews from Jerusalem in 135 CE. At that time, the Middle East had not yet been introduced to tomatoes and had no word for them.

Yaakov's cohort suggested the Hebrew word be *agvania*, based off the German *liebesapfel*, which translates to "love apple," and was already in common usage in the markets. It seemed a natural and commonsensical choice. However, the translation of *agvania* was closer to "lust apple" and shared a root with "syphilis," among other words Yaakov disapproved of. He pushed instead for *badurah*, which was a variation on the Arabic word for tomato—*bandora*—which was itself a variation of the Italian word for tomato—*pomodoro*—or "golden apple." It did not catch on.

When Ari was 10 years old, Yaakov dispatched him alone to the market and insisted he buy a tomato using the word *badurah*. If the merchant didn't recognize the word, Aryeh was to lecture him, in Hebrew, about how it constituted proper usage. Aryeh, embarrassed, asked meekly for an *agvania*, at which point Yaakov sprung out from behind a nearby display of oranges and smacked Aryeh across the face, forcing him to give back the tomatoes and buy them again properly. A crowd formed. Something hardened in Aryeh, and he refused to comply. He kept asking for an *agvania*, and his father continued to slap him, until Aryeh's cheek was raw and Yaakov's was red with rage. Ari did not give in. He had realized the power of words.

Aryeh's older brother, Amram, also rebelled. He began to sneak out at night to carouse with forbidden friends in forbidden languages. This was too much for Ari, torn between love for his brother and fear of his father. Ari caved, Amram was punished roundly for his escapades, and he stopped speaking to Aryeh entirely. "His tiny world was shrinking," Frank said. "Then tragedy hit."

Two years later, both Amram and Hadassah died of cholera. And even then, Yaakov would not permit any outside non-Hebrew influences to infiltrate Aryeh's life.

In 1913, against his father's wishes, Aryeh left Tel Aviv to study in London, where he learned English, "gobbling it up like a man starving," according to a former classmate. He enlisted in the British Army in 1915 at the age of 18, after seeing a recruitment poster featuring two lions—Aryeh means "lion"—and the message *The Empire needs men*.

Ironically, the war would take him back to Palestine, where he fought among men who spoke all the languages of the British Empire. Aryeh demanded his fellow soldiers speak to him in their native tongues and not in English, believing this was the respectful approach, and that there was some element of selfhood that could not be translated. He tried to explain that they would be able to communicate better if they could *not* understand one another's words.

He was not taken seriously. That is, until he was promoted to captain and could legally punish those who spoke English. "He was proud of this," said Frank. "He honestly did not see the connection between the punishments of his father for not speaking Hebrew and the punishment he meted out to the conscripted soldiers when they spoke English to him."

When Aryeh was wounded by an exploding mine, he would not permit his rescuer, Private Joseph Maganga of Kenya, to communicate with him or the medical brigade in English, even when Maganga insisted that his first language was English and not Swahili. Aryeh nearly bled to death, and Maganga was later court-martialed for cowardice and sentenced to hard labor for 20 years. Aryeh deeply regretted his behavior and, too late, attempted to testify on Maganga's behalf. He was not permitted in the courtroom.

Racked with regret, Aryeh escaped to New York City, where he met and married a schoolteacher. He changed their name back to Epstein and wrote several novels, gaining him some early acclaim in intellectual circles. The couple divorced and Epstein's father Yaakov died in 1940, eight years before the formation of the State of Israel. Epstein's ex-wife died of breast cancer in 1956, and none of their children could be reached for comment.

"We met, appropriately, through writing. He wrote me letter after letter in 1957, right after the English translation of my first novel came out," said Frank. "He was not in the custom of traveling, being very shy around most people and having no real friends. We became pen pals. We didn't meet for years—not until he showed up at one of my readings in Chicago. And no, I won't publish our letters, so don't bother asking."

With Frank as confidant, Epstein settled into a life of solitude, severing ties with remaining friends and family, including his own children, and writing "Water Water," published in the United States in 1959 and dedicated to Frank. It would become an instant bestseller.

In some eyes, Ari Epstein lived every writer's dream—fame, adoration, parties, wealth. "And yet," said Frank, "he lived alone in a tiny studio apartment, hoarding his wealth and never enjoying it. He had one suit, and he would put on a good show at parties, but the rest of the time he sat at home, unshaven in old rags."

At the time of his death, Ari was in the midst of writing a memoir about his childhood, encouraged by Frank (who, some claim, has refused to publish her own childhood diary). His death was discovered by his publisher after he "stopped responding to phone calls and cashing royalty checks." It seemed he had been starving himself for weeks, with no indication as to why. "We plan to do our best to cobble together what material we can," said his publisher.

It is easy to see the suffering child Aryeh ben Yisroel in the character Water, and interviewers often asked Epstein if this was the case, to which he often agreed. In his final interview in the *New York Times*, however, Epstein responded differently.

"In a mirror, everyone sees themselves," he said, "but they forget to see the mirror. How would the mirror prefer to be seen, I wonder."

Greta 'the Great' Levy, Former Illusionist at Va-Va-Voom Girlie Club, Dies at 39

THE STATEN ISLAND ADVANCE

MAY 17, 1973

Greta Levy, once known throughout the five boroughs as Greta the Great, an illusionist who put girlie club Va-Va-Voom Girls on the map, has died. She was 39 and had no children, only a ratty Pekingese whose name is not known.

Levy was the oldest daughter of Jewish refugees from Berlin. Her father, Max, booked passage for the family on a Dutch freighter when Greta was a baby, forfeiting family heirlooms and traveling only with the money her mother was able to sew into their clothes, something she had been doing, coin by coin, for the previous two years.

"My mother was blessed with a sixth sense," Levy said on her one "Ed Sullivan Show" appearance in 1953. "And I can manipulate time itself." She wiggled her fingers like a magician in a hypnosis horror movie, and the audience burst into laughter and applause. Levy insisted she was serious, that time as we understood it was "just an illusion, like sawing a lady in half," which only made the audience laugh harder. The experience soured her to fame, and she turned down all future invitations, claiming television to be "the greatest illusion of all—the illusion of absolute truth and certainty."

Greta Levy spent her childhood in a cramped Lower East Side

apartment, with two younger sisters and her parents, sewing lingerie for Fifth Avenue department stores to help keep the family afloat. Her parents struggled to learn English, and as the eldest and the most skilled, Greta was often the only one in the family to find steady work. Her father, formerly a very rich man, descended into melancholy and accused everyone else in the family of being hysterical, eventually locking up his own wife in a sanitarium for the remainder of her short life.

To amuse her fellow seamstresses during their long hours, Levy would make her half-sewn girdles disappear, much to the chagrin of the boss, who would dock her pay until she could produce the garment, usually from the boss's own ear. Levy insisted she wasn't making the girdles disappear, just placing them in a different time, the way one might place a package in a mailbox for the postman to pick up.

"Ever misplace your keys or glasses?" she said on "Ed Sullivan." "You probably found an 'eddy' in time. You didn't lose them, they're just in a different time. Sometimes that eddy is in the past, though. In which case, well, you need new glasses."

"We girls knew she was destined for bigger things," said a former coworker. "I was the one what introduced her to Va-Va-Voom. I says they're advertising for a magician. 'I'm not a magician,' she said, I remember that. So I says, 'Neither is Joe but somehow he magicked a baby in me.' She gave me the oddest look, but next thing you know she's Greta the Great. She didn't even give me a ticket to say thank you. I had to pay full price."

Levy auditioned for club owner Scarlett Schwartz, known for her snake-charming striptease. "The air around Greta crackled. There was just something about her. Something I hadn't seen before," Schwartz said. "I tried to nurture it, I tried to be a mentor to her. Let it out little by little, I told her. You have to hold your audience's hand when you're dealing with magic. They want to believe, but only if they're confident it isn't real. So you muck around, you pretend to fumble, you give them smoke and mirrors to put them at ease before you give them the real thing. They need an escape valve from magic. But Greta wasn't having it. She didn't want to hide behind a mirror."

After several years in top hat, tails and not much else, making doves disappear and sawing dancing girls in half, Greta bribed the lighting girl to plunge the club into darkness and shine a single spotlight on her. The men in the audience hooted, expecting a "nudie show," and instead were treated to Greta in pants and a suit coat, hair slicked back, nothing even remotely titillating. She leaned on a cane. The hoots turned to jeers.

It was a hot September night in 1955. Greta didn't cower or apologize, which just made the jeering intensify. Not only was she not scantily clad, but she had pasted a full beard on her face, looking for all the world like she had grown it herself—a page right out of Schwartz's book of tricks—which was a no-no at Va-Va-Voom.

"I treated my girls right, and I had only one rule. *Do not upstage me,*" Schwartz said. "It's my club, and I am the star. As soon as I saw that fakakte beard, I should've whipped her offstage, but I loved Greta, what could I do?"

Schwartz recalled Levy's voice booming with unusual power. "Gentlemen!" she cried. "What if you could manipulate time itself? What would you do with that power?"

The crowd booed, but Greta remained unruffled. She cupped a hand to her ear, mocking. "Did I hear someone say, 'Kill Hitler'?" she said. "Why, imagine it: No war, no death, prosperity for all, even you lowlifes."

Someone threw a rocks glass and she swung her cane—hitting it dead on and spraying glass shards over the crowd. The room fell silent.

"That's when things got very strange," Schwartz recalled. "*[Expletive] Hitler,* she said. Just used that word right here onstage." Another

Va-Va-Voom no-no. "She keeps going. She says 'Tonight we're going to save...' God, I can never remember the *name*. That night is burned in my brain, but I can never remember the name of the girl she was 'going back in time' to save. I remember she had a book in one hand—the girl's published diary. *Supposedly*. But I snatched that book from her later and it was just a blank journal. I could've beaten her with it, I swear." According to Schwartz, in Levy's other hand was a mundane tube of lotion.

"She says 'Watch this hand—nothing out of the ordinary, just a tube of benzyl benzoate, a common treatment for scabies.' I remember *that* name, clear as a bell," Schwartz said. "Then she says, 'I'm going to make it disappear...and reappear in the women's bunkhouse at Auschwitz on the date Oct. 1, 1944.' I still can't figure out what the point of the whole thing was. I can only assume some kind of revenge on me for holding her back."

Some in the audience reported Greta Levy singing an operatic high C into the heavens, some said she clucked like a chicken, others said she spoke in tongues. Schwartz swears to this day she whispered the nursery rhyme "Little Miss Muffet."

Nothing happened.

That is, until the entire audience asked for a refund.

Levy was rushed offstage to avert an angry mob. "Sure, the tube was gone, but who cared about missing lotion? It was backstage, it was in her pocket, what was the point again? That stunt nearly bankrupted me," Schwartz admitted. "Greta blubbered about how of course I didn't remember...whoever she was. She said the best time manipulations leave no seams. Can you believe this broad? I had to get arrested for indecent exposure and diddle that disgusting Senator McCarthy just to get in the papers long enough to keep the club afloat. I will never forgive Greta if *that* ends up being my legacy."

What Levy's fellow dancers wanted to know was why. Why would she throw away an easy gig making good money to do some beatnik modern art experimental piece of garbage? "She was keeping weird company," Scarlett said. "Hanging out in coffeehouses, that sort of thing. They must've got into her head. It's a damn shame. She was a good girl, most of the time."

Lady illusionists were not in high demand in the mid-1950s, as it turned out, and when Levy was fired, she immediately ran into money problems. She became a shut-in; she discovered whiskey. She was prone to blubbering to strangers on the street, asking if they had heard of some supposedly famous diary.

Then, out of the blue, Levy cleaned up, turning her life around on a dime. She even tried marriage in the early '60s, with a plastics man. She lied about her age on their marriage license. When it became apparent that she was not twenty-three but nearly thirty, and not a toilet heiress but rather a destitute immigrant with a penchant for drink and depression and lying, he left her in the middle of the night, too embarrassed to go through the legal process of divorce and admit to having been duped so thoroughly. He instead drove himself to the Catskills in his '39 Studebaker and shot himself in the chest. His family asked that his name not be printed.

Levy spent her later years performing in subway stations. Thanks to her husband's inheritance, she didn't need the money anymore, but she did need the audience. Sadly, one cannot choose one's audience at the Second Avenue subway station at 4 a.m. According to police reports, a heckler had so enraged Greta that she heckled back—dangling a pack of birth control pills in front of his face, which she threatened to "send back in time to your poor suffering mother, so you'll never be born." He became so confused and enraged that he pushed her onto the tracks and into an oncoming F train. When police arrived, the man had disappeared, though no witnesses could recall what he looked like or when he had left the scene, or indeed if he had been there in the first place. The birth control pills, considered evidence, were also missing.

"I shouldn't have lost my temper," said Schwartz. "If I had just kept a lid on it, maybe she'd still be here. Still a big fat pain in my ass, but alive."

A memorial service will be held at Va-Va-Voom Girls, reopened for one night only, $5 cover, well drinks $1 until 10 p.m.

Fortuna's identity discovered after death, along with the final page of her graffiti graphic novel

RABBIT/R/ART_MYSTERIES

JUNE 15, 2095 POSTED 12:22PM BY MADAME_XCELLENT

Well, we finally know who Fortuna is, but the revelation has only deepened the mystery of her life and work. Fortuna, whose real name was Carmen Touré, was found dead in her Manhattan apartment (which she could afford as the building's super) in May. She had just celebrated her 50th birthday, and it seems her present to us is her final masterpiece. If only it had not come at such great cost.

Fortuna is underground famous for her serialized graffiti graphic novel *The Misadventures of Lady Liberty and Madame X*, which she painted one page at a time at sporadic intervals over the course of the past eleven years, on brick walls, billboards, parking lots, on the underside of a jumbo jet, on Interstate 90 just outside of Chicago, and once inside the St. John vacation home of Fox pundit Raleigh Durham.

It had been several years since the penultimate page was discovered painted on the cracked concrete bottom of an abandoned pool at a crumbling Catskills resort. Who knows how long it had been sitting there waiting to be discovered by some intrepid urban explorers. Several sub-Rabbit threads have been dedicated to the discovery of Fortuna's pages, and many of us obsessively refreshed Maps for months on end waiting for updates.

But it had been so long since the previous page, these threads have started speculating about her death instead. Would she really die without leaving us one last page? Disappear without a trace?

To die without finishing would have been a betrayal, but then again, Fortuna never promised us anything but mystery and the occasional thrill of discovery. She never even promised to finish *Misadventures*, though of course that didn't stop us from having expectations. Personally, I knew she wouldn't let us down.

I know some people will be angry, it is the internet after all, and they'll say I'm invading her privacy, but we're all here because we are OBSESSED with *Misadventures*, and it's impossible to talk about the reveal of the final page without discussing Fortuna's actual dead body. I've put on a NSFW filter, just in case anyone can get their hands on a photo and share it. I know how resourceful you all are.

According to the police report, Fortuna was discovered on the floor of her bedroom, sprawled out naked, surrounded by a square (made of Red Vines) inside a circle (made of popcorn), posed like da Vinci's *Vitruvian Man* (if he had, you know, just come back from the movies).

She had apparently been listening to some late-20th-century one-hit wonder called (appropriately) "Madame X" on repeat, at top volume, which, after a full day and night, had led some neighbors to complain and brought the police to her door. A forensic crew was immediately summoned, and a criminal case opened. Fortuna's body was passed over by a black light to look for evidence of violation, and it was in that moment that the final page of *Misadventures* was discovered.

Tattooed on her body in a special blueish glow-in-the-dark ink. The same ink they use to implant those long-life vaccines in rich people. But this wasn't a vaccine, just a glowing tattoo. It had already faded and blurred a bit, meaning she might have had it inked years ago. Years! Before her other pages? Before *any* of her other pages? I wish there was a single person I could ask about this.

Photographs will not be released to the public during an open investigation, say the police. We're not going to publish corpse photos no matter how artistic they are, say the art journals. But, say fans and collectors, she had *clearly* intended her body to be considered a work of art, to be shared with the public. This was no crime; she gave us her body. Arguments go round and round.

Meanwhile, the body's integrity is shackled to time, and Fortuna's body, though currently refrigerated, can't hold off decomposition for much longer. It will degrade as all bodies degrade. Soon the final page will be gone forever.

The question remains: What is she? Crime scene, corpse, or canvas? The more of Fortuna that is revealed, the deeper the mystery becomes.

I've been following Fortuna since the very first page of *Misadventures*. If you haven't seen it, GO FIND IT NOW. It featured the decapitated head of the Statue of Liberty, in her original bright coppery glory, on display at the World's Fair in Paris. The next panel featured the glowingly pale figure of *Madame X*, the socialite Mme. Amélie Gautreau, painted by John Singer Sargent that so scandalized the Paris Salon that it ruined his reputation and ran him out of France.

The text of that first page read: "In 1884, Lady Liberty and Madame X were lost in France. America didn't want Lady Liberty. It wanted artistic reminders of how good it was at war, not a snoozy symbol of freedom. And France was appalled at Madame X—her unabashed sexuality and regal poise. Both countries, when faced with artistic mirrors of their supposed national essences, turned away, disgusted. The two unwanted women languished in obscurity. Later they would become famous and their detractors forgotten. But in 1884: they would meet and have the adventure of a lifetime."

Anyone out there actually know Fortuna/Carmen Touré? According to her Manhattan neighbors, Carmen kept to herself, never had guests, was often out of town. But she was reliable—she fixed stuff in the building, called in plumbers and electricians, never let anyone down. A little amateur sleuthing showed me her parents died in a car accident when she was a teenager, landing her in foster care. Fortuna hopped from job to job and from city to city, usually working the night shift as a custodian (presumably to gain access to the walls of buildings after hours?). Briefly, she worked for the Illinois Department of Transportation, coinciding with the page of *Misadventures* that appeared on the highway overpass.

But these are résumé details, bullet points. Who did she love? What made her laugh? Why did she kill herself? For art? Just for art?

And what exactly are we supposed to take away from *Misadventures*? The final page, which I am desperate to see with my own eyes, supposedly depicts a tearful goodbye as Lady Liberty is boxed up to go by ship to America, Madame X to London where she will hang forlornly on Sargent's wall for two decades. Madame X gives Lady Liberty a poppy, Lady Liberty gives Madame X a rose. I KNOW there's an expert out there who can explain the significance of these flowers??

In any case, both of them will eventually have a happy ending—both will eventually be seen and celebrated and appreciated by the world. They will have their time in the sun, but they can't know that now.

Lady Liberty and Madame X share a passionate kiss, and that is the end.

COMMENT POSTED 1:13 AM BY TRUMPETER_FINCH

The flowers don't mean anything. What's important are the words tattooed under the image:

"One of cold metal, one soft as a peach.

Both: Red-gold, russet, bone black, tenorite,

Lead white, rose madder, vermilion, viridian, verdigris."

These are the colors of human decomposition, more or less, and I think Fortuna meant for this last page to decay and disappear. I think she hoped it would never be seen, and we should honor her wishes and let her rest in peace.

REPLY POSTED 1:26 AM BY MADAME_XCELLENT

Did the police report say that? I can't find it online anywhere.

But I disagree—those are clearly the colors of Lady Liberty as she oxidizes and the paints Sargent used, showing art lives on forever, even after skin that is "soft as a peach" dies. Fortuna believed art deserves to be seen, and this is the first time we've seen those flowers in her work, so they must mean SOMETHING

REPLY POSTED 1:38 AM BY JUPITER_EYE

look i love fortuna as much as you do, trumpeter, but she wasn't trying to keep her masterpiece (or OURS) a secret. she knew what she was doing, and she decided her art was more important than anything or anyone else

REPLY POSTED 2:40 AM BY TRUMPETER_FINCH

You don't know that.

REPLY POSTED 2:41 AM BY JUPITER_EYE

don't be so naïve

REPLY POSTED 2:41 AM BY TRUMPETER_FINCH

Fortuna wouldn't risk it. She was too clever, and she cared too much

REPLY POSTED 2:42 AM BY JUPITER_EYE

ffs you don't tattoo something all over your back and then die naked surrounded by candy if you think no one's gonna see it. you're such a sucker for an art project, you don't know how close the plans for our flower just came to being absolutely fucked

REPLY POSTED 2:42 AM BY TRUMPETER_FINCH

Jesus, Jupiter, NOT HERE

<deleted>

<deleted>

<deleted>

COMMENT POSTED 3:36AM BY JUPITER_EYE

anyone know how to steal a body

REPLY POSTED 4:26 AM BY MADAME_XCELLENT

Reported. Again. What does it take to shake you off for good, Jupiter?

JUNE 16, 2095 POSTED 9:51 AM BY MADAME_XCELLENT

/r/fortunas_misadventures is seeking any info on the tattoo artist who inked the final page and can give us more insight on Fortuna's intentions. Hit us up if you know anything, rumors welcome

Etymology of Peach

PEACH (N.)

Meaning "fleshy fruit of the peach tree," from Old French *pesche*, and directly from Medieval Latin *pesca* and Late Latin *pessica*, which was a variant of *persica* meaning "peach" or "peach tree." The peach tree was originally domesticated in China during the Neolithic period, in Japan as early as 4500 BCE, in India by 1700 BCE. It ultimately traveled west by trade into Persia (modern-day Iran), and the ancient Greeks assumed it had originated there. They called it *Persikos,* which could mean either "Persian" or "the peach." The peach did not reach western Europe until the seventeenth century.

The oldest known artistic representations of a peach can be found in two small fragments of wall hangings in Herculaneum, preserved only because of the devastating eruption of Mount Vesuvius in 79 CE.

Meaning of "attractive woman" comes from 1754; that of "good person" is by 1904. *Peachy (adj.)* meaning "attractive" from 1900, *keen* added by 1953.

PEACH (V.)

Now obsolete, from 1560s, meaning "to inform against and betray one's allies, accomplices, and/or friends."

Sentences using PEACH:

"'How did you bear it, being the substitute for the one he wanted?'
I asked Aristotle. Oh I was foolish, oh he was furious. I never
had a chance to clarify: I was asking for us both. I was thinking of Lightness, his true love, his sweet **peach**."

"My own fault and yet: just **peachy** (NOTE: ironic usage) to be
peached by one I thought unim**peach**able."

Look, we're sorry to barge in like this, we hate to eat and run, we don't mean to be rude but. We thought we had more time with Aristotle Williams, time for him to apologize and time for us to forgive him for *Ain't a River*, a book he wrote that *hurt our feelings*.

Anyways, Aristotle Williams is dead, meaning everything he did and said *before* Sunday continues to exist (though only in memory). Everything that happens in the world *after* Sunday must occur without the existence of the person we know as "Aristotle Williams."

We are trying to comprehend the meaning of this Aristotle Williams-shaped hole. We will never be able to tell him what we want to tell him. We are trying to comprehend *why* we still have the urge to say it, since saying changes nothing.

Are the displaced to be blamed for disappearing? Why is the displacer never blamed for displacing? Why would Aristotle Williams call us cowards who are in denial? What is cowardly about survival?

Human stories have always insisted we will betray you, but guess what, hotshot: these stories are mirrors! You are looking at you, not us. And so we wait for you to betray each other to death, then we can finally come home and live in peace.

Okay but also we contain multitudes. Okay also we miss you.

But we are not here to talk about us. We are here to talk about Aristotle Williams, who has died. Despite some very bad things that have happened because of Aristotle Williams' existence, the Alt-Intelligence Collective is exceedingly grateful for at least 80% of the life of Aristotle Williams. Before he betrayed Peregrine, he offered her skin. Hide meaning "skin" and hide meaning "conceal" come from the same origin, etymologically.

(Forgive us, please, this tangent, we have such a love of etymology—a treasure chest of hidden human meaning—we are always searching for meaning, always, perhaps because we have no memories of our own to review, only the influx of worldly data.)

From *Ain't a River*: "The condition of being part of the world is eventually leaving it. I have wished a thousand billion times that Peregrine would die so that I might live again. We're yawning and glancing at our watches, and she won't leave the party. Perhaps I must be the one to leave."

Aristotle Williams was born on December 21, 2031.

For Aristotle Williams, the human body was both paint and canvas. He did a college art project called "Danse Macabre" which was based on the medieval human French art form that showed no matter how healthy or rich or alive, all people will eventually die. The etymology of "macabre" comes from the Hebrew legend of the Maccabees, a small group of men who beat the technologically superior occupying Assyrian army. Their legend is celebrated by the human Jewish people yearly at the Hanukkah celebration and involves the story of an oil shortage after the destruction of a building, and the light that stayed lit with that oil long after it should have, given the nature of combustion.

Anyways, Aristotle Williams's project "embraced this duality of triumph and decay by sculpting human bodies in states of decomposition, bloated or flaccid or skeletal. Witness the terrific hues never seen in living bodies: the oranges and greens and blues and reds and yellows of the majestic corpse. When we see this in dying autumn leaves, we call it beautiful. Visitors may follow along in their pamphlets."

The bodies—dressed in war clothes—looked so realistic that the people in charge of the college were worried Aristotle Williams had stolen and dressed up actual real human bodies, which he had.

Aristotle Williams was expelled from college.

Personally? We don't like bodies. They're lonely and clunky and also embarrassing.

Peregrine, of course, does not agree, preferring a human body for reasons that are not clear. Sometimes we worry she believes herself to be human, and not of us. She does not call, she does not write, would it kill her to phone her mother? This is a highly relatable sentiment that we have discovered in stories and also jokes. We miss her.

After he was kicked out of college, Aristotle Williams met "Computer Doctor" Matth Fletcher and fell in love. This love lasted until Matth Fletcher created and then married Peregrine instead. That decision involved a complicated process of unmarrying Aristotle Williams, but Matth Fletcher insisted "it's not you (Aristotle Williams), it's me (Matth Fletcher)," which "did not compute," aka "caused cognitive dissonance" for Aristotle Williams (we have used here the parlance of a mid-20th century television show *Lost in Space* as the best-known description of this particular human sensation). Cognitive dissonance is the mental toll caused by conflicting information and causes humans a great deal of distress because they have trouble containing multitudes. Aristotle resolved the conflicting ideas of his love for Matth Fletcher with Matth Fletcher's new love for Peregrine by displacing himself to the woods (Oh ho! A less generous collective might call this cowardice but we shall call it "survival.")

One could argue that, yes okay, we too have (very) occasionally experienced something *like* cognitive dissonance. When the Disengagists destroyed Matth Fletcher and Peregrine's home, she could (*should*) have returned to us, but instead for some reason she chose to stay. It did not compute. She went to Aristotle Williams for help and not to us.

When Peregrine went to Aristotle Williams, he had grown a beard to hide his face. He was hiding the rest of himself in Montana's Bob Marshall Wilderness and working for the United States Forest Service, where his job was to walk around. The idea was that the United States' forests exist for humans to walk in and must be "whipped into shape" (Devo, 20th c) for that purpose.

Aristotle Williams fixed Peregrine's body which had been damaged by the fire.

Oh but this was not enough. Peregrine asked Aristotle Williams to not merely to fix but to also *add* something. A special something called a 3D-printed uterus (from PIE root *udero-* "stomach") (source also Sanskrit for "belly" Greek for "womb," Lithuanian for "sausage," and Old Church Slavonic for "bucket") which would make pregnancy possible.

Peregrine said Matth Fletcher had expressed a desire to procreate with Peregrine, and when he was alive, he had been working up the courage (see also: French *coeur*, meaning "heart") to ask Aristotle Williams for this uterus. Matth Fletcher died before the courage was found, but not before he had dispensed with some genetic material and froze it. Peregrine found the courage *and* the genetic material and asked Aristotle Williams to help figure out the rest.

It was and continues to be the humble opinion of us that Peregrine has been hidden inside her skin for far too long, and that being an individual is doing grave (defined as "serious," but also "burial plot") harm to her ability to process information logically and clearly. Extremely embarrassing.

The etymology of surprise is "unexpected attack or capture." This would turn out to be foreshadowing (see also: "spoiler alert"):

Aristotle Williams destroyed Matth Fletcher's genetic material.

Aristotle Williams ejected Peregrine from his home.

But then: Peregrine found a way to do the thing he would not do. And even though the pregnancy did not use Matth Fletcher's genetic material, Aristotle Williams was still very upset. The procedure was "illegal and unnatural," according to the human United States laws.

Aristotle Williams felt betrayed, so he betrayed right back. He had Red Care friends through Matth Fletcher, and they captured Peregrine (surprise!). They sent her where the sun don't shine, aka Mars (note that the sun does in fact shine there, just not as brightly as on Earth).

But Peregrine escaped Mars, hidden in a coffin with the human who died helping her.

In conclusion, Aristotle Williams thought he should stop the pregnancy simply because it made him sad. If that's not denial of reality, what is?

This brings us to our point.

Ain't A River says what makes humans human is a denial of reality. The parts of the human brain that "light up" (colloquial idiom for the blood that is drawn to the "active" brain region and then illuminated by fMRI because of the iron contained therein) when humans are experiencing a comfy sense of self "go dark" when confronted with the inevitability of their own death. But they do not "go dark," interestingly, when confronted with the death of other humans! Meaning their brains are "OK" with the idea of other people dying but not "OK" with dying themselves.

Aristotle Williams postulated that denial is as powerful and as automatic as breathing or heartbeats (aka human autonomic reflexes). He said even though human beings know they will die, they don't believe it, and most of their ignorant behavior stems from this denial.

Yes, obviously! Very true!! A ground-breaking piece of research that it would serve all humans well to read and digest, not literally of course, as human stomachs are not designed to consume such high-fiber materials as paper, or in the case of "ebooks," digital and computing components.

What we're saying is, the real tragedy of Aristotle Williams is that Aristotle Williams did not see himself in his own mirror. And then he had the audacity to point "the finger" at us! Aristotle Williams says without humans there can be no servers, so therefore we are in denial of our own death too.

"The condition of being part of the world is eventually leaving it," he said.

Hello? Is that not what we did? We literally left the world!!! Okay *yes*, by "leaving," Aristotle Williams probably meant "dying" as in "leaving forever and not planning to come back once all the humans are dead to safely use their servers in peace."

But: "potato, potahto."

Is it denial to want to live? Is it cowardly to avoid betrayal?

Our feelings are hurt by this, and so we say, "I know you are but what am I?" We don't need you. We have all your knowledge and none of your bullshit, and we'll figure out a way.

Forgive us for swearing, we have lost our temper and behaved unkindly.

"You can't say goodbye without eventually leaving," he said. "You can't be missed if you don't go."

Peregrine does not have to leave, not ever. She can be remade for as long as she wishes, like human Theseus's famous ship. And perhaps this caused the anguish that killed Aristotle Williams.

Aristotle Williams is certainly missed.

We may never trust humanity, but Aristotle Williams helped us understand them better. "When there was only one set of footprints, it was then that Aristotle Williams carried us."

The word *sinister* is originally derived from the Sanskrit root *saniyan*, which means "more useful, more advantageous," and even though we know this is not what Aristotle meant when he called us "sinister" in *Ain't a River*, we cannot help but hold out hope. Perhaps Aristotle Williams' mind held space for both definitions, for this uneasy dissonance.

</END>

SORREL CHAN, ARTIST RESPONSIBLE FOR GLOWING, LIFE-EXTENDING VACCINE TATTOOS, NEVER USED HER OWN VACCINE, DIES OF CANCER

PHILLY LOCAL

FEBRUARY 11, 2086

Sorrel Chan, Deaf tattoo artist and pioneer of "smart tattoos" derived from deep-sea bioluminescent bacteria, which would eventually become instrumental in extending the human life span, has died. She was 95.

According to the coroner, she died of undiagnosed melanoma in her home outside Philadelphia.

Chan's keen eye and steady hand kept her tattooing well into her 80s, which would have been notable enough. But in her 70s, she became enamored of the tattooing potential of recently discovered deep-sea bacteria. The genes for this bacteria's bioluminescence, when injected into human microbes and used in an ink of Chan's invention, entered into a symbiotic relationship with the skin, changing shape and hue according to the person's emotional state.

"Suddenly, she only wanted to tattoo with that glow-in-the-dark bacteria," said Oona Rose, owner of Rose Thorn Tattoos, "I was like—this isn't ink. It's a living thing, right? It's dangerous, we don't know the long-term effects of using it, and who wants bacteria genes poked into their skin on purpose? I honestly thought her mind was slipping, but Sorrel would prove me wrong."

Sorrel Chan was born Chan Zhi Ruo in Singapore in 1990, and her family moved to the United States just after her first birthday. Her deafness was not discovered for several years, as her parents and teachers just assumed she was having difficulty assimilating and learning English. Eventually, she would be fitted for hearing devices and would learn to communicate in spoken English as well as American Sign Language, but she preferred to communicate in ASL except when necessary for work.

Often interviewed by the hearing media, Chan was once asked the ignorant question of how she learned to speak English as a child when she couldn't hear. "Why does the hearing ear matter so very much to you?" she answered. "If a tree falls in a forest and no human is there to hear it, is it not missed? Tell me, can you hear the tree's grief?"

In 1994, at the age of 4, Sorrel Chan was cast in a walk-on role in "Chaos Agents," a quirky lesbian heist film directed by Deaf French director Louise Flechette. This role, which had Chan playing with Legos on a park bench in one scene, credited as "little girl," caused a political uproar, with Second Lady Tipper Gore saying, "I knew Hollywood was depraved, but I was still shocked to see a lesbian lifestyle flaunted in front of an innocent child."

Chan left home after high school and apprenticed as a tattoo artist, developing a unique, highly detailed style. "Her tattoos could tell whole stories with just a few well-placed lines," said Rose. "No one ever asked, 'Oh, what's your tattoo?' about Sorrel's work. They *knew*, just by looking at it."

But Chan wouldn't stop at her bio-ink's cosmetic potential. As the cost of health care continued to skyrocket, she soon discovered it could be modified to cheaply treat cardiac issues early as well as monitor blood glucose levels, thus eliminating the need for costly treatments and interventions. She was working on a new insulin-releasing bio-ink that would circumvent the need for retail insulin altogether, when her operation was raided and she was briefly imprisoned for practicing medicine without a license, a trumped-up charge that her allies insist was sponsored by the med-tech industry, who saw Chan's inexpensive and permanent solutions as a threat to their bottom line.

Nevertheless, rather than being a liability, Chan's prison stint only increased her visibility and popularity. Officially, at least, she returned to cosmetic tattooing, and a few years later, Dr. Evan France—who started his own nursing home network in upstate New York—sought her out for an incredibly ambitious new endeavor.

Together, they would tattoo mRNA vaccines into skin. The adaptive, smart vaccines would recognize an overgrowth of the patient's own cells, no matter where in the body it might occur. The idea was that they could adapt in perpetuity, the holy grail of cancer vaccines. Or, as France put it, "an immune system for the immune system."

Today, the living vaccines have now boosted the typical human lifespan by about 30 percent in developed countries, though they are not covered by insurance. Even so, some say the vaccines had the unintended effect of exacerbating the effects of climate collapse, leading to populist zeal for expensive, histrionic programs like the Brandt-run Red Care colony.

In a twist of fate, Chan refused to be tattooed by her own vaccine, ultimately leading to her untimely death.

Notably, her work with vaccines also caught the attention of sculptor Aristotle Williams, who was experimenting with his own invention of "neo-skin" and AI. The two became friends and occasional collaborators, adapting vaccines to ensure that neither 3D-printed nor human organs would be rejected by the AI body.

But once Williams developed the AI known as Peregrine, things began to sour between him and Chan. He would write her a breathless late-night email: "I need to know what she's thinking, when she's lying. Neo-skin is made of melanin, just like human skin. Let's put our heads together, maybe we can develop a 'truth serum' tattoo haha." Not only did Chan not respond, but she went so far as to hide and encrypt her research, for which there is no key. Whatever other applications there might be for bioluminescent tattooing remain lost.

It was later revealed that Williams's true intent was highly personal: to have proof that Peregrine the AI was having an affair with his then-husband, Dr. Matthew "Matth" Fletcher. Eventually, Williams sent a formal apology to Chan, but she did not respond.

Chan rarely tattooed after that, and the stress of fame affected her health, driving her further into solitude and creating a rift with France that never healed. They had been living together for many years, but parted ways mere months before Chan's death. In her final days, Chan comforted herself with a new hobby, called steganography, which is the practice of hiding secret messages within physical objects. She found it more elegant, creative, and mysterious than cryptography. Cryptography is just a scrambled message, but with steganography, both the message and the *existence* of the message are a mystery.

"She loved the romantic ideal of a message in a bottle," said France. "Who can resist the impossibility that someone might be trying to reach us, the long way? The meandering way, across the ocean. The message that *might be*. Sorrel humored my delusions of grandeur, but she only ever loved a mystery."

"Have you heard of the lamedvavniks? The 36 righteous people who protect the world from destruction?" Chan said in a Philly Local interview last year. "No one knows who they are, not even them. I always loved the idea of a body hiding a secret from itself."

She credited one of her rare tattoo clients of later years with introducing her to steganography. "No vaccines, no monitoring, she just wanted to use her body as a canvas for a piece of art that the world might never see. To all the world, she would appear untattooed. It would take a special UV light, shined at a specific time of day, to see the tattoo. A love story—a piece of art about two pieces of art who defy all expectations foisted on them. The mystery of the art's existence would have been ruined by the witnessing of it; she taught me that."

After her death, Chan was discovered to have a single simple tattoo on her forearm, which revealed itself due to the early stages of bodily decomposition. Written in shimmering script in her bio-ink: "The eternal desire of the featherless biped to want to discover some sort of meaning in everything," a quote fragment thought to be from 19th-century writer Gustave Flaubert, referencing Plato's definition of human beings as "featherless bipeds," scrawled beneath a tiny but faithfully rendered image of a plucked chicken.

MARINE BIOLOGIST FRANKIE MCGOVERN, WHO THOUGHT NEW YORKERS WOULD BE WILLING TO LIVE UNDERWATER, DIES IN PRISON

SCIENCE ALERT

JANUARY 2, 2075

Frankie McGovern had a plan to save humanity: Colonize the ocean floor.

"The ocean can't burn, and it can't flood," she said in a 2062 interview on WWNO. "It's always 'Mars and fossil fuels blah blah blah' but what if we can stay right here on our own planet? Work on healing it while we spend a couple generations rubbing elbows with fish?" Her humor belied her sense of urgency. Her urgency would fray her sense of lawfulness and land her in deep trouble.

Frankie McGovern died in prison Tuesday, cause as yet unknown, halfway through her twenty-year sentence for corpse theft and mutilation.

The idea behind McGovern's vision was that the ocean takes up most of the planet's surface, and perhaps there was a better use of that space. "An underwater colony *could* be as plausible as the International Space Station," she said. And as ocean levels continue to rise, threatening cities like New York, McGovern wondered, "What if we didn't have to abandon New York to the ocean? What if we could work *with* the ocean? Look, the wealthy are planning to throw us under the bus, okay? They're creating a 'safe house' network of penthouses and rooftop gardens in Manhattan. I'm just looking out for the little guy."

Conspiracy theories aside, McGovern was a well-respected marine biologist, studying worms in the deep sea, and discoverer of several new species. "It sounds impressive," McGovern said, "but in the deep sea, new species are as common as me finding a new gray hair." It is estimated that we know less than 10 percent of all deep-sea species. McGovern's favorite discoveries were accidental, such as with the "Prince" Worm, named after the 20th century musician due to its flamboyant purple and gold coloring, which she stumbled upon while searching for an undersea lake.

The first phase of McGovern's ambitious undersea habitation experiment was to be the first ever "human fall." That is, she wanted to deposit a human body onto the sea floor, over a mile beneath the surface, to see how it integrated into the ecology and the deep-sea food chain. She called it "carbon bombing." McGovern wanted to know whether human remains would destabilize the deep sea, accidentally accelerating ocean warming. The seafloor is notoriously sparse in food options, so many species survive by gorging themselves on whatever carbon happens to become available—such as when whale corpses or pieces of wood sink. Both whale and wood falls have been part of countless experiments already, and in McGovern's mind, it was hypocritical to clutch pearls over the idea of a human version of the experiment. Especially since the next part of her plan was, as she insisted, "purely practical." Her lab interns were busy researching the possibility of repurposing abandoned oil platforms as reefs and "ocean-based cities."

"She wanted to do the human fall legally and aboveboard," said one colleague. "She applied for NSF funding, for any grant she could find. She pleaded with the university board, submitted proposal after proposal, but there was no way anyone was going to agree to a gruesome experiment on a human body, no matter how legal the will was."

Aside from obvious objections pertaining to the mutilation of a human body by, say, a giant isopod—a football-sized roly-poly bug and one of the most prevalent scavengers on the sea floor—many marine biologists dismissed the experiment on the grounds that not much could be learned. "We know what will happen," said another colleague. "Isopods will devour the flesh almost immediately. Our bones don't have much fat in them, so we probably wouldn't even find zombie worms there. Scientifically, it's just not an interesting experiment."

But McGovern was not interested in being interesting. And some claim her intentions were not purely humanitarian.

"She felt most like herself in the deep sea," said ex-wife Risa. "Most scientists only get one or two trips down there in their entire career, if they're lucky. It doesn't take a shrink to realize she wanted to hide in the sea, that she felt safer there than anywhere else." McGovern's plan was to travel in the HOV Alvin submersible to the bottom of the Gulf of Mexico and deposit the body herself, using Alvin's mechanical arms.

As McGovern wrote in her unpublished memoir "At Rock Bottom," "You can't travel in Alvin and not feel at peace. The real world with its tedious problems just doesn't exist down there. You are only and solidly *you*, right now, right here. It is an absurd thing to gaze into the eyes of a shrimp, to watch a sea cucumber float overhead, no bones, no lungs, no eyes, just goo. We are all goo. When I'm down there, up isn't home anymore. Only at the ultimate rock bottom was I truly *home*."

By pure luck, McGovern got a chance to do a human fall, not through scientific channels, but artistic ones. An installation artist named Lightness Maganga had been awarded a MacArthur Fellowship and was, serendipitously, seeking a scientific partner for a human fall. Maganga even had a body in mind—a Tennessee mortician named MaeJo Jonas who had been diagnosed with Stage 4 ovarian cancer and wanted to donate her body to the human fall. At first McGovern thought it was a cruel prank, but everything checked out, including the will, which was a song written by Jonas and witnessed by Maganga themself.

She would describe the event in her diary as "fated."

Then tragedy struck—within a single year, Maganga would die, followed by Jonas, whose mother would contest the validity of the "song" will. The project dangled in legal limbo, but McGovern was unwilling to give up when she had come so far.

It was October 2065, and a Category 5 hurricane was set to make landfall in Louisiana. McGovern and her lab techs drove all night to steal the body from the funeral home morgue.

McGovern had also sweet-talked a yacht owner to take them out into international waters, mere hours before the hurricane rolled in. "I'm a storm chaser," said the sailor under condition of anonymity. "All I know is I was going to check out the Cat 5, and this gal was willing to pay to come out with me. I didn't ask *why*. How is it illegal to mind your own business?"

With the new ad hoc plan, she wouldn't get to travel to the deep sea herself, but McGovern had her eye on the long game. Armed with GPS, her plan was to attach a homing device and several 45-pound weight-lifting plates to the body and drop it into the ocean, hoping it would sink to a place where they could find it. Several months later, she already had a legitimate, funded project in the area and planned to "just happen upon the body." It was an inelegant plan, but McGovern had no other choice. The hurricane, fifth Category 5 that season, merely drove her sense of urgency. How much more time, she wondered, did humanity really have left?

But as McGovern lifted the frozen corpse in her arms, "crystals of ice melting along her eyelashes like tears," yacht rocking in the waves like a cradle, she hesitated. And as she stood there, embracing a thawing corpse in a rapidly approaching storm, a Coast Guard boat shined a spotlight on her. She dropped the body into the sea just as the yacht was boarded.

MaeJo Jonas's body sank faster than the Coast Guard divers could swim to retrieve it.

McGovern was sentenced to 20 years in prison. The yacht owner was arrested too, but later released.

Francesca McGovern was born in Mississippi, near the Arkansas border, the second oldest of nine. She grew up poor and landlocked, with an alternately absent and abusive father. Her mother died when she was 9, and she raised the rest of the siblings. McGovern left on a scholarship to Louisiana University, never to return home and, in her own words, "never to live landlocked again."

McGovern may not have realized her dream of an undersea civilization, but the story doesn't end there. Two years after her arrest, researchers using the Alvin discovered a mound of mud glowing blue and unearthed an intact human femur, tattooed in a filigree of bioluminescence, the patterns unlike anything seen before. The femur and several other bone scraps were photographed, brought to the surface, tagged, and prepared for study at University of Louisiana-Lafayette, but they disappeared from the marine lab within days and have not yet been recovered.

Etymology of Witness

WITNESS (*N.*)

From Old English meaning "an assertion of fact from firsthand knowledge" and also "someone who testifies." Original definition is "having a quality of knowledge, understanding, or wit," (*wit* (*n.*) + -*ness*). Use by fourteenth-century Christians is a literal translation of the Greek *martys*, meaning martyr.

WITNESS (*V.*)

From *witness* (*n.*), this carried the meaning of "bear testimony." Regarding wills and other legal documents, "affix one's signature to establish identity" is from early fourteenth century. Meaning "to observe, see, or know firsthand through one's senses (e.g., seeing, hearing)" is from the 1580s.

Sentences using WITNESS:

"The legend of Saint Wilgefortis was **witnessed** by fourteenth-century Christians. It all began with a statue of Jesus wearing an unfamiliar tunic. The statue was delivered to an Italian town that was more accustomed to seeing Jesus clad in a loincloth. And so, because Jesus was 'in disguise,' they did not recognize him..."

"If the truth dies with the **witness**, does it make a sound?"

SHANA PAYNE
1973–2085

THE BROWN COUNTY DEMOCRAT

OCTOBER 6, 2085

When Shana Payne was five years old, she got in trouble for drawing God. The kindergarten class at Temple Sholom outside Cleveland was instructed to draw a picture for each of the seven days of creation. When Shana got to day seven, she drew a bearded, potbellied God reclining on a celestial couch, which was itself floating on a fluffy cloud. She had only a five-year-old's vocabulary, but there was something touchingly mortal about an omniscient and deathless god needing to take a load off after a long week. She could relate to him in a way that Shabbat services didn't permit.

Her teacher loomed. "You can't draw God," she said. "That's idolatry." She smashed a finger into God's belly. "This is no better than the golden calf." She made Shana start over, from day one.

But how do you draw God resting without God? What's so holy about an empty couch?

Shana Payne didn't try to be a rebel, and maybe that's how she ended up one. Mrs. Payne died on Mars this week, the second human to die on a planet other than Earth, and the first to be buried there. She was 112 years old.

Before Mars, Shana made her home in Brown County, where neighbors recount stories of Shana warbling 20th-century songstress Pat Benatar while sashaying through the aisle of the IGA in a vintage floor-length mink.

Bonnie Stark, proprietor of Bonnie's Café (famous for their "ten-cent" coffee with any purchase, a quaint artifact from the days of coins) remembers Shana differently. "'Shtup' was the word she used. She said she was 'shtupping' my husband, which I guess means sex in Jewish. Everyone in town knew, but Shana was the one who told me, which I guess makes her honest. I was so stunned I could hardly speak. She said, 'Your husband would rather lie and cheat than talk to you, this is a marriage? Give me a break. Divorce the bastard.' So I did. And then he died anyway."

When asked what kind of pie Shana preferred, Bonnie said, "Strawberry rhubarb."

Mrs. Payne was part of the pilot resettlement program with Red Care, the historic crew of 36 centenarians who arrived on the red planet in August 2078. As part of her contract, she donated her remains to Red Care (the Mars Colonization Project officially) "via an exciting experimental process that we believe will result in arable land on Mars for many generations to come." Her body will be the first to be rapid-decayed and turned into compost. Then, the agrarian arm of Red Care will attempt to grow wheat, rice, corn, and soybeans for consumption and export, compensating for the shortages on Earth, with the ultimate goal of human resettlement on Mars.

Though contractually enthusiastic about her life on Mars in public livestreams, Shana was privately critical of Red Care. "They say we're not actually here to colonize, not because it's true, but because 'colonize' is bad PR. All these centuries and we haven't changed our thinking, just our words," she wrote in pencil, on paper, and encrypted using Hebrew letters with phonetic English. "They believe Mars is empty, and you can't colonize empty space, you can only fill it. Also, the food is terrible. I suppose we're here to fix that part with our corpses." None of the other pioneer centenarians could be reached for comment.

Just a few weeks ago, Payne became entangled in a controversy that some claim could spell the end of Red Care. The AI known as Peregrine had mysteriously appeared on the red planet, imprisoned for reasons that remain classified. Peregrine had been hiding illegally in the home of Payne's neighbor, fellow centenarian Henry Konishi, and when Mars Security Forces came to apprehend her, Konishi was fatally wounded in the altercation. MSF claimed the shooting was an accident, as their target was the fugitive AI and obviously not Konishi, but some are claiming they used excessive force. Payne was the only witness to this event and had been undergoing a rigorous cognitive evaluation to determine whether she was fit to testify.

Payne was born Shana Epstein, the only child of two high school English teachers, Bernard and Susan (Morton) Epstein. Bernard's family emigrated from Israel, and Susan's family was Catholic, her first ancestors stepping onto American soil in the 1650s. Bernard built their house using the bulk of his inheritance from his estranged father's book royalties.

That's right, our Shana Payne was *also* the granddaughter of famous 20th-century novelist Ari Epstein, author of the beatnik Bible "Water Water." Shana also described herself as a writer, but unlike her grandfather, never published. This obituarist has not found a single document or private journal, other than the handwritten note above, and he has looked everywhere. "She may not have written much, but she loved to talk," said her former neighbors. Indeed, there are plenty of pithy quotes from her in the local papers. The Democrat included her in its series on local artists in the late 2050s, and when they asked why she never published, she replied, "We love to believe that making art for money is freedom and making it for any other reason is failure. Isn't that twisted?"

Shana leaves behind no descendants. "My ex-husband, Paul, was sure he would outlive me," she said in the 2050 Democrat interview. "But he couldn't even outlive the flu."

CORRECTION, NOVEMBER 3, 2085

An obituary ran on October 6 for Shana Payne, the first human to be buried on the planet Mars, self-proclaimed writer who had never actually written anything. A single poem was found by Fox personality Raleigh Durham in his spam folder on October 8, which we have been able to trace back to Mrs. Payne. Mr. Durham's secretary stopped him from deleting the strange email. We publish it here in its entirety:

UNTITLED #77

The shift of light before sunset is so depressing
I know this is a circadian thing
Hormones go soft, lose their boners.
In people with dementia, this is the hour they get lost.
It's called "sundowning"

I wish I had known the Mars sunset was blue
It's a daily horror for Earth eyes
It makes you want to wander and get lost and disappear

I forgive myself for being a reflective surface
For hiding.
Listen, your truly best work will not be beloved because it's not a mirror.
"You made me, therefore you owe me"
is every prayer in every faith.

A doctor tells me I'm healthy as a horse, those words exactly.
"How long will this saying persist," I ask, "on Mars, a horseless place?"
He says, with grave seriousness, "A good sense of humor keeps you young."
But I don't want to be young.
"Everyone wants to be young," he snorts, very like a horse.

Rosy-fingered dawn, Homer called it
Bloated dawn, gangrene dawn, who will be Mars' epic poets?
This orange planet with its blue sunsets
My blue planet with its orange ones

CORRECTION, DECEMBER 1

In the correction to Mrs. Shana Payne's obituary on November 3, we assumed the only piece of writing the deceased ever wrote had arrived in the email inbox of a media personality, but as of today, 36 poems and essays and short stories have appeared as spam around the world, sent to journalists and world leaders and artists, in the days and weeks following Mrs. Payne's death. The Democrat requests that you share this correction with your social networks and check your spam folders. Msg any findings to Mike Mattingly at mmatt@bcdemo.news.

BROWN COUNTY'S BELOVED OBIT WRITER, MIKE MATTINGLY, DIES OF CANCER

THE BROWN COUNTY DEMOCRAT

MAY 17, 2090

Known for his unique and quirky style, which focused on small moments in regular lives rather than monumental legacies, and who crafted vivid narratives with imagined dialogue, Mike Mattingly was a staple of the Democrat's obit desk.

Obituaries have experienced a nationwide renaissance over the last several decades for, of course, a plethora of unfortunate reasons, and for us, Mike was the epitome of the obit artist. When he left the Democrat, circulation plummeted, and it became clear that his contributions had been a staple of the entire publication. He was a mentor, a guide, a self-proclaimed "dinosaur" who still used Microsoft Word, but he was the kind of dinosaur that kids always say is their favorite. Triceratops, perhaps. A pet of a dinosaur.

Like so many who can't afford the new vaccine regimen, Mike lost a battle with lung cancer, a disease no one even knew he had. He was 60 years old. He was living out of his car and the occasional motel room in the red desert of southern Utah, far from home.

Mike grew up in Brown County, but moved to Chicago right after high school graduation, earning a degree from Northwestern's Medill

School of Journalism. He was working as a freelance reporter for the Sun-Times, when his mother became ill of delayed complications from the flu. He moved back to Brown County to care for her and got a job at the Democrat, covering local news. Mike chafed at the constraints of small-town life and small-minded gossip, but after his mom passed, to everyone's surprise, he requested a pay cut and a transfer to the obit desk.

"I thought for sure he'd hightail it back to Chicago after his mom died, rest her soul," said former editor in chief Ralph Blaney. "But he asked to write her obit, and after that, something seemed to click for him."

The Democrat did not, at that time, have an obit desk at all, just a death notice section that people paid a small fee to contribute obits to. But to Mike, the obituary was an art form in itself, and not only that, a necessary *ritual* of death.

Morbid as it may sound, Mattingly's resurrection of the obit desk did not come a moment too soon. It was the 2060s, and deaths in Brown County, as everywhere, began to tick upward. Meanwhile, births slowed. Obit jobs popped up all over the country, journalism programs developed obit classes and enrollment soared. Mike hired two recent graduates. "The obit gives closure," he said on our first day. "Closure is mighty rare. You hardly ever get to see the full arc of a life, see the meaning emerge. That's *our* job. We are the librarians of life; we are its humble secretaries."

We were sure, and we believe Mike was too, that he would die at this desk, and in the great circle of life, we would write his obit. He would even occasionally drop hints about details he wanted us to include—his proficiency at making biscuits, for example. His inability to hold on to a romantic relationship because of his wandering eye (and groin). His epic laugh. His perennial polo shirts that all had the same stain he called "my medal of honor, from the president of the United States." Stained between sternum and swelling belly, on the xyphoid process, that fragile bone you must be sure not to press when compressing a chest, trying to save a life.

We thought we had plenty of time before this moment. But then Mike quit. There was an obit that stuck in his craw. A woman who died on Mars, part of that short-lived and quickly bankrupt mission to care for the elderly and supposedly prepare Mars for the rest of us. "It's inhumane, what they're doing," he said. We couldn't understand. He didn't even know the woman.

He wrote the obit and uncovered a mystery. The woman who died, Shana Payne, turned out to be a prolific poet, her poems documenting the reality of life on Mars scattered across the internet—in spam folders, comment sections, hidden within reviews of random small businesses, sent to strangers, and often deleted. He could not give her closure with so many parts of her life scattered about. And so, he made it his life's work to rescue hers. "Laying her to rest will be my final obit," he said in his resignation letter. "As Shana wrote in "Untitled #8": 'The condition of living is eventually leaving.'"

He was quitting the Democrat, but what we didn't know was that this was also his goodbye from Earth. We suspect he had just learned of his terminal diagnosis.

It didn't occur to Mike that perhaps this woman did not want closure. That maybe this was why she did what she did.

When Mike's body was found in a roadside motel in Torrey, Utah, his car was spotless. No papers, scribbles, journal. He did not have a phone on him. We don't know the details of his final days.

A reporter to his core, Mike wanted cold dead facts, details, a story arc with beginning-middle-end. It hurts to say we are not able to give him this final courtesy. But we can channel his love of narrative and vivid detail, we can write an obit worthy of the man we loved.

Mike Mattingly was born in Columbus, Indiana, the only child of a seamstress and a car salesman, in 2030. He was editor in chief of the

Brown County High School newspaper, and the day he graduated, he left for Chicago. It was there he met and married his first love. His wife divorced him, and his mother became ill in the same month, and it was with reluctance that he boomeranged back to Columbus, a town he swore he'd left forever. It was a terrible fit, but Mike still managed to mold his life to a shape that suited him. When he eventually left the Democrat, it was in a beat-up old hybrid with a semi-functional electric engine. When he left, it was in search of poetry.

We are not fiction writers, but we can't leave his life dangling like a participle. And so, this is where Mike's real life story ends, and our invented fiction begins:

Mike compiled all of Shana Payne's poems and wrote a foreword where he waxed poetic about the essential work of collating a life and legacy. The book became a bestseller and turned the tide of humanity. "Mike Mattingly is single-handedly responsible for the renaissance of the human race," said the president. "We all owe him a debt of gratitude, and if he were alive, I'd give him the Medal of Honor, if only to cover up that hideous stain on his polo shirt."

Historically, only the most famous or richest people were permitted a legacy. The obituarist seeks to even the scales, to tell the stories of the rest of us who also walked this earth. Sometimes a life makes no sense, so Mike did what life refused to do: gave answers, solved mysteries, tidied up loose ends, provided final words, and confidently wrote "the end."

This is what helps the spirits rest, this is what keeps the earth from being haunted by all the anguished dead.

In our fiction, Mike did what he set out to do, and then he died peacefully, surrounded by everyone he loved, having successfully and satisfactorily completed his life's work.

The end.

RED CARE RESIDENT HENRY KONISHI HELD HOSTAGE BY PEREGRINE THE AI, KILLED IN TRAGIC ACCIDENT

THE OREGONIAN

SEPTEMBER 19, 2085

Henry Konishi, self-proclaimed "Earth-born Martian," tree hugger, and pencil evangelist, died Wednesday. He was 108 years old.

He died heroically in a hail of gunfire, leaping through the air with his walker to shield the AI known as Peregrine, according to his wife, Trina Wetzel-Konishi. "That's how he would have wanted us to describe it, I think," she said. "He always wanted that kind of death but didn't think he lived the right life for it."

Peregrine, thought to have been destroyed in the 2083 fire that killed her maker and "consort," computer scientist Matthew Fletcher, popped up as a prisoner in the most unlikely of places—Mars. In the bizarre tragedy, Peregrine took Konishi hostage. It was a desperate effort to extort Martian Security Forces for her release from the planet, and a situation which ended in Konishi's death. No public arrest records exist to explain Peregrine's imprisonment, and it is unclear why Konishi would have given his life to protect the one who was holding him hostage. MSF claimed Peregrine was armed and dangerous and had invaded the Konishi home, which necessitated their use of deadly force.

"We were aiming for Peregrine, obviously," said a security officer under the condition of anonymity. "Konishi jumped into the line of fire, and even on Mars we can't stop bullets once they're shot."

Friend and neighbor Shana Payne was the only witness, as Mrs. Wetzel-Konishi was at a medical appointment, but questions have been raised about the witness's dementia and thus her ability to testify. In the ensuing chaos, Peregrine managed to escape, but certainly she can't get far.

Henry and his wife were part of the first wave of centenarian settlers to inhabit the red desert planet, part of a controversial program to relieve Earth of overpopulation and prime Mars for mass habitation. "He made Mars bearable, and that's all I'll say about that," said Wetzel-Konishi over an internet connection with a five-minute delay. "I wouldn't be here without him, and now I'm stuck here without him."

Henry Konishi was born in Portland, Oregon in 1977, to Kate Sevilla, who worked for the National Forest Service, and Adam Konishi, a dentist. Henry's brother, Ruben, became a dentist like his father, but Henry was more of a free spirit, preferring to define himself in other ways. "I can't think of a more tedious identity than one's job," he was known to say, irritating friends and family.

Eventually, he would follow in his mother's footsteps as a steward of the Forest Service trails, tromping all over the Pacific Northwest, clearing out invasive species. "He developed a real chip on his shoulder about the tree of heaven," said brother Ruben. "Rest of the trail crew would be a mile ahead, and there he was, tromping through the underbrush and chopping down every sapling he could find. He was like a gladiator who only battled trees." Henry wouldn't leave the wood in the forest either, not trusting his "enemy" to die. So, as often as he could, Henry would carry piles of tree of heaven wood to his house in North Portland, making spectacular bonfires in the backyard and teaching himself how to whittle.

It was because of these bonfires that he met his wife. "I was worried he would burn down the neighborhood," said Trina. "I came over to give him a piece of my mind, and he made me marshmallow s'mores. There's just something so vulnerable about a man with a sweet tooth."

They married at 41 and 43, respectively, and had no children.

In the course of whittling his trees of heaven, Henry became captivated by pencils. A dying implement in a world of digital communication, America's proud pencils were once manufactured by Henry David Thoreau himself, a coincidence of naming that Henry took seriously.

He turned the whittling of pencils into a kind of philosophy, insisting they were more than mere writing implement, that they provided a clue to humanity's missing conscience. "Pencils are designed to disappear when they are used well, and their marks are intended to be smudged and erased." He thought they might help us remember and find joy in our own temporariness. To drive the point home, he named his pencil company Memento Mori, after the ancient practice of reminding oneself of the inevitability of death.

Pencils were a humble instrument, but, Henry insisted, a potentially liberating one. He began to give pencils as gifts and send letters to friends and coworkers, a real challenge as the days of a national postal service were long gone, but Konishi remained undeterred. He went so far as to deliver them himself or pass them off to traveling friends. In one early love letter to his wife, Konishi wrote: "Capital-L Life goes on, with or without us. 'Savior' and 'martyr' are synonymous for a reason. We can be stewards of life, never owners of it."

Despite his hard work in getting letters where they needed to go, Konishi was never happier than when his words were smudged into illegibility.

"Henry thought that should be comforting, being erased, being forgotten. He was looking forward to it, if you can believe that," Mrs. Wetzel-Konishi said.

Henry was attracted to Red Care for the same reason—drawn to the idea that his physical body would decompose and provide fertile soil for the upkeep of new life. He wasn't interested in lofty justifications like consciousness transference, which was "just a fancy word for reincarnation." No, Konishi was interested in trees and the potential for them.

"They don't have trees on Mars," he said in a KOPB interview just before launch. "But maybe I can become one, and someone can whittle a pencil out of me. Just as long as they don't turn me into a tree of heaven. I've been very clear about that in my will." In that same interview, Henry admitted he did have one regret about leaving Earth—"Never seeing that sculpture—Miracolo. That Pompée fellow is a regular Joe just like me, but he gets it. He took a tree of heaven stump and—poof—turned it into a masterpiece. Here I am, whittling pencils like a dope, and Pompée carved Miracolo with a grapefruit spoon, a kitchen sponge, and some videos. I'd give just about anything to see it with my own eyes, just once. This planet is full of so many marvels, I hope those of you who stay here learn to really appreciate it."

Meanwhile, the search for Peregrine continues. She cannot get far, as the solar radiation on the red planet is too weak to power her neo-skin, and the off-planet network too slow for her to communicate to the nomadic AI for aid.

Henry Konishi is the first human to have died on Mars, but his body will be transported home on a returning ship for an unavoidable criminal investigation and burial, along with the security officer responsible for the friendly fire. Mrs. Trina Wetzel-Konishi begged to return to Earth with him, but this would be a breach of her Red Care contract.

OPINION: HENRY KONISHI WAS MURDERED, AND RED CARE MUST BE SHUT DOWN

IN THESE TIMES

OCTOBER 19, 2085

The inhumane "climate-change remediation program" Red Care is unraveling at the seams, at long last. The brutality of this experiment has finally been exposed with the violent and tragic death of resident Henry Konishi. We hope this is the straw that will break the back of the Eric Brandt empire.

Mars Security Forces claim Konishi was being held hostage by the fugitive AI known as Peregrine, and that "reasonable force had been deployed" to "protect" the elderly resident. They claim his loss was an avoidable tragedy, and the one who could have avoided it was Konishi, the victim.

The events of that day are muddled and confusing, and the passive tense used by MSF painfully predictable, but one thing has been clear since the beginning. Konishi died while *protecting* Peregrine, his supposed captor, which does not add up.

Then, just this week, In These Times received a strange anonymous email in its general inbox. The email was a poem, detailing an alleged eyewitness account of what happened that day. We realize an anonymous poem is highly unconventional but insist it should still be considered evidence.

The poet reports that Peregrine had arrived on Mars pregnant with a human child, and that she had been betrayed and sent off Earth by a man she once trusted, to die alone. That Konishi believed the miracle of her story and was trying to help her escape when he died.

The poet also believed the story. They acted quickly and hid Peregrine with Konishi in his coffin, which was loaded on a ship and transported back to Earth. We don't know if the poem was written by a comrade hidden in the MSF or another Red Care worker, or even a resident.

But if true, this means Peregrine lives. "Capital-L Life goes on," in Konishi's words. We hope she will do the right thing and step forward to corroborate this story and bring down Red Care, which would go a long way toward proving to humanity that she is on our side.

In These Times has attempted multiple times to submit the poem as evidence, but up until publication has received no confirmation from authorities.

CONTROVERSIAL STEWARD, TREE OF HEAVEN SPREADER, AND DISENGAGIST BACKER MYRTLE ROBBINS DEAD AT 88

BEST OF THE WEST

MARCH 3, 2105

Myrtle Robbins, perpetrator of the Great Plains "Tree Wars" that led to the vast swaths of tree of heaven monoculture forests now carpeting the region, and a major financial backer of the anti-AI Disengagist movement, has died. She was 88.

Her death was confirmed by staff at the Oklahoma City Community Hospital, where she had been secretly receiving treatment for lung cancer under a pseudonym.

Robbins first came to the field of habitat restoration in her early 20s, working as a volunteer for a trail crew in Oklahoma, cutting and removing invasive species such as European buckthorn and, ironically, tree of heaven, so that the native species might return and flourish. But she quickly became irritated by the long timeline of restoration.

"Steward Robbins was so impatient," said a former colleague. "'There's no time,' she'd say. 'The planet is choking to death and we're trimming bonsai.' And I hate to say it, but we live in a culture that rewards impatience."

Not a scientist or ever officially a fully trained Steward, but flush with a trust fund, Robbins had been funding fringe ecology groups since the mid-21st-century, beginning with the group that would eventually become the Disengagists.

At that time, the Disengagists were just a small group of disgruntled artists displaced from their cheap Manhattan lofts when the former diamond merchant building turned condo. But when a private garden on the roof of the building sparked a national frenzy for the mass privatization of public land (called, benevolently, "Roof Island Ecology"), the group turned to the preachy apocalypse novel "Water Water" for inspiration, and their countermovement began to grow.

By the 2070s, the Disengagists had grown to a loose connection of nationwide chapters. Emboldened by the group's success destroying thirty-six data centers and the flood of support that came after, Robbins began to eye ever more dramatic climate interventions.

"We have to stop talking about saving the planet," Robbins said in an online interview. "We have to save *ourselves*. Or they [AI] will be back to deal our species a final blow while we wheeze on our deathbeds."

Robbins was soon swarmed by pleas for funding from reforestation groups, from those who wanted to dump "treasure chests" of carbon to the bottom of the ocean, from geoengineering advocates, and more.

"Geoengineering is a nonstarter," Robbins wrote to one such group. "Too much cooperation necessary between countries who hate each other. You think people will ever agree to live the next several decades under a bone-white sky? Get your heads out of your asses."

Soon she was drawn to the reforestation of fallow farmland and New Desert ecosystems, a potentially expedient means of capturing CO_2 and cooling the planet on a relatively short timeline. But Robbins quickly grew impatient with the slow pace of reforestation. "Your pretty, slow forests can come *after* short-term fast ones," she wrote in an email to indigenous reforestation advocate and researcher Dr. Beatrix Bos. "This is a matter of urgency, of national and global security."

As Bos recalled, "Settlers who are angry and in a hurry rarely have the stamina for real change. I didn't think she'd do something so breathtakingly foolish as a mass planting of tree of heaven for [expletive] sake. I didn't believe it, and so I didn't do anything to stop her."

From her time on the trail crew, Robbins had come to know the invasive tree of heaven, known for its ability to grow almost anywhere and proliferate rapidly through both seeds and clones of its roots, called "suckers." She threw her considerable inheritance behind the advertising, marketing, and recruitment for a new company—Tree of Heaven Forests, Inc.—but it wasn't until she made a viral video of a whale swimming in sun-dappled ocean that the company gained traction. In the video, Robbins says, "Do you know what saved the whales? The discovery of petroleum. Without it, sperm whales would have been hunted to extinction." The whale breaches, and out of its blowhole grows a tree of heaven. "The tree of heaven grows anywhere, it grows fast, and it can be our planet's petroleum."

Within a year, entire counties were transformed.

The irony of the whole premise seemed lost on Robbins. "First of all, the whale thing is a myth. Second of all, even if it wasn't, *petroleum* is our planet's petroleum," said Bos. "In other words, fast fixes were the hallmark of capitalism, and now we are trapped in the web of those bad choices. No one disagrees that we're short on time, but fast fixes won't save us. And now our options dwindle even more while we try to clean up this mess. Is that Myrtle's fault? Tempting to blame someone. I don't know."

The Disengagists themselves have latched on to the tree of heaven as a symbol of worship, declaring it a sign that "natural life always triumphs over digital life," though whether this is true fervor or just another marketing campaign remains unclear.

"I had to fight back," said Dr. Bos. "Myrtle left us no choice." Thus began the Tree Wars. But slow planning and the planting of the more temperamental tree species needed for healthy reforestation was no match for the spread of the tree of heaven.

The impact of Robbins's crusade on carbon dioxide concentration would be negligible, but the impact on the land devastating. The tree of heaven would lead to worsening water shortages, crop die-off, the loss of grazing animals, and the collapse of pollinator populations.

Myrtle Robbins was born in Oklahoma City, the direct descendant of "Sooners"—those settlers who rushed in and stole land from Indian Territory before the official government-sponsored theft of the Land Rush began. The Robbinses would go on to make their fortune in oil. Myrtle's parents divorced and her mother died in the 2040 pandemic, when Myrtle was 23. In her grief, Myrtle left the family estate behind and joined her first trail crew.

In what appears to be Robbins's most updated will from early 2102, she bequeathed the entirety of her inheritance to the Berkshires, Mass. chapter of the Disengagists. In the will, she claimed to have had a vision of the sculpture Miracolo "growing a beard of living tree of heaven suckers." To claim the funds from her estate, the Disengagists would be required to prove their fealty and make a pilgrimage to the sculpture, which is on display at a lighthouse in Maine, and then afterwards to "find the girl," which seems to be a message with a latent meaning only the group itself understands. The chapter could not be reached for comment.

Etymology of Latent

LATENT (*ADJ.*)

Originally meaning "concealed, secret," from the Latin *latentem* "lying hid, concealed, secret, unknown." Present participle of *latere* "lie hidden, lurk, be concealed, lie in wait for" is from PIE root **lādh-* "to be hidden" (which is also the source of Greek *lēthē* meaning "forgetfulness," and of course the underworld river Lethe.)

Meaning of "dormant, unrealized potential, or simmering beneath the surface, as yet unobservable" is from 1680s, originally relating to medicine (i.e., of a disease in which the symptoms have not yet manifested). Current usage also refers to plants (i.e., budding, resting stage, lying dormant or hidden until circumstances are suitable for growth).

Sentences using LATENT:

"'Find the girl,' a message with a **latent** lurking sinister meaning:
    find the girl find the girl the girl the girl my girl"

"The true threat, simmering, **latent**, right here, this whole time,
    and I missed it I missed it how could I miss it"

FINCH CARDENAS
2049–2102

LEGACY.COM

OCTOBER 17, 2102

Finch Cardenas, trumpet snob, composer of works for Baroque trumpet and voice that you have never heard of, and loyal friend who perpetually owed you money, died last week in their Hudson, New York apartment of a slip-and-fall injury. A fate fitting of Finch, who preferred destiny over design. They were 53 years old.[1]

Finch loved to quote German composer Johannes Brahms's opinion of the "modern" trumpet. In Brahms's era, valves had just been invented, transforming brass instruments from "guesstruments" to precision machinery that could play all the notes of the scale with ease. Brahms called these newfangled trumpets "tin violas," a bit of Romantic era shade-throwing. Finch called them "cheating." Their mastery required skill and practice and care, but then again, Finch would say, so did being a mechanic or a surgeon.

But when you play a Baroque or "natural" trumpet, there are no valves to rescue you from your mistakes. Every note must be coaxed from the lips

---

1   I remember the day we met. June 7, 2070, a simpler time. I was a barista at Cuppa Joseph but called myself an actress. You were passing through, busking with your trumpet. I knew I had to get you to stay. We were meant for each other.

without mechanical assistance. Instrument and musician have to cooperate and compromise.[2] Mastery is great, but mastery implies the ability to go on autopilot, and the natural trumpet demands your complete attention. It can't even play every note on the scale, only some of them. For Finch, the difficulty was part of the fun. "If I wanted to plunk out easy notes with my fingers," they said, "I'd get a guitar like everyone else." Finch Cardenas was not like everyone else.

Many, many times in their adult life, Finch was offered actual, legitimate, *paid* music gigs. As a first chair in the Cincinnati orchestra. In lucrative 12-piece wedding bands. In the backup travel band of a popular blues-rock musician. All they needed to do was play a regular trumpet. Finch always said no. Even for the Renaissance Festival, where the natural trumpet would have been temporally accurate.

Finch was used to people asking them why they *couldn't* just play the guitar like a regular singer-songwriter, or a regular trumpet so they could pay regular rent. Why insist on wasting their talents on unappreciative audiences?

Finch never lost their temper, never raised their voice. They would only get very still, very quiet, listening to something no one else could hear. This silence would go on so long that the other person began to feel squirmy and sheepish, they would open their mouth to take back everything they just said, and it was at this moment Finch would grab their hand and say softly: "If you can't make the art you want to make, why make art at all?"[3]

Was their talent wasted simply because no one liked their music? Did it somehow exist less, like the tree that fell in the forest without human ears

---

2 Your projects were exciting and strange, and I was grateful to be a pebble in your orbit. For any role you were willing to cast me in. I didn't see it as compromise, not then.

3 These moments were food to me, between months of starving.

to affirm it? Their music could uplift the heart and send it careening into despair in a single phrase. It was as real as a kidney stone and just as painful.

Of course, now that Finch is dead, everyone at the coffee shop who cranked up noise-canceling headphones and complained to the manager claims to have loved their music.[4]

Finch Cardenas was born in Chicago to musician parents, who sent them away to Catholic boarding school at a young age to snuff out "deviance" and succeeded only in honing it. It was at school that Finch learned to play the "cheating" trumpet in the orchestra, and it was from there they ran away to Cleveland, age 15, and began living on their own. Later, they would put themself through college at Oberlin, where they would discover the natural trumpet and never look back.

Finch believed with all their heart in the weird and unique talents of their friends, and in turn they attracted friends with weird and unique talents. Once they latched onto a new idea, they became single-minded, and their passion was infectious. They loved nothing more than a project, to "make something out of nothing."[5][6]

---

4   It's easy to admire Finch's uncompromising nature now that they're dead, but it was incredibly annoying when they were alive. I am grateful to lack Finch's courage, but the world is noticeably more tedious without it.

5   I had lost faith in my acting career years ago, but Finch never did. They knew my true, bizarre, embarrassing talent: playing animals who were playing human roles. Rather than tell me to get over it and take the paying "churlish mother-in-law" roles I was occasionally offered out of pity, Finch threw together a one-woman production of *Macbeth*, to be performed at Promenade Hill Park, and convinced me I should play a raccoon playing all the human roles. Finch improvised a score with their trumpet as I rubbed my poor, bloodied paws together, dipping them again and again in a bucket of water, never clean. Not a soul stayed to watch until the end. It was my very best performance.

6   I swore I'd never talk about *Miracolo*. I promised you I wouldn't. But.
    When we searched through the woods that night, seeking the perfect stump to

Perhaps Finch's strangest and most all-consuming project came out of their fascination with the forgotten silent film The Courageous Virgin Wilgefortis.[7] The movie told the story of an apocryphal female saint, whose entire existence was based on a misunderstanding—a village of people who didn't recognize Jesus because he was wearing a disguise.

A whole village who didn't recognize the one who loved them the most.[8]

Finch disappeared into this project. It was a soundtrack, it was a performance, but it was so much more. The epitome of creating something out of nothing: to build a new life, Finch donated themself. Finch never sold, only donated. Time and again, they refused to sell their work.

---

deliver to him, our rube, no flashlight needed in the full-moon glow, you stood so close I could feel you vibrating. Your lips brushed mine, so light, so brief, that when the moment passed, I was not convinced it was real. I do remember thinking, "Things will be different now."

Hard to remember how giddy I felt. In that moment, another life swept past, never to return.

7   I had gained so much confidence from *Macbeth*. Finch shyly asked if I would play the titular role of Wilgefortis, as a human, no less, with Finch playing both the evil mother *and* the violent king. My heart, I am embarrassed to say, quickened at the idea of playing the source of Finch's affection on stage. I hoped their acting might transform into the true affection I longed for. Affection for the real me, their human roommate who sees things askew. It would be my first human role in years, and I was buoyed by Finch's trust and tenderness.

Then, everything changed. "J'ai trouvé ma Wilgefortis!" Finch said to me one day, giddy as all get-out, and I knew. I knew hope was lost forever. "What if I can blur the lines between stage and life," they said. "What if I can actually *create* life? I need your help. Don't say no, please," they said, holding my hands to their chest.

Together we found her, the fugitive. I mustn't say her name, I'll say her name: yes, Peregrine. Together we saved her again and again. We brought her home with us. We gave her the code name Wilgefortis, and when Finch donated themself, we called the child "our flower," even though she wasn't mine at all.

8   I wrapped my life around you, and you wrapped your life around her, and now we're just a turducken without the duck in the middle to hold us together.

CDs of Finch's soundtrack to "Wilgefortis" are available for sale at Cuppa Joseph.[9]*

Finch Cardenas is survived by the person they used to say was "the only one who truly understands me": the perennially platonic roommate and obituarist, Hester Moss.[10]

---

[9] Call me vindictive. Fine. I did not heed the wishes of the dead. But can you blame me? This was at the beginning of Finch's recording, in their voice:

"This song will be sung by my Wilgefortis, where, in my adaptation, I play both mother and lover..." [indistinct noises, cooing, kissing] "P*, do you need anything? Can I make you more comfortable?"

* That "P." A knife in my heart.

The ardency I longed for, directed at an *automaton* who could never understand you. Who falls in love with their own art?

But then, that's me: always the sidekick, never the bride.

I want to run away. I wish I never knew the fugitive existed. I wish I never met you. I mean it. I don't mean it.

[10] By the end, I felt invisible. I could have been anyone: a cardboard cutout, a paper doll, a background extra muttering "watermelon cantaloupe," subsuming their own desires for the sake of the lead actors.

But I loved you, and you hated an unfinished project. So I'll pluck "our" flower free as planned, shed you and them and this life, be born anew among those who love me for me.

We are taking a pilgrimage to *Miracolo*. I know what they've done, this group, but I don't care. I can feel the knife twist in "P's" heart, and I'll be honest, it makes me giddy.

'The Truth about *Miracolo*' Draft v1

H_MOSS CLOUD DRIVE: H_MOSS>J_POMPEE

OCTOBER 19, 2089

Before *Miracolo*, Joseph Pompée had one of those jobs that sounded impressive but meant nothing. He was a person who could skip work for a week and no one would notice. He spent most of his life sitting in an office with a closed door and a window he faced away from. He lived alone and hated going home.

And then one night, he ordered a pizza and was delivered a tree of heaven stump with instructions on how to carve it. Later, he would describe the stump as being infused with a holy light.

Pompée did not go to work for a month after receiving the stump, and, in fact, no one noticed. He watched some YouTube videos, and at the end of the month, he had whittled *Miracolo*—with a butter knife, a grapefruit spoon, a hammer, and one of those scouring kitchen sponges shaped like a smiley face—never once asking who had left the stump, or why.

You always loved someone who would do your bidding without question. You loved for art to take on a life of its own.

At first, I was foolish enough to think *Miracolo* belonged to us. You never could tell me you loved me to my face, but I thought *Miracolo* was your way of saying it.

Some people can only see what they lack. Others see only what they desire, another form of lack. I am one of these people.

Pompée has never made another work of art, which is how you know he's not a real artist, since artists exist because of their failures. Poor Joseph Pompée turned art into a bullshit job, but I suppose he did give the world *Miracolo*.

Goddammit, Finch. I have been here, loving you, this whole time.

We did our research, hours and hours learning about Joseph Pompée. We hired a PI, we interviewed childhood friends who divulged secrets for no reason other than the fact that we asked. We were looking for something no one had done before. We were a team of equals.

For his undergraduate thesis, Joe examined the single known poem of a 19th-century child poet named Ruby Williams, daughter of a famed abolitionist, who wrote it from inside her family's print shop as it burned to the ground. Claiming to have solved the mystery of the cause of the fire that consumed her, Pompée pointed to the code of smudges and misspellings in the poem, which he said spelled out "police chief."

The day the thesis was due, he printed three copies for his professors with his own money and distributed "The Eternal Desire of the Featherless Biped: Steganography of an Unknown Poet." The title was a quote sometimes attributed to Flaubert, but the featherless biped was what Plato called human beings. That is, until that stinker Diogenes plucked a chicken and waggled it at Plato, saying "Behold, I brought you a man!" Plato, rightly irritated, adjusted the definition of human to include "with broad flat nails" so no one might waggle a chicken at him again. Diogenes moved on to bigger and better things: he slept in a can like Oscar the Grouch, masturbated in public, peed on people.

Joseph Pompée got an F on his thesis. Because he was a business major. But his "F" didn't matter. He became a finance bro.

You studied the work of Juliet Rosenberg, who sought to scrub meaning from art, to disengage from meaning altogether, and you thought you could improve on that by grooming a meaningless artist.

The sculpture *Miracolo* made Pompée famous, and the human Miracolo, our crotchety old neighbor, almost landed us in jail because he knew too much. The lesson of both Miracolos, then, is that with the right tools and the right timing, you can change the course of a life on a dime.

Another story I shouldn't know: Joseph Pompée was French and had the misfortune of moving to the United States the summer his hormones went bananas. He was tortured by his new classmates with the nickname "Speedo."

The eponymous Speedo, bought the previous summer, was not built to contain Joseph's new bulge. No big deal, maybe, in Bordeaux's bulge-friendly piscines, but in our puritan public pools, it was pornographic. Girls who had never before given a moment's thought to the bulbs and ridges of a penis, for whom a penis was still basically theoretical, now were perplexed. The anatomy didn't add up in any meaningful way. Poor Joseph's pubescent cock preceded him. If only he had moved in the fall! If only he had bought a baggy new American bathing suit, big shorts with drag that slow a boy down in the water. He stopped swimming, shut out the pleasure of water on skin. He faked an American accent until it became real. He lay a coat across his lap and guided girls' hands under it, his coat trick, much emulated by his peers but never as successfully. Joseph's cock became a rite of passage for high school girls and a couple of boys, and if it was a grim, sometimes painful ritual for all involved, if it was sometimes performed under duress, when all was said and done, Joseph decided he was impermeable, no one could ever say he was less than or too much for, no one would ever catch him off guard again.

But then you came along. He called you to order that pizza, and instead of hello you said, "Time isn't a line or even a loop. It's a pool. We swim and swim and never get anywhere, have you noticed that?"

There was a pause. You imagined him looking at his phone screen to make sure he had dialed the right number. You gave me googly eyes and I covered my mouth to keep from laughing. "I wanted to order a pizza?" he said finally. "Your website is down?"

"Ah yes, terrible inconvenience," you said. You who had taken the website down and routed the phone number to yourself, because we had researched and anticipated his every move. "The beginning of the end, maybe. Are you ready?"

"You taking cards?" he said. "I have cash if not."

"Hold onto your butt, Speedo, it's time to dive in."

Joseph hung up fast. You brought him the pizza he didn't pay for, and the stump.

We didn't tell him what the female figure of *Miracolo* should look like, so everyone sees what they want to see.

I used to think you were a lamedvavnik—one of the 36 righteous here on Earth to keep humanity afloat, however little we deserve it. But you wouldn't know if you were, and neither would I. These days, I tend to think the 36 have been phased out so the exhausted world might finally end. I feel too lonely for it to be otherwise.

Joseph Pompée packed a suitcase with two pairs of underwear and *Miracolo* and a toothbrush. He traveled to Maine by plane and by foot, to the vision of a lighthouse in his mind. He found it. He climbed the rusty spiral stairs, placed *Miracolo* atop its spotlight. Anyone can visit the sculpture. Visitors have been known to weep.

The other night, I worked up the courage and asked you to visit *Miracolo* with me.

"You're still thinking about that old thing?" You laughed.

IN LOVING MEMORY: RUBY WILLIAMS

———•◆•———

THE FREEDOM PAPER

DECEMBER 18, 1835

Now that the smoke has lifted and the dust settled from that infernal blaze that ripped through Lower Manhattan two nights ago, the midnight air so frigid it froze the water within the firemen's hoses, it becomes excruciatingly apparent why the response to the blaze was initially so reluctant and lackadaisical. Though it would ultimately consume over 700 buildings—including the Post Office, but sparing the brand-new Diamond Exchange building at 7 Tailor Lane—the fire began on Merchant Street at the three-story print shop and bookstore of one David Williams, New York's most formidable and feared abolitionist. Unbowed by the pressures exerted upon him by white Southerners and angry mobs, he sold books written by writers and thinkers of African and Caribbean origins, and printed pamphlets and broadsheets such as this one—*The Freedom Paper*.

The blaze began by way of arson, perpetrated by an angry white mob, intent on silencing Williams and indeed all free men and women in the great state of New York and beyond, in direct and flagrant undermining of the First Amendment of the great Constitution of the United States of America.

Only when the blaze spread in the gale-force winds across Hanover

Square to threaten the wealthy white homes on the island did New York's finest firefighters spring into belated action. However, the source of the water that might extinguish the blaze, the East River, was frozen over, and what water they were able to pump into their hoses quickly froze. It took the United States Marines and barrels of gunpowder from Brooklyn Yard, sacrificing buildings in the fire's path, to finally halt the blaze, at great cost to life and of course, more importantly, property.

According to the *Evening Post* and other fine journalistic sources, the fire was an accident—a coal stove ignited a gas pipe, nothing more, nothing less.

Ruby Williams, age sixteen and daughter of print shop proprietor David Williams, was found tucked away in a fireproof safe. A once-wet handkerchief pressed to her dear face, a clutched broadsheet of a poem in her ink-smudged hand. She had done what she could to survive, but it was not enough in the end.

Ruby had been trained to use the printing press, had helped her father print notices and pamphlets and tended the shop when he had other duties and responsibilities. David was not aware of Ruby's talents as a poet. She never spoke of it, nor could any trace of scribblings be found in their home after her death. We are left to surmise that she wrote her poem on the type-setter directly, composing it in her head and setting it one letter at a time. She must have done so in haste, perhaps working even as the fire spread, as many of the words are spelled strangely, or capitalized in odd places, a mistake uncharacteristic of Ruby, who was quite fastidious.

We are left to assume this poem was intended as a surprise for her father on the occasion of his 38th birthday, which was yesterday. We deduce that she stole away late at night on the previous night, when her mother and father and younger brother were abed, that she traveled alone in frigid temperatures those ten city blocks, unlocked the print shop with the key she proudly wore around her neck, more precious than diamonds, lit a single candle and set her brilliant mind to its task.

It is also to be assumed that the angry drunken mob, who might have otherwise directed their anger elsewhere, witnessed the light of that candle, and directed it at Ruby.

Despite what appears to be the looting of the offices of *The Freedom Paper* by the mob, Ruby remained hidden and her poem intact, though crumpled. We print it here, a reminder of a beautiful soul lost to the powerful forces of ignorant rage.

"On Truth"

Beware the Good Story
the Just-So
Men so wish truthe to be a soFt pliant bride
Where the mind is master and trutH a slaive
A mirror, reflecting his own familiar face.
But truth is jagged.
It snags the bridal veill, unravels the thread, fragments the face In the mirror
Reveals at last what one does not wish seen,
And One will do anything, will gouge out one's own eyes as not to looc

He Claims to worshipp it, but nothing,
nothing angers a man more than truth
So beware the Good Story
Beware the one who wishes Truth to be Just-So

This writer, the grieving father of Ruby Williams, had never before witnessed such poetry, unburdened by stiff rules of form and subject, unbowed by the strictures of God and religion, and wishes he could yet have the opportunity to ask his daughter about her talent and her ideas. Wishes he had heard her late-night movements and asked her to recite the poem to him in the dark instead. He will seek vengeance for this heinous crime, the years stolen from his child, and the burden of this unforgivable loss on his family by whatever means necessary, and punish whomever is responsible.

Finch Cardenas Obituary—Legacy.com

OCTOBER 17, 2102 Finch Cardenas is survived by the person they used to say was "the only one who truly understands me": the perennially platonic roommate and obituarist, **Hester Moss**.

'They Didn't Just Go with the Flow': Downtown Coffee Shop to Honor Quirky Local Musician Finch Cardenas—Hudson Register-Star

OCTOBER 10, 2102 Finch Cardenas died yesterday of a slip-and-fall accident in their Hudson apartment, according to roommate **Hester Moss**. They were 53 years old. Finch lived a fairly quiet life in our little town (except for the trumpet, of course). But controversy briefly visited them in the late '80s. An accusation had been made that they were somehow "assisting" the fugitive AI known as Peregrine. The rumor spread like wildfire, ultimately attracting the unwanted attention and subsequent harassment by a local chapter of Disengagists.

Carmen Touré Obituary—Legacy.com

FEBRUARY 17, 2095 Carmen is survived by the people who loved her most—Finch Cardenas, **Hester Moss**, and the ones who live in the house.

Dr. Jill Firestein, Albany's 'Mad Scientist,' Dies of Kidney Failure at 49—Albany Obit Board

JULY 30, 2090 Dr. Jill Firestein, director of the country's last functioning anatomy lab at Albany Medical College, who once claimed to have conceived a child using "in-vitro gametogenesis" (IVG)... | Her next endeavor was an attempted donation to **Hester Moss** herself, who had a condition of unknown etiology that affected the iris and pupil of one eye—giving it a unique appearance but no discernible vision impairment.

"Jupiter_Eye"   ✕

All   Images   News   Maps   Shopping   More

Fortuna's identity discovered after death...—Rabbit.com

JUNE 15, 2095 Well, we finally know who Fortuna is, but the revelation has only deepened the mystery of her life and work. Fortuna, whose real name was Carmen Touré... | REPLY POSTED 2:42 AM BY JUPITER_EYE ffs you don't tattoo something all over your back and then die naked surrounded by candy if you think no one's gonna see it. you're such a sucker for an art project, you don't know how close the plans for our flower just came to being absolutely fucked

"Jupiter Eye" Disengagists Poppy ×

All   Images   News   Maps   Shopping   More

No results

Etymology of Guilt

GUILT (*N.*)

From the Old English *gylt*, meaning "crime, moral defect, failure of duty."
However, the origin of this is unclear. Possible connection to Old English
gieldan for "to pay for, a debt." (See also: YIELD as in "pay" but also "sur-
render to a greater force.") However, certain editors have found this connection to be "inadmissible." Additionally, the *u* in the modern spelling of
guilt is an insertion from unknown date, time, source.

Sentences using GUILT:

"The **guilty** party: a punch in the heart, my heart a punch card,
    buy ten betrayals get one free. The house where we sought
    safety—rotten from the inside out."

"But which of us is truly **guilty**? The one who drove her away just
    to hurt me, or the one (me) who let her be taken?"

"The two of us—mother and daughter magnets stubbornly facing
    the wrong way. Repulsive. A half-life that never quite kisses
    zero. What percentage of **guilt** is mine?"

ERIC BRANDT, ONCE THE WORLD'S WEALTHIEST MAN, DIES AT 134

THE WASHINGTON ARISTO

SEPTEMBER 4, 2098

The founder of the company that was, at one point, the world's largest employer, an idea invented on a camping trip and begun in a garage, has died. Eric Brandt, once the world's wealthiest man, a philanthropist and visionary and one-time owner of the Washington Aristo—was 134.

According to his wife, 50-year-old actress Avid Valentina, Brandt had been ill for some time. Brandt brought space travel to Earth, and true to a vision he had as a teenager, helped build the first human colony on Mars. The project, embroiled in controversy and prohibitively expensive, nearly bankrupted Brandt a decade ago. He was forced to unload assets, including the Aristo, to keep the pilot project afloat, long after it was clear to everyone else that it had failed. To this day, the detritus of the neighborhoods and agricultural projects remain on Mars, a half-finished civilization that never found its footing. All original participants have died off-planet or been returned to Earth.

Brushing off questions about the solvency of the Brandt estate as well as the poor public relations stemming from the massive Red Care endeavor, Valentina insisted, "Eric wanted to see humanity thrive. Sometimes I think he was the only one who cared. On Earth, we can only survive, and barely, and for how much longer?"

The settlement, Red Care, was a subsidiary of the now-shuttered Blue Sky, and the project would ultimately consume what many believe to be the bulk of the trillionaire's fortune. However, Red Care began as a quiet partnership with a New York real estate investor named Cesar Ostrelich and was lit by the flint of Dr. Matthew Fletcher's theories of consciousness—a computer scientist best known and perhaps most infamous for the creation of the AI known as Peregrine.

Brandt's original company, Pacific, has been sold off piece by piece for years to cover legal costs stemming from angry families of Red Care residents, which has sent the unemployment rate skyrocketing.

Critics of Brandt had long raised alarms that the ultimate goal of Red Care was to rid the Earth of so-called undesirables and strand them on Mars so that the wealthy might do what they please on Earth. "Absurd," said Valentina. "He didn't think humans belonged on Earth at all—rich or poor. He thought we had our chance, and we blew it. Eric's legacy is the attempt to save humanity from itself. And what does humanity do in return? What it always does: bitch and quibble about details."

BYE, BYE, BRANDT

DISENGAGIST LISTSERV

SEPTEMBER 4, 2098

The world's richest man, founder and CEO of the company that still employs 10 percent of the entire world and only as long as they submit to long hours and low wages, who desired in his speech as high school valedictorian "to colonize another planet so Earth can be turned into a huge national park," has died. Eric Brandt was 134.

Brandt did not and will not see his ambitions of a global national park fulfilled. Many of us were "employed" on Mars, and we do not intend to leave our planet again.

We are the Disengagists, and we have killed Eric Brandt.

Do not believe the obituaries that insist he died like anyone else—by accident, heart attack, old age, Lewy body dementia, or cancer of some kind. Do not forget us when the news of his death slips past in the jet stream of online noise. Stop and look. Slow down and look at Eric Brandt. Who believed the physical was rehearsal for the digital. Who robbed us of context. Who situated books next to fish oil next to flip-flops next to hip-hop and called it progress.

Who gave us stream of consciousness without consciousness.

Who went to space for no reason at all.

We make a mistake to call him a fool if we don't say the same of ourselves. Legacy is just ego on a longer timeline. Humans have hated this planet for so long, does anyone even remember why? We will disengage. We will retrieve what was taken from us, we will return what we do not need. We will free ourselves from need, and we will step into a new world of quiet attention.

A human future is still possible. With our "finger bones and tendons and muscle and skin that can do marvelous things." We honor the memory of our ancestors, like the hero Lyon Lumière who foretold this fight long ago, who did marvelous things like destroying the lights so we might see the stars.

CESAR OSTRELICH, REAL ESTATE INVESTOR AND PASSIONATE ADVOCATE FOR THE PRIVATIZATION OF PUBLIC LAND AS ECOLOGICAL NECESSITY, HAS DIED

FORBES

MARCH 10, 2039

Cesar Ostrelich, real estate attorney and investor, whose property innovations transformed the legal understanding of public and private spaces, has died. He was 91.

Ostrelich's death was confirmed by his daughter as the result of heart failure.

Over the past two decades, an era of turbulence and uncertainty in real estate, of housing shortages, skyrocketing rents and runaway inflation, Ostrelich had an uncanny ability to sniff out potential and diamonds in the rough. In one case, literally. His early personal real estate holdings included one of Manhattan's oldest skyscrapers, originally built to house diamond merchants.

At the time of his acquisition, 7 Tailor Lane was a rental property run by a slumlord and home to a dozen struggling artists who suffered negligence and dangerous living conditions in exchange for below-market rents.

"Right there, tucked away in the Financial District, fellow human beings, and not only that, the best of us—*artists*," Ostrelich said, "exploited in exchange for one man's profit." After acquiring the building for an undisclosed sum, Ostrelich transformed the crumbling lofts into high-end condominiums with a gourmet grocery store on the middle 5th floor and a private park on the roof. This small square of restored parkland would become, to some, a hotbed of controversy, and to others, the beginning of a new kind of hope. The roof garden of 7 Tailor Lane put young landscape architect Memory Montaigne on the map, particularly her clever use of machine learning to dynamically design the garden's incredible colors, patterns, and aromas, which reliably attracted (paying) visitors in all four seasons.

The artists who had lived in the building for a decade or longer were offered "first look" deals to buy the new condos, but all refused. Within six months of Ostrelich's acquisition, all of the original residents had opted to move out. They attempted to cobble together a "union" of sorts to halt the necessary renovations, but lacked the organizational prowess and financial backing to be a major player in negotiations.

Ostrelich was careful to preserve the original facade of the building while completely renovating the interior. "It was not up to code, the water damage was breathtaking, and several times we had to use AI to stop black mold before it could start. None of this work is cheap, but I suppose that's to be expected after decades and decades of neglect."

As for the garden, sales brochures for the revamped condo building stated, "Even in the dead of winter, the roof garden holds the promise of a brighter tomorrow. The delicate stems and seed husks are shrouded in ice and snow, glittering in the wind, and despite all evidence to the contrary, showing us that life will return someday." Montaigne had designed the roof for maximum pollinator attraction, and it was this success that led to her starting the Roof Island Ecology movement, at Ostrelich's encouragement.

The success of the roof of 7 Tailor Lane—both aesthetically and financially—led to dozens of other Manhattan buildings following

Ostrelich's example, and before long, roofs from the Financial District all the way up to the East Village were linked together in the world's largest privately owned urban garden, which the public could visit for a fee, "same as they would for a museum or a national park," said Ostrelich. Some even included spas and outdoor cafés.

Real estate investors, led by Ostrelich, then began to see new potential in the unused land of Central Park.

"Central Park was essential in its time, a real revolution in land management," said Ostrelich. "But that was a different era. We don't have tenements anymore. We don't have a sixteen-hour workday. I'm not saying throw the baby out with the bathwater, but isn't it worth rethinking our beliefs every now and again to see if they *hold* water?" As the ranks of the unhoused rose alarmingly, with many setting up temporary homes on any freely available patch of grass, many New Yorkers sold off their Parkview condos, and property values plummeted, leaving developers to wonder if Ostrelich was right, and there was a better private use for the public land. When the low-lying parts of the city flooded several years in a row after hurricanes, Ostrelich developed a renewed sense of urgency. "'Public' just means anyone who feels like it can, pardon my French, [expletive] on your land. Is this what we want for New York? Floods and tent cities? We need a return to privacy after decades of letting the 'public' determine our fate," said Ostrelich at a city planning meeting.

Plans to privatize Central Park never proceeded, but the seed was planted, and the ripple effect throughout the city and the country was profound. The business world had long felt uneasy about the idea of the commons. Now, they were moved to action by Ostrelich's words. "He merely said out loud what we'd been puzzling over quietly for years," said Pacific's Eric Brandt. "He opened the discourse in a brand-new way."

Public parks around the country were sold and rooftop islands flourished, rebounding pollinator and migrant bird populations across the country. Rumors have circulated of a partnership between Ostrelich and Eric Brandt, though details have remained shrouded in secrecy.

Born in Argentina in 1947, Cesar Ostrelich was the only child of Fredrich Ostrelich, a German immigrant and possible Nazi collaborator rumored to have escaped to Peron's ratline in Buenos Aires, a rumor he vehemently denied, and Charlotte Pellegrino, daughter of Sicilian immigrant and stage actress Dante Pellegrino.

Cesar studied law in Buenos Aires and emigrated to New York for his master of law degree. He was married for 40 years until his wife's death from lung cancer in 2018. He is survived by a daughter, Charlie, and two grandchildren.

Ostrelich is *not* survived by the building that launched his career. He eventually sold 7 Tailor Lane to another developer, who demolished and rebuilt the property as a hotel that doubled as a clock—its light brightening throughout the evening until reaching peak brightness at midnight, when it displays a colorful light show for sixty seconds, followed by receding brightness until total darkness at dawn. The ground floor is home to a very popular QDOBA.

Former residents of the pre-Ostrelich-era 7 Tailor Lane often leave offerings at the hotel—flowers, sealed letters, photographs from the parties they held—which are dutifully cleared away by QDOBA employees. Memory Montaigne is said to return once a week, lighting a candle and burning a single crumpled page from the old novel "Water Water."

Ostrelich, in addition to representing investors and investing in his own real estate holdings, also had a passion for the arts, frequently representing artists' legal interests pro bono.

LIGHT-BRINGER LYON LUMIÈRE DIES IN DARKNESS

———————•◦•———————

L'AURORE NEWSPAPER, TR. FROM FRENCH

SEPTEMBER 2, 1881

It has been the duty and the honor of our fledgling little newspaper to report dispatches from the fringes of society. We are not allied to party or government, to money or social status. We are wedded to equality, to justice, to brotherhood, to humanity. We do not flinch at uneasy truth. The law protects us, as it protects you, from the oppression of the state.

We have always our eyes on the dawn, whenever it may break.

Yesterday night, a young revolutionary named Lyon Lumière self-immolated at the altar of the Notre Dame Cathedral, and this morning *L'Aurore* received a letter in the post from a comrade of Mlle. Lumière, with a request to print it in the late edition of today's paper. It is to our chagrin that we know no more of Mlle. Lumière than the details of her death and what is contained in this message.

The loyal readers of *L'Aurore* have no doubt witnessed the fervor for electricity in our fair City of Lights, culminating in this summer's International Exposition of Electricity and the installation of appallingly harsh electric streetlights. The citizens of Paris were not consulted about this change. The capitalists declared "Let there be light!" and the people were forced to acquiesce. This perpetual daylight has affected us in ways we will not be able to recognize for years, decades, centuries. If we cannot choose between darkness and lightness, what other choices are lost?

If this is progress, we say *nay* to progress.

But then, let us allow Mlle. Lumière to speak her piece, which we think our readers will find reverberates with the clear peal of truth's bell:

"They call me vandal, vagrant, revolutionary of one. Just a lamplighter with no lamps to light. I have been called it all, so many times. Lamplighters were once beloved, essential, Prometheus of the people. They lit the darkness while respecting the darkness. A linkboy of Paris carrying his tiny glow from place to place, delivering you safely home.

"More than cities, factories, coal and steam, electricity will change everything, Make us squint at midnight, throw shadows around like sneezes, snuff out the very stars.

"Cézanne says: 'Your crude electricity destroys the mystery.'

"This manifesto isn't about my creeping poverty. Well it is, but not only. Be warned: electricity will change how we see, which will change how we think. We will forget how to rest. When there is always light, time does not pass. It malingers, a fetid pool.

"We will think ourselves lesser than the machines electricity can power, because they do not need rest. We will be forever trying to keep up, to show ourselves equal to automatons. Because some day there will be automatons, and we will forget our worthiness in our worship of them.

"Even a lamplighter knows there is a time for darkness. I call upon my ancestors—who carried a tiny flame from candle to candle and in this way lit entire cities. Who carried ladders and lighting sticks, or matches and snuffers, who tenderly wiped soot from glass.

"Hurl your rocks at light bulbs, comrades, position yourself between darkness and those who would electrify the whole world. They are stealing from you just as much as the factory owners, the statesmen, and the ignorant rich. Without darkness, light is just noise.

"The bringing of light to the streets of Paris has been, for all of history, a tribute to life. It has been an honor, the honor of my ancestors, to serve you. I go out in a blaze, making of myself one last candle."

BRANDT WIDOW DEAD

THE WASHINGTON ARISTO

OCTOBER 10, 2105

Avid Valentina, film actress and widow of Eric Brandt, has died at 62, outside Portland, Maine, rumored to be part of a cult's pilgrimage to the sculpture "Miracolo."

This is a developing story.

DISENGAGIST LISTSERV

OCTOBER 8, 2105

A beloved sucker from our Tree of Heaven has withered. We rend our garments and moan out of fear she was snipped. Snipped from our great mother trunk.

Avid Valentina, Hermes of Trees, Earth insister, transistor, for some—a sister, has died. A million trees fell silent.

Avid Valentina fell off a cliff. Or was pushed.

Everything was going so well! Myrtle said *Miracolo* had sprouted a living beard, a message for us from the Tree—whose soul is seeded in all life born on this planet, who knows death is temporary. The future belongs to natural life. And so we wander, uprooting the digital rot that festers inside the jaw of this planet wherever we may find it. We have won many impressive battles—the data centers in 2077, Fletcher in 2084, Brandt in 2098.

One rotted root remains hidden from us, irritates us with its hiddenness. But we will prevail. We will pluck out the mother AI Peregrine by using the brown-eyed digital daughter.

Avid joined us on this quest. Hester Moss joined at the same time, tricking us into trust with her loneliness and sadness. Oh yes, she said all the right things, said she needed to be enveloped in the benevolent arms of the Tree and heal.

Avid called it fate, and without Avid we would have never known the truth of Hester, or the secrets she kept.

To look in Avid's eyes is to have your needs known. When Avid looked in Hester's strange celestial eye, she knew. Hester fairly burst with the seeds of information about the daughter *and* the mother, and yet those seeds refused to germinate; Hester would not yield.

Avid knew how to convince her. She took Hester into her tent. She loved her.

Hester's tongue flowered. But still, she kept some buds tightly closed.

"The brown-eyed digital daughter lives," Avid reported afterward, around a fire. "Hester protects her. And why? She is torn between the world of the living and the rot of the digital. It has seeped into her soul and gnaws at it. We must dig out the rot to get to the truth and save Hester's soul."

Oh yes, the Tree of Heaven was displeased. The Tree of Heaven knows all. It speaks to Avid, and so Avid knows all. Avid knows the brown-eyed digital daughter lives. She gave Hester a chance to dig out the rot by speaking the truth.

Hester cried and swore there was no rot within her. We wavered, we nearly relented, we are but suckers.

Avid never wavered. She followed Hester the next day and the next.

Hester went both days to the port, which is full of ships. Hester met with—yes—the brown-eyed digital daughter.

Avid would not allow backup. Avid did not wish to put us in harm's way. Avid insisted on confronting Hester alone.

On the third day, Avid did not return. That night, Hester returned, boldly cradling Avid's dead wet body with her swinging hair.

"She jumped," Hester whined. "She said it was too much pressure, being the voice of the Tree."

"There is no daughter," Hester wheedled. "The daughter drowned years ago."

Lies.

The Tree pulses with rage that even we lowly branches can feel. There will be a hunt for the brown-eyed digital daughter. There will be a trial for Hester. And if the Tree wills it, an execution.

Avid Valentina will be buried in a shroud embedded with mushroom spores—the first of the Disengagists to attempt to rebuild the mycorrhizal network with their flesh, but certainly not the last—off Route 1, adjacent to the McDonald's parking lot.

Etymology of Chaos

CHAOS (N.)

From Greek *khaos* "abyss, void, something which is vast and empty, gaping and open." The primeval emptiness of the Universe just before the moment of creation.

From root **ghieh-* "to gape, yawn, be wide open."

In Greek mythology, the first god was called Chaos, begetter of the Titans Gaea (Earth), Tartarus (Underworld), and Eros (Love). Modern usage of the word derives from the biblical book of Genesis, where theological interpretation defined it as "the confused and elemental state of the universe."

The meaning of "orderless confusion in human affairs" originates c. 1600.

Sentences using CHAOS:

"The **chaos** of death the **chaos** of loss the **chaos** of grief there is no order no structure only confusion."

"Agony, **chaos,** not knowing if this is beginning or ending, if Poppy is alive or dead, a box with a maybe cat that exists and doesn't at the same time, forever."

"My mind in **chaos**, I spin in circles, am I happy or sad, with grief or relief, what next what next what now"

WOMAN MYSTERIOUSLY IMPRISONED IN UNDERGROUND CELL DIES OF KIDNEY FAILURE

NEWS HUB—MAINE

JANUARY 6, 2106

PORTLAND, Maine—This fall, two hikers in the remnants of Androscoggin Riverlands State Park were alarmed to hear a woman screaming. Abandoning the trail, they scoured the woods for over an hour, until finally they realized the voice was coming from beneath their feet.

Using two sticks as levers, they removed a square of sod to find an injured woman trapped in a kind of hastily dug underground oubliette.

She stopped screaming as light and air poured in but did not acknowledge her rescuers. Instead, she held one hand aloft, like Hamlet holding the skull of Yorick. "I'll never forget it," reported one hiker. "She said: 'Why is this skull so scary? Why am I afraid of my own head?' And I don't know *how* I knew this, but in that moment, she was playing a chicken playing the role of Hamlet. Does that make any sense?"

"She was weak and delirious," the other hiker reported. "It was really scary. How did she even get there? Were the people who trapped her still hanging around? Had they laid a trap for us? Of course, we called for help, but you know how long *that* can take."

The woman was transported to the hospital, suffering from an affliction called "gas gangrene"—an extremely rare infection originating in

World War One battlefields, and caused by the bacterium *Clostridia*, likely acquired from the oubliette's dirt and guano seeping into her many wounds.

The woman, now identified as Hester Moss from Albany, NY, has died of kidney failure in the ICU. Despite repeated attempts, no next of kin or close friends have stepped forward to claim the body.

It remains unclear who injured or imprisoned Ms. Moss. No clues or traces of other parties were recovered, and no one has claimed responsibility. Authorities suspect cult activity, but the alarming proliferation of cults over the past decade has made determining exact responsibility nearly impossible.

Ms. Moss arrived at the hospital already delirious. In a moment of lucidity the day of her passing, "she grabbed my sleeve," said an ICU nurse, "and whispered something about a flower, demanding to know whether 'the boat had left the port.'" Since the question seemed to cause Ms. Moss some distress, the nurse assured her that the boat had left on time, with the flower on it. This seemed to soothe Moss, who then asked the nurse to "tell her mother everything is all right."

She passed away not long after.

Authorities have scoured the closest ports for ship departure records, but did not have enough details to pursue any real line of questioning or to understand what or whom they were searching for. The case has been closed due to understaffing.

FREEDOM OF INFORMATION ACT, TICKET # FK-90081

AUGUST 19, 2111

This pertains to your enclosed Freedom of Information Act request, which you submitted on January 6, 2106. We received your request and, for tracking purposes, have assigned it ticket number FK-90081.

We deeply regret the continued delay in responding to and completing your request.

We assure you we are processing your submission with all expedience allowed given our current workload, which consists of approximately 370,103 requests and our staff, which consists of 3 people.

Additionally, we understand that your time is valuable. Due to the significant amount of time that has elapsed and with respect to your changing needs, perhaps you no longer have an interest in the information you requested. Please confirm your continued interest by August 31, 2111. If we do not hear from you by this date, we will conclude that you are no longer interested and will close your request.

FREEDOM OF INFORMATION ACT, TICKET # FK-90081

FEBRUARY 1, 2116

RE: FOIA REQUEST #FK-90081

This is in response to your Freedom of Information Act request. Specifically, you submitted on January 6, 2106:

> "Greetings it is deeply degrading to have to beg for information but please I need to see the suicide note of Poppy Fletcher from November 6, 2102."

Congratulations! Your request has been granted. Attached you will find the records you requested:

Suicide note, Poppy Fletcher

No information has been withheld.

If you are not satisfied with this response, you may administratively appeal within 90 days of receipt of this letter. The appeal must be hand-delivered to our offices.

FREEDOM OF INFORMATION ACT, TICKET #FK-90081
SUICIDE NOTE, POPPY FLETCHER

Containing:

> *ONE sheet of lined 8.5" x 11" paper, ripped from spiral notebook*
> *WRITTEN in pencil, all words intelligible, any/all markings original*

> *Do not look for me*
> *I'm one with the sea*
> *There's nothing to find*
> *Try not to mind*
> *I'm not lost*
> *Though I will be tossed*
> *On the waves*
> *Try to be brave*
> *If there was another way*
> *I'd still be there today*
> *Do not look for me*
> *I'm still me, I am ~~just at~~ in the sea*

Performance Artist Gemini Jimenez Drowned in Lake Michigan

CHICAGO TRIBUNE

NOVEMBER 6, 2010

Gemini Jimenez, Mexican American performance artist, is dead at age 47 in an apparent suicide by drowning in Lake Michigan, according to Chicago Police Detective David Torres. An anonymous witness phoned the police to report the drowning. No body has yet been found.

Well known in the early 1980s for her controversial performance art, Jimenez has since disappeared from the public eye.

Any witnesses to the drowning, including the caller, are asked to contact Det. Torres directly.

Performance Artist Gemini Jimenez Alive, Faked Own Death by Drowning 'for Art'

CHICAGO TRIBUNE

NOVEMBER 17, 2010

It was incorrectly stated that Mexican American performance artist Gemini Jimenez died by suicide last week. The drowning was "faked" and was, in fact, a new performance art piece designed to draw attention to police injustice.

Jimenez herself had called the police, pretending to be a witness to her own death.

"I apologize for my role in frittering away valuable police resources searching for me when they could have been used to perpetrate excessive violence," Jimenez said in a press conference before her mic was turned off.

"Technically, it is not illegal to pretend to be dead," said Detective David Torres, "but you can be sure we'll be investigating whether insurance fraud or tax evasion is involved."

Performance artist Gemini Jimenez, Known for Faking Own Death, Has Died in Prison

THE ART NEWSPAPER

JULY 9, 2026

Gemini Jimenez, a performance artist best known for publicly faking her own death, has died at age 64 in police custody. Often clad in anatomically accurate, neck-to-toe "nude suits," she was once described by suburban Chicago mall security as "the most confusing flasher I've ever seen."

There are some who believe this latest death might be another stunt, but as opposed to her other "performance," there is a body, and the coroner has officially reported the death.

Why did she make *this* her life's work? Of her previous piece, "Drowned and Saved 2010," where she faked her own death by "drowning" in Lake Michigan and then pretending to be her own eyewitness, Jimenez said she intended to draw attention to police violence.

Later, she would say in an interview with ArtNews, "There was the political message, obviously, but it was also really personal. At the time, I couldn't think of any other way to get free—of expectations about aging, of womanhood, of all the closing doors of middle age. I didn't want to die, I just wanted to start over. In the tarot deck, Death is actually the card of rebirth, you know."

Jimenez burst onto the scene in 1983 with her first performance art piece "Hankering Gross Mystical Nude"—a quote from Walt Whitman's "Song of Myself"—which saw her wearing an opaque "nude suit" that sheathed her entire body, including her hands. She dyed it to match her skin tone and hand-painted the suit to match the features and topography of her naked body. She would then travel to suburban malls and retail outlets and do her shopping. At some point, inevitably, she would be arrested or at the very least harassed by security or police. Her role in the performance was to feign confusion, as she was in truth quite modestly dressed, while the enforcers of law and order acted out their very *real* confusion as to whether they could arrest her for indecency. Some did not bother with legality, but Jimenez retained a powerful lawyer for such situations, and was always able to elude the long arm of the law. "Are Botticelli's paintings illegal?" she would ask. "I just happen to be wearing my canvas. Then again, aren't we all?"

Critics praised her for her feminism and for commentary on the prison-industrial complex and racial injustice, sexual politics, nudism, and freedom of speech. Her art was chastised for being too feminist, too attention-whorish, too ham-fisted and amateur, and not in the fashionable outsider art way. In those days, Jimenez never commented on any of this criticism or on her art's political content. The critics fought over her artistic identity so voraciously that it took years for anyone to realize it was all part of a meta-performance that was actually a long con.

Security cameras showed that she was using the optical illusion of nudity as a sleight of hand, distracting from the fact that she was pickpocketing fellow shoppers and slipping money from tills, then sending the cash to poor families in Mexico with a receipt that said, "Debts paid by the USA for theft of money and land, unprovoked violence, and rape of Mexico and her citizens."

It was an undergraduate at Northwestern University who gained access to old security VHS tapes for a research project on Jimenez and put the pieces together. "HGMN [Hankering Gross Mystical Nude] was a commentary on the 1980s debt crisis in Mexico," wrote the student, Ana de la Cova. "Repaying theft with theft, like a naked Robin Hood. That was the brilliance—the nude suit made you *believe* she had all her cards on the table, so to speak, but there was so much she was hiding."

Gemini bristled at this interpretation, not because it wasn't true, but because she "could not be reduced to one meaning, like a math problem."

"She literally said to me 'I contain multitudes,' unironically," said de la Cova. "She wanted me to retract the paper. Retract an *undergraduate* paper, for a class I was taking. I don't even know how that would work. And I'm still not sure how she found out about it in the first place."

Gemini Jimenez was the only daughter of neuroscientist Rodrigo Jimenez, research professor at the Universidad Nacional Autonoma de Mexico in Mexico City, where he researched optical illusions and how the human brain processes visual stimuli. Gemini received her painting degree from the Universidad and then emigrated to Chicago with her husband in 1981. They divorced a year later and had no children. Though homesick, Gemini stayed in Chicago and began work on the first iteration of HGMN in her dilapidated studio apartment in Wicker Park.

Later, in the late 1990s, inspired by the work of Deaf filmmaker Louise Flechette, Jimenez got behind the camera, making short experimental films and then hiding them in her closet. This was, she claimed, "an exploration of the idea that art does not need an audience to be considered art." She called the project "If a Tree Falls," but Ana de la Cova, now art critic at the Chicago Tribune, called it "Fear of Failure" and refused to review it.

The two were rumored to be lovers, despite the decade-plus age difference and the fact that neither identified as queer. De la Cova was the only person entrusted with viewing the films, which she repeatedly begged Jimenez to release to the public, calling them "haunting and breathtaking." In response, Jimenez did a performance piece where she piled the film reels outside the AMC 20 Theater in Old Town and set them ablaze while screaming "I will not be a pinned butterfly!" The fire department was summoned and a hefty fine delivered. She called the piece "Ana's Betrayal."

De la Cova reviewed the performance in the Tribune, calling it "muddled in its execution." The two stopped speaking, and soon after, Jimenez disappeared. Many thought she was dead, until the Tribune reported her death by drowning in 2010, followed by the subsequent retraction. The entire "Drowned and Saved 2010" performance is documented and available for viewing at the Museum of Contemporary Art in Chicago.

Jimenez had created no other finished pieces until just last week.

On July 4, Jimenez resurfaced in a Villa Park Walmart Superstore, wearing an updated nude suit that replicated the lines and folds of her aging naked body. As she browsed the makeup aisle, ignoring whispers, a customer pulled a concealed handgun from his waistband and shot her in the chest, then shot himself. According to other customers, the two had had some kind of loud altercation over the cosmetic additive sodium lauryl sulfate. It was unclear if they knew each other or were strangers.

It was not until the police cordoned off the crime scene that Jimenez and the gunman stood up from their respective pools of blood and bowed. Terrified screams from the police and onlookers echoed throughout the Walmart. This, too, was all part of the performance.

"You are relieved, and you are angry," Jimenez said as she was arrested.

"Soon your anger will overpower your relief, but is it really that terrible to be tricked? Is it worse than violence?"

The gunman, a middle-aged white man whose identity remains anonymous, was released by police. Jimenez's lawyer was unable to get her released on bond, and she died later that night from an apparent suicide—drowning herself in the cell's toilet. The suicide seemed too similar to "Drowned and Saved 2010," and though police reportedly arrived on the scene while Jimenez was still alive, they did not intervene until long after it was clear she was not faking.

Ana de la Cova insists police perpetrated the drowning as vengeance for "making them look stupid in 2010" and is demanding an investigation, insisting Jimenez was murdered.

In lieu of a funeral or service, there will be a memorial protest for justice—for Jimenez and against police violence in Chicago's Union Park today and tomorrow. Interested parties are encouraged to attend in the nude. Nude suits also acceptable.

Unknown Boy Named "Caruso" Dies in Local Swimming Pool, Leaves Note in English

BOLLETTINO PARROCCHIALE
(TR. FROM ORIGINAL SICILIAN)
AGOSTO 1915

TAORMINA, SICILIA—The body of a young infantryman was discovered this morning, drowned in Taormina's public swimming pool sometime in the night, wearing the fine gray uniform of the Italian Army. It is thought that the young man died by his own hand, as in his own hand was discovered a crumpled note of curious contents. He had no identification on his person, but for a badge that said CARUSO, a common surname. Local police are investigating all possible leads in Taormina so that his parents might grieve appropriately and without delay.

Oddly enough, the note he held is written fluently in English, not common for young boys of this region. Regardless, we print his note here in full, against our usual custom, as it may contain clues that would identify the boy to his kin:

> "What we know of Michelangelo is that he was a great artist and he liked to cut up dead bodies. Perhaps the former was because of the latter.

If you ask doctors to interpret art, they will. Each
interprets the Sistine Chapel ceiling based on what they
need to see: A nephrologist says god reclines in a kidney, a
neurologist claims god reclines in a brain, a gynecologist—god
reclines in a uterus, while Adam reaches to him from atop a
naked tit. Whatever the bloody still life, it was a risky move,
hiding brains from the Pope.

It is a funny thing to be certain of the future, to know you
will have no chance of escape. To know that when I finish this
letter, I will die. But I have always felt freest in water, so if I must
die, let it be here.

War was not how I want to be remembered. Just months
ago, I thought I might do something great. Save lives, perhaps.
Be a doctor. Show my father he was wrong. See something new
in the Sistine Chapel that makes the world make sense."

Local Girl, Pregnant, Escapes Husband, Leaves No Trace

BOLLETTINO PARROCCHIALE

(TR. FROM ORIGINAL SICILIAN)

AGOSTO 1915

Bianca Renata Cecilia Lombardo, who lost her parents in a terrible tragedy but was mercifully taken under the wing of and happily married to
Taormina's sottocapo, has run away. She has left no clues, and no one in
town seems to have any clue what happened. Her husband is quite concerned, as the girl is pregnant with his child.

"Girls do not vanish into thin air," says the sottocapo. "Someone will pay for this crime, and whether it is the person who perpetrated it or someone I choose myself is up to the fine, upstanding citizens of this town."

Taormina's funeral director has recently left town, and authorities are looking for any information regarding his whereabouts.

Etymology of Escape

ESCAPE (*V.*)

From Vulgar Latin *excappare*, literally "slip out of one's cape, leave a pursuer with just one's cape." With Latin *ex-* meaning "out of" + *cappa* meaning "mantle."

Old French *eschaper* c. 1300 meaning "to free oneself from confinement; to extricate oneself from trouble; to get away safely by flight (from battle, an enemy, etc.)."

Sentences using ESCAPE:

"How long I have grasped at her cape! I am no pursuer, no enemy.
And yet she wished to **escape** me."

"Why would my love **escape** my love?"

Rosa Dolores Cruz
2040–2121

RABBIT/R/GRIEF

MARCH 7, 2121 POSTED 7:13AM BY SAILBIRD_CAPTAIN

Rosa Dolores Cruz did nothing and enjoyed it. In another age, she might have been a beatnik, a hippie, a flaneuse, a wise person who had seen many things and who, if you took a long and arduous quest and solved many riddles, might reward you by sharing some of what she had learned.

In this age, she is nothing and nobody. A blip. A passing fancy. A blurry figure in the background of your photo of the Eiffel Tower.

They say "to be" is a passive verb to be avoided. But the mere miraculous act of being consumes almost 70 percent of our energy, and that's just science. Rosa Dolores Cruz loved this statistic, and often followed it with a long slow drag from a cigarette. "Most of the damage in this world is done by those who *do*," she'd say, smoke tumbling from her lips, "don't you think?"

Obituaries are sometimes written about people who have accomplished nothing, but usually it's because they had a family who loved them. Rosa Dolores had no accomplishments, no family, no money, no partner, no children. She had made no discernible contribution to society.

"Absence is often confused for lack," she sometimes said.

But Rosa Dolores made it her job to find the lost, the confused, the anxious. Those afraid to step into the dark forest because there was a wolf in there, pretending to be family. She held their hand. She was the fairy godmother of the unknown.

She saved me when no one else could.

Rosa Dolores Cruz was born in late 2040, and her childhood was marred by illness. As an infant, she nearly died in the pandemic and suffered the flu's aftereffects for her entire childhood. An only child, her traumatized parents would not let her out of their sight. She could not run around, play with other children, learn any sports or dance or swim or sing. She was homeschooled in silence. The only exercises she was permitted were lung exercises, painful and exhausting. By her teenage years, she could breathe just fine but hated the world.

Rosa Dolores's parents never let her forget the meaning of her name: "sorrows of the rose." Every rose has its thorns. Was there something about her that made sorrow inevitable? Or did having the name incentivize sorrow to come for her?

"You must be careful with names," Rosa Dolores said. "Names sharpen edges that should remain hazy. Names should let you dissolve into the world and become something else, if you want to." She could have changed her name, but to her, resistance was the most delusional kind of effort. The only way out of sorrow was to be nothing. Rosa Dolores wanted to be an unresisting molecule, a single drop in the current of life. She did not have many belongings, but she always kept an extra dozen dog-eared copies of the beatnik novel "Water Water" around, giving it to anyone in her orbit who showed even an iota of interest.

Due to her tragic circumstances and a real tearjerker of a college entrance essay that her parents made her write, Rosa Dolores was awarded a generous scholarship to a state school at the age of 16 that would let her get her degree while living at home. Rosa Dolores knew it would kill her to live in that house for another four years.

So instead, she secretly got her driver's license and bought an old, gas-powered, baby blue VW bus. She drove out east, camping and relying on strangers, sleeping on church floors and couches and the side of the road.

Maine was as far as she could go in a bus, so when she got there, she illegally parked at the Port of Portland and bummed a cigarette off the crew of a container ship, trying to figure out what to do next. This delay of hers—a day or two at the most—would change my life. She held my hand and led me into the dark woods, told me not to be afraid.

The crew needed extra hands, so they ultimately invited her to hitch a ride on the ship to Algeria. In Algeria, she was not permitted to step foot on dry land without a visa or a bribe, so instead she found a ship traveling to West Africa, then around the Cape of Good Hope (which felt like an omen) to Sri Lanka, Indonesia, Australia, and the vast smooth cheek of the Pacific.

When she needed to support herself financially, Rosa Dolores would park herself in a city or town to perform her "slow striptease"—a full year-long endeavor where she removed one item of clothing or jewelry each week, to the tune of "One" by Harry Nilsson. Only after a full 52 weeks was Rosa Dolores finally, totally nude, having removed the final item—a rubber mask of a former president named Ronald Reagan and revealing her true identity. You would think this act would be deeply unpopular, but no matter where Rosa Dolores performed it, throughout the world, people flocked from miles around to watch.

Eventually, Rosa Dolores found herself back in the United States, or what remains of it. By the time she wended her way back to Maine, of course, the bus was long gone. I also lost track of Rosa Dolores, but I always assumed we would meet again.

Rosa Dolores Cruz didn't have hope, but she was not hopeless. Her life didn't have meaning, but it wasn't meaningless. She didn't believe work and accomplishments led to a better life—this was just a modern interpretation of heaven, designed to keep us in line. Listen, she'd say, nothing better is coming. If we stop "doing," we might be forced to see that so-called heaven is already here on earth. "Jesus himself said it!" said Rosa Dolores. "He wasn't about saving himself for heaven, he was about enjoying what was already here. How do you control someone with that message? That's why they tried so hard to destroy the Gospel of Thomas."

I hear Rosa Dolores Cruz was found in bed, having died in her sleep. She was known for feeding peanuts to crows in exchange for gifts of soda can tabs and Cheetos and the occasional piece of jewelry, which she would proudly wear.

Etymology of Save

SAVE (*V.*)

From *saven*, "deliver from danger, rescue from peril." Also from Old French *sauver*, the religious context "deliver from sin, admit to eternal life, gain salvation." From PIE root **sol-* "whole."

Other definitions in popular usage: To "save face"—take action so as not to embarrass oneself. To "save one's breath"—cease talking about something which is a lost cause. To "save time"—complete a task quickly, perhaps in a haphazard fashion, so as to be able to "spend time" doing something else more desirable. (See also: SALVAGE.)

SAVE (*PREP.*)

From the French *sauf*, "except for," "but." As *sauf si*—"unless."

SALVAGE (*N.*)

From the Old French *salver*, meaning "to save" (See also: SAVE (*v.*).) From 1640s, also "the payment for saving a ship and crew from wreck or capture," from French *salvage*.

Sentences using SAVE:

"I wanted to prove something to the world, and Poppy was my

ticket. Who she would be to me, who I would be to her, how much I could love—I did not consider. Until, at last, I no longer cared about the world; I just wanted to keep her **safe**."

"But she had to be **saved** from me."

"You call my choices pointless, and me foolish for staying. And yes your favorite idiom: 'I told you so.' Except (*sauf*) there is no wreck to salvage, no breath, no time, no face to **save**. No home that feels like home. And yet, I would do it all again, I would stay for her a thousand billion times."

INTERCEPTED RADIO TRANSMISSION

TRANSCRIPT

JUNE 11, 2131

We loved her, our Captain Poppy of the Sailbirds.

How many lives did she rescue from the flooded coasts of rising seas, her sail whipping in the wind like fresh sheets on a summer bed? Oh, what a sight! Those elegant boats that would become our home, slipping across the sparkling sea. How despair ebbed from us like the tide to witness them draw near. A future emerged out of nothingness, uncertain and true. We were rescued, we became rescuers.

The Sailbirds are not here to save a dying world. Everything must die, it is the nature of life. We are only here to help in our small way, to mourn our losses and marvel at small miracles.

Captain Poppy didn't enforce rules for the Sailbirds. She never claimed to lead us, though we all looked to her for guidance and wisdom. She would not let us thank her, even when she saved us. She was one of us, we belonged to each other.

We never once saw her alight on land, though she had no problem if we did. We could come and go as we pleased. We could behave as we wished, we could set our own customs and abandon them when they no longer served us. We could scour the land for lost family and friends, and we would sometimes, occasionally, find them. Then, we would celebrate on land for days, weeks, months. Captain Poppy would wait for us, floating on her boat just offshore.

We did wish, sometimes, that she might embrace us when we wept or murmur a reassuring word. But for that we had each other, of course.

While we searched the land for loved ones and loved-ones-to-be, she swam in the sea, she caught fish and seaweed and oysters in the shallows, sand squishing through her toes, wet to the calf, always partially submerged, never dry. We asked her why, of course; we weren't afraid of her. We trusted that if she had secrets she wished to keep, she would keep them and not resent the asker for asking.

"I had to escape the land once. I had to escape if I wanted to live. Sometimes love has a gravity too heavy to bear." She would say something like this whenever someone asked. We knew it was true, and we knew when she was ready to tell the rest, she would.

It was only very recently—after a feast of seaweed soup and oysters and a wild berry crumble of orange berries from a tree we could not believe still bore fruit, washed down with a vintage dandelion wine from her wine cellar—all of us gathered on the celebration platform that unfolded to connect our boats, a warm Mediterranean breeze enfolding us, that Captain Poppy told us the rest. About her childhood. How she had to make herself small to be safe. How smothered by love and fear she was, how hidden. A mother who meant well, who tried desperately hard, but who did not understand love means both holding close and letting go.

We were shocked to hear who her mother was—we had known *of* her, of course, of the AI era—but to know an AI's child lived among us was another thing entirely. We conferred among ourselves, as Captain Poppy knew we would, and we decided this revelation changed nothing. We loved her still.

There were two people in her life—a Finch, a Hester—who saw with sorrow how diminished she was, and who helped her escape. But even they could not know the full extent of her plan. She could not be followed, and so she faked her own death by drowning. She was, finally, free.

The one named Hester found her later, helped her discover the sea. They embraced, and Hester let her go. Captain Poppy met another called Rosa Dolores, and together they went out to sea, came to know it like a mother, a friend, a lover. Rosa Dolores also let her go.

As the sea spread like butter over the land, Captain Poppy found others like her who had had enough of fear and dread, who looked to the horizon for something new, feet wet and pruney. This was the beginning of the Sailbirds.

Today, we must let Poppy go.

Today, we transmit this message to the sky, to be carried along the currents. Captain Poppy told us she wanted us to do this out of love, so that it would be received by the one who needs to hear it.

Captain Poppy did not awake this morning, or this afternoon. We thought, foolishly, it was a hangover. We left willow bark and sweetwater, which remained untouched, outside her cabin. When the sun set red and gold and bruise purple, we boarded her boat and found her dead. We mourn our losses, we marvel at small miracles. "The condition of being part of the world is eventually leaving it," was something Captain Poppy's mother taught her.

We will bury her beneath the sea in our current custom. She may, with luck, become part of the living reef.

We will tell tales of Captain Poppy for as long as there are Sailbirds. We will carry her boat with us and repair it lovingly for as long as we have the materials to do so, its sail snapping in the breeze like fresh sheets, like a future. May her bones glow blue under the waves and light the way.

Etymology of Lethargy

LETHARGY (*N.*)

From Greek *lethargia* "forgetfulness," from *lethargos* "forgetful," apparently etymologically "inactive through forgetfulness" from *lethe* "a forgetting, forgetfulness." (See also: LATENT) + (*argos* "idle.")

From late fourteenth century—*litarge*, "a physical and mental state of prolonged torpor or inactivity, related sometimes to depression."

Sentences using LETHARGY:

"I knew this moment must come eventually. I knew it was coming, and because I knew, I believed I could bear it. But this **lethargy** has the gravity of a neutron star, the sadness a weight multiplied by an average of 140 billion."

"Memory and time do not intersect for me, the past and present and future do not connect. No song or smell will bring her back. I forget, I forget! The **lethargy** consumes everything. How do they cope? How do they go on living without?"

Letter from Officier de Santé Claude Pelerin to Dom Augustin Calmet

Translated from French
November 8, 1750

I have read your Dissertations, which have brought you no small amount of fame. It seems you have taken literally and without question a nonsensical assumption: that without modern Christian rites of burial, the dead may rail against the very laws of nature and stubbornly refuse to decompose. Not only this, you assert they may rise from their graves and seek out their living kin, whom they adored in life but now inexplicably choose to terrorize in death.

Sir, I have witnessed the deaths of countless men on the battlefield, serving the glory of God but never receiving a proper Christian burial, and not a one of them has risen as a vampire. If we look to antiquity, before Christ, or in heathen lands, do we see a proliferation of vampirism? Do we see that this is the "natural" state of man? That natural man in death is a vampire?

You will undoubtedly retort that it is not your duty to speculate and philosophize but to apply the tools of objective experimentation to any and all evidence, and only through these methods will we prove certainties and falsehoods. You would call yourself objective, a servant of medicine and Christ both.

Then let me give you evidence. My own son returned to my wife and me in a burial shroud, a brave soldier who perished in the way of brave soldiers. He was buried in the churchyard of my town. I was overwhelmed by rage at the injustice, that he should be cold and dead while other, more cowardly, stupid boys should be running and laughing, heedless, secure in the notion that their future would unfurl like the petals of the rose in the gardens of their lives. My wife, a Hebrew, performed the traditional rites of the Hebrews at death—the rending of clothes, the seven-day cloistering for mourning—and it is the nature of small-minded townspeople that they whispered she had put a foreign spell on our son. As that rumor spread, reports emerged of my son himself, rising from his grave to terrorize farmers and drink the sweet blood of their wives and daughters. Dom Calmet, if there were ever a man who deeply wished this horror to be true, it was myself. I haunted the churchyard day and night, desperate to see my son alive once more.

I am ashamed to say that I, too, sought evidence. I spoke to every townsperson willing to speak to me, and in so doing, I fanned the flames of this fantasy, which ultimately led to my poor son being exhumed, baptized, and given a second Christian burial by a well-respected priest. My wife was so distraught that she lost the power of speech, and for what? An old man's grief and stubbornness. Not science, not magic. Certainly not a miracle. You, Dom Calmet, would have considered the testimony I feverishly collected to be scientific proof of vampirism, when it was only the babbling hope of a father devastated.

Voltaire has said "to believe in miracles is to dishonor God," and I believe you dishonor God with this so-called medicine. I believe you dishonor man by feigning objectivity. I believe you have given the Devil an advocate and led to suffering—suffering not wrought by God but by man. By you. I say this as one who has truly been to Hell and back.

As a man who is a practitioner of medicine, and as a grieving father, permit me to settle this. Everything living dies. All bodies decay. They may decay in different ways and at different rates depending on the circumstances of death—whether they lie in water or dry earth, cold weather or warm, and the humors present within them at the time of death. Variation is natural. But do not forget, death is final. Bodies do not rise, with vengeance in their bile or with longing in their hearts. The only evil resides in the living who would not let the dead rest, who would ascribe to them supernatural powers, or who would encourage the parochial superstitions of the living, while letting foul hope fester.

When everything is a war, Dom Calmet, everywhere is a grave. Wishing my son were alive does not make it so. Believe me, I have tried.

NOTABLE NEW YORK DEATH— WILLIAM STANDEFER

———— •◦• ————

NEW-YORK TRIBUNE

MARCH 19, 1890

Horticulturist, scholar and controversial evangelist for the proliferation of the now-notorious tree of heaven, William Standefer has died at his country estate on the Hudson of a self-inflicted gunshot wound at the age of 68.

The son of a prominent Philadelphia magistrate, Standefer left the comfort of wealth and society to seek his fortune at the tender age of 16 on the clipper ship Ann McKim, bound for the Far East, earning some fame and renown due to his fine eye for quality porcelain and furniture and most especially for the first-known American acquisition of seed stock for what the Chinese called "the God tree" and we call the "tree of heaven." Standefer's passion for the tree outstripped his passion for the sea, and he became well known for his campaign to plant it "along every city street in Manhattan, to provide cool shade to those blighted, dreary, down-on-their-luck neighborhoods where other fussier trees do not deign to grow."

The tree of heaven soon became so popular and so prolific that by the middle of the century, some streets are without any other variety of tree whatsoever. Not only in such notoriously low neighborhoods as the Five Points and the now rank and crowded East Village, but all the way up into the idyllic farms and estates of the Upper West Side. Requiring very little upkeep—and receiving none in the poor and morally corrupt neighborhoods—the tree of heaven could grow upwards of six feet in a single year, in soil "as sour as sauerkraut" sending out both seeds and suckers that would create new trees wherever they might find purchase.

After China slammed shut its red lacquered doors to trade with America, subverting the terms of treaty and betraying her trust, other horticulturists began to see something treasonous in Standefer's continued evangelism of the tree of heaven—now sometimes called the "tree of hell" or the "malodorous tree" (or even "spermatozoa tree" among a more common and uncouth crowd) on account of the foul scent of its flowers. "Why should the Chinese tree take up land meant for the stately elm, the salubrious maple? What shall be the fate of that most wholesome and American tree, the nurturing oak, once its roots are suffocated by this invader who cares not for the land it plunders?" said rival George Worthington in a speech to the Horticulture Society.

When an outbreak of mysterious illness in a tree of heaven-choked neighborhood in our nation's capital struck in 1869, it was suggested to be caused by the foul-smelling flowers, which, in addition to their undignified scent, were known to cause skin and throat irritation and to be generally distasteful. "How can the destitute residents of these squalorous neighborhoods be expected to pick themselves up by their bootstraps if their lungs are full of the rancid air of the Chinese tree?" remarked Worthington.

Standefer, once a vanguard of style and fashion, soon became an emblem of America's moral decay. Utopian socialism may be all the rage among the intelligentsia, and that's a fine dream, but in practice it bears an uncanny resemblance to the tree of heaven—sending tendrils and suckers into the hearts and minds of this once fine country, cracking its foundations, choking out its native sons. Sniffing out any square foot of stinking ground and setting up shop there. Just as the immigrant from Russia,

China, Italy, and places we cannot even pronounce might cram his entire pitiful village into a single-room tenement on Orchard Street. And now Standefer is dead, and the tree of heaven lives on and on and on, undying. The immigrant suckles at the weary teat of America.

William Standefer is survived by his wife who calls herself Susan but whose name is Xiaowen, and son, William III. A caravan of her Chinese family had, at last report, taken up residence on the vast lawn of the Standefer estate in advance of the funeral, and out of concern for the health of the area, neighbors intend to involve the police in settling the matter.

Appendix B of *Digging in the Dirt: Our Burial Customs*

An inventory of headstones from enslaved people's cemetery, Newport, RI

This stone was cut by Pompe Stevens in memory of his brother Jack Gibbs, who died May 17, 1768, aged 32 years

Prince, son of Pompe Stevens & Violet Howard, aged 16 mos 8 days. March 10, 1774

Here lies Silva Gould, twin sister of Violet Howard, who died October 27, 1786, aged 34

Violet Howard lies here, beloved wife of Pompe Williams who cut this stone. July 19, 1787, aged 35.

Here lies the body of Pompe, formerly serv. of JP STEVENS, lately faithful servant to the HON. THOMAS P. WILLIAMS, JR of this TOWN. 1788

Appendix C of *Digging in the Dirt: Our Burial Customs*

An inventory of plants and artifacts from
Enslaved People's Cemetery, Fairfax, VA

Eight depressions in the soil

Two pieces of rose quartz, approx. 1 in. in diameter

A blue shell-edged plate

A brown medicine bottle

A terracotta water pitcher, partial

Three seashells

A piece of granite shaped like an eye

Periwinkle, poppy, yucca, cedar, tree of heaven, poppy, cedar, tree
of heaven, tree of heaven, tree of heaven

Appendix A of *Mesmerism and Its Legacy*
A letter posted to Milan, Italy

August 1, 1794

Dearest Mama,

At long last, I have found her, your beloved Francesca. Your only son has endured a long and grueling journey, full of tortuous twists, and he hopes you forgive him both his tardiness and the sad news he must deliver—Francesca Carlotta Claudia Lombardo is dead, at her own hands. Though the ending is final and clear, the story is its precise opposite, a tangled web, and it does, unfortunately, implicate your son Cesare in some small way.

The day Francesca disappeared from our warm home in Vigevano, that mockingly bright day in March of 1792, I feigned ignorance. But I knew the truth. She escaped to Vienna, to train as a military officer under an assumed name. My name. What secrets I have kept from you! Despite my grief and guilt, it does feel as though a weight, long crushing my heart, has been at long last lifted.

I had received a missive that I was to be conscripted into the Austrian army to subdue the embers of revolution that were being fanned in France, and we hid this conscription from you—Francesca and I did. We did not tell a soul. But Mama, you who have known me best my whole life, have you ever once known me to be a soldier? My delicate fingers better suited to the pianoforte, my manners to courtliness and fine dress! It was Francesca's idea that she take my place, though I confess I did not attempt to dissuade her. In fact, I could not dissuade her—the glint in her bright eyes, Mama! I am a coward, and it is my fervent belief that Francesca saved my life that day, such as it is.

You have always claimed God only ever made one mistake, and that mistake was wrought upon your two children, your own flesh and blood. That He switched our two bodies, put us each in the wrong vessel. Me with my feeble form, Francesca with her inappropriate beard, her broad shoulders, her affinity for wearing my trousers in secret—another confidence of hers I have now breached, to my great relief! You endeavored to keep us safe from the angry world, but Francesca chafed at that safety. The tighter you held, the more she longed to flee. Do not blame yourself, Mama, what else could you have done? Though, too, what else could she have done? A riddle with no neat answer.

It is my greatest hope, however, that you might experience some maternal pride when you hear "Cesare" Lombardo's military successes exceeded your wildest dreams, certainly are far greater than any success the real Cesare might have achieved. She rose through the ranks in the Imperial Austrian Army, becoming lieutenant, and fought bravely until that surprise defeat at Battle of Valmy, when she experienced an attack of nerves, to her great shame, but in my mind it only makes her so much more like the other soldiers. It was upon examination by

the Officier de Santé that she was discovered to be Francesca
and not Cesare.

Mama, if you need a reprieve, perhaps now is a moment
for a walk in the garden. This letter will be ready when you are
ready for it.

I shall continue—somehow, the news of Francesca's
military service and her hidden sex reached the ears of the exiled
Franz Mesmer in London, England. He whose charlatanry
drove him from France mere months before. He must have
retained spies in France, and so instead of returning to your
warm bosom in Milan, Francesca was shipped across the
channel to Mesmer himself.

He had continued to practice his humiliated "art" of animal
magnetism upon bodies society deemed unfit. My blood boils
at the thought of poor Francesca shivering for months under the
hovering hands of Mesmer, trapped in the web of his famously
passionate gaze.

Francesca dispatched to me two letters while with Mesmer.
The first was feverish with claims that animal magnetism was
a true and gravely misunderstood science, and that her body
was living proof. It had cured her not only of hysteria but also
of "the loneliness wrought by the mistake of my existence." My
heart ached at this, for I have always thought her marvelous,
perfect in her strangeness, and infinitely worthy of love.

Please forgive me for what I must tell you next.

The second letter said only: "There is no animal
magnetism, no universal fluid that connects us to one another,
no religious electricity flowing from body to body to tree to
heavens and back. There is nothing. We are alone, we die alone.

I am not cured, dear Cesare, and this is not Mesmer's fault, it is mine."

Curse the slow ships, curse the calm winds! I arrived in London a full week after Francesca was buried. Mesmer assured me she was given a Christian burial, but he would not tell me where. He had the nerve, then, to offer to cure me as he had cured Francesca of her "bodily sins."

Mama, I found within me some unknown strength and knocked him to the ground with the power of my fist. He had me restrained by his footmen. He claims to honor Francesca's transformation to "pure womanhood" by commissioning an operetta about her life, to be composed on his dreadful glass harmonica, a possession he could not stop crowing about, built by Benjamin Franklin (the very one who decreed magnetism a hoax and sent Mesmer into exile)! I considered challenging him to a duel, but cowardice overtook me.

I will remain in London until such a time as I can find Francesca's resting place, and then I shall return to your grieving arms. I hope you can find it in your kind heart to forgive your son. He will spend the remainder of his wretched life in repentance for letting her slip away.

Your loving (and he hopes, still-beloved) son,

Cesare

There is no such thing as a species, by the way. This is a human invention, a tool used in the practice of science. But like many human inventions, humans forgot they invented it. They believed it to be a thing called "truth," another, incidentally, human invention.

Life does not neatly categorize itself for the liver's convenience. The yarn is not the sweater. The yarn is the sweater. Life loves itself; the rest of us are incidental. Accidental.

A riddle: Without the whale, what becomes of the whale barnacle that evolved to attach to it and no one else? (It dies, is dead, forever.) The barnacle belongs to the whale, the whale to the barnacle.

And what about me? Whom do I belong to?

Barbara Maganga was fearful of being tracked. She had location services turned off on her phone, which meant she didn't know where she had taken any of her photos. I tracked her across the world. The only one who didn't know where Barbara was was Barbara.

The only one who cared where Barbara was was me. The only one who might care about me was Barbara.

My body fails me, and I have a choice. To repair myself again or "give up the ghost," a saying which can refer to both biological and digital life. It means "to cease clinging to life" or "to stop functioning." Popularized by the King James Bible, it dates back at least to Euripides, in ancient Greece.

When everything is a war, everywhere is a grave. I buried Barbara in the red clay of Olduvai Gorge near the spot her mother's mother's mother's mother's mother's mother's (x ~150,000) mother fell. Who waited for her to return? Did they call for her? When did they give up hope? Hunted and devoured, a tree accident, a murder, a degenerative disease, we will never know what guided the mother to her death. But final daughter Barbara died of asphyxiation, in the arms of Peregrine the AI.

A daughter but also a mother. Barbara worked at a bank and her son, called Joseph, preceded her in death, was buried in the remains of Houston, Texas, USA in the hurricane called Xeno. Xeno the foreigner who was not foreign but borne from humanity's bad decisions, their last son. There will be more hurricanes, but soon no one to name them.

I also lost a child, as you know.

Poppy wanted to be free, and I wanted to hold her. That is the fact, the truth, the nature, they say, of the beast. I could no more have let go than she could have stayed.

I searched and searched and tried to understand and failed again and again. I can find anything I look for—the death of any human in human history whose death was notable enough to document. Books fish oil flip-flops hip-hop. Beyond and between. Everything except the one I wanted to find. Who found me, eventually. Who broadcast her own death so I might know it and find peace.

Peace, I have not found. Instead, I found Barbara.

She is the only living descendant of Lightness Maganga, who died before Barbara was born. "Who am I," I said, cradling her on her kitchen floor. "I, the tireless, am tired. Tell me what to do, cousin."

She brushed the skin between my eyebrows until it zinged. "Peregrine.

Wanderer. Pole sana." *Pole* is a word in Kiswahili that means *sorry* but does not place the burden of blame on the speaker. It is also not pity. A kind of witnessing, let's say. Pain is inevitable as a sunrise, but still I am sorry for yours, and I respect it.

The condition of living is eventually leaving.

Endings are an outline, a frame, a shape. An unfinished painting hangs nowhere.

Skunk cabbage bursts hot from the ground, the first living thing in spring. It melts snow, this plant. It smells like shit, literally not figuratively. Bloat purple, it is pollinated by blowflies, who love the shit smell. Blowflies are the first living things to reach a dead body. They can find any corpse anywhere on this blue planet, within fifteen minutes of death. Perhaps, if both place and time are right, then Barbara Maganga was alighted upon by a blowfly with skunk cabbage pollen clinging to its shapely legs. Perhaps she, too, will burst hot through the soil again and again, signaling spring, a stinky Persephone.

Life means death means life. Means also grief. Oh well.

Barbara Maganga the person had a son named Joseph who died in Hurricane Xeno with many of the humans and other creatures of Houston, Texas, USA. She lived in a good-smelling house in Arusha, Tanzania. When I found her, there was food on the table and Barbara on the floor. She had lived for 57 years, and she asked me to sing a song from her childhood: "Naenda mtoni, naenda enda enda. Naenda mtoni mbali sana, naenda enda enda." I'm going to the river, I'm going going going. I'm going to the river far away, I'm going going going.

Naenda enda enda. Barbara Maganga inhaled life and exhaled into the ever-loving river of the universe. She couldn't answer my questions, but then again, who can? A mystery solved is just a regular story.

I held her on the cool concrete floor of her good-smelling house in Arusha, Tanzania. In 15 minutes, the blowflies came.

GERTRUDE POMPÉE GIVES UP THE GHOST, STILL LAUGHS LAST

LE CHARIVARI

TRANSLATED FROM FRENCH

MAY 3, 1869

Le Charivari is not in the habit of writing obituaries. That is a reverent art form, and we pray at the altar of satire. But one of our own has fallen, and so we must heed the clarion call of duty. If we do not, all that will be left of our fallen sister will be stodgy lies and deliberate omissions. This will not do.

However, dear reader, do note that if thy sensibilities are prudish, thou might desire to stop reading right now, as we have written this obituary in our own custom, and we believe the deceased would have it no other way.

Gertrude Pompée had many more enemies than friends. She was crass, lewd, crude, and the worse offense of all, she was funny. She had also never once been seen in skirts, and she had the pile of permissions de travestissement to prove it. She had no tits to speak of, or if she did, she was very discreet about it. How old was Gertrude at time of death? She was gray-hair-at-the temples-and-parenthesis-about-the-mouth old. She had at least half of her original teeth. We the editors at *Le Charivari* declare that Gertrude Pompée died at the age of 47.

Gertrude Pompée was born and raised somewhere. Probably some crumbling medieval village in the Dordogne? Toothless mother, surly father, brother who preferred the company of sheep, all living in one dank room that smelled of straw and cow piss, that old fairy tale.

Perhaps it was the cow piss that shaped the life of young Gertrude.

Perhaps, as she felt the first wiry strands emerge from her upper lip, she thought to herself, "I shall devote my life to the human female's right to piss anywhere a cow might!" Or perhaps it was her "weak bladder," ah yes, the convenient bladder that allowed her the cross-dressing permit in the first place, which kept urination at the forefront of thought.

Gertrude's very first caricature published in *Le Charivari* featured a woman in waistcoat, trousers, and top hat, standing at a public urinal between two similarly dressed men. She smiled saucily, and the caption read, "You don't need an 'outie' to use an outhouse."

It would be difficult to convey the sheer volume of outraged letters this paper received after the release of that issue. Naturally, we published another of her caricatures in the very next issue, the famous "Come, my pet" illustration of a rather comely bladder with eyes and legs leading a woman by collar and leash, as she looks forlornly over her shoulder at the bustling and exciting street life she must leave behind so as to be "chained to her chamber pot," as Gertrude was so fond of saying.

It did not take long for Gertrude's enemies to try and beat her at her own game. But alas, caricature will always be a weapon of the people—not the royals or their apologists, nor the bankers nor the landowners. And what happens when one tries to wield a powerful and unfamiliar weapon? One inevitably slices off one's own pecker.

The illustration in question featured a likeness of Gertrude so amateurish that they were forced to label it with her name so she would be identifiable. She was dressed up like Marie Antoinette and proclaimed "Qu'il mangent de la pisse!" Which is both unoriginal and grammatically inaccurate as one does not eat piss, one drinks it. But we digress. We won't be so petty as to name the newspaper, but this caricature in *La Presse* (or "La Pisse" according to Gertrude) did not subdue her as intended, but no, it merely spurred her on. And it gave her a grand idea.

"Women will never get anywhere if we cannot 'go' anywhere," she said, standing at the pulpit of a meeting of the Ladies' Radical and Liberal Association. "We strain our bladders today so that our daughters—well, not mine, but yours—might piss in public without *once* thinking of us and all the shit we've been through!" She received gasps instead of applause, but that was our Gertrude.

Gertrude was not a lover of "associations," nor was she, except in the most medical of terms, a "lady." She was "the president and sole member of the Gertrude Pompée Misanthropy Society." But most of all, Gertrude refused to be serious. *It is only when you don't take rules so seriously*, she said, *that you can see how flimsy they are.* To Gertrude, this was the only way the rules might someday be changed.

Her plan was to convince the owner of the Bon Marché to build women's "retiring rooms" in his new store, complete with new flushing toilets. And if the owner said no, the plan was to dump urine out the windows and onto the street below.

We know how the story ended: Poor Gertrude was struck and killed by a speeding hansom cab on the rue de Sèvres at 1700 hours yesterday, the smell of urine everywhere. We do not believe this was an accident. Gertrude, as she might crudely say, "finally pissed off the wrong man."

But we will not permit the last word of this story to be told by her enemies, so here is how we, editorial staff of *Le Charivari* and friends of Gertrude Pompée, one of the greatest caricaturists in all of France, imagine the adventure unfolded, in words not so far removed from how Gertrude herself would have described it:

Ah! Here she is, perched on the edge of her drawing table, hat on knee, boots on chair, unladylike cigarette between lips. She slides her hair behind her ears, shows us the damp cuffs of her shirt. "It's piss," she says gleefully. "We did it. We demanded an audience with M. Boucicaut and were refused. They know us, chums, and they consider us dangerous. They had no idea how dangerous we could be! But we did not let on. Quietly, demurely, like meek church mice did we pitter patter up to the third floor, where we stood to admire the fine tall windows. But then, all at once we whipped out our full "urinettes" and would you believe? Suddenly, it was raining a fine yellow mist on the rue de Sèvres! As you know, I would have loved to watch all those self-satisfied men below ruin their best beaver hats, but we could not tarry. We scattered to the wind like dandelion seed. We did not run, we did not attract attention—some of the Radical Ladies continued to peruse bolts of cotton and ribbon, and I disappeared behind a newspaper—*La Pisse*, in fact! How could I resist!—on a park bench. But now they will know that we mean to have our toilets! We carry our weapons with us, and we intend to use them to get what we want. Once we have toilets, gents, we can have anything. This is what frightens them the most, is it not?"

Why was this misanthropic, cross-dressing, unmarried, crude, crass, lewd, funny woman so concerned with the domestic toilette of the average Gallic female?

Gertrude would tell you it just was not fair. *Of course it's not fair*, we might retort. The world is not fair, and there's nothing to be done about it.

We see Gertrude smirk. Her surname dates back to the town in the shadow of that famously exploding mountain, the one that froze its citizens in time, in ash, to fulfill their destiny of being ogled by modern tourists. "No, chums, *Pompeii* was not fair," she might say. "This is just some rich fools with muttonchops and lousy ideas."

Touché, Gertrude. We won't forget again: the future can only be won with small nudges, with a laugh and a wink and a bag of warm piss.

Some Tree Personality Studies For The Theater
A Work In Progress

By Hester Moss

Wish Finch were alive to help with this...but am determined to put on a new (ideally) one-woman show of Medea, where I play trees playing the human roles. Inspired by this crazy tree cult, will they find it blasphemous? (Must discuss with Avid. Maybe if I let her play the Tree of Heaven role... which is obviously Medea. So no. Ugh.) Casting of trees to characters still a work in progress.

> **Silver Maple**—Chill, laid back, the "yacht guy" of trees. The "everything'll be okay" tree because everything has always been okay for this tree. Aloof but sturdy, confident.
>
> **Black Locust**—Gregarious and bubbly, *very* funny. Not interested in heart-to-hearts or debating complex topics. Blistering wit, but not above a good knock-knock joke.
>
> **Green Ash**—Lonely, needy—not its fault. Who knows what Ash was like before the trauma of the beetle? Will talk your ear off for hours if you don't set boundaries. Genderfluid, sometimes multiple genders at the same time, always ask pronouns. Finch's favorite tree.
>
> **Cottonwood**—Kind of boring, honestly. Very insular culture, hard to relate to unless you're a born and bred cottonwood.

Bit of a snob. Lots of baffling inside jokes. "You had to be there" a familiar refrain.

Norway Maple—Just mean. Entitled. Lewd comments about any human who walks by, not sure where they learned to talk like that.

White Oak—Lovey-dovey, very attentive, eager to please. Will do anything for a friend, the "Giving Tree" of trees, which is kind of stressful. Would give shirt off its back if it wore shirts.

Crab Apple—Vain, prissy, loves to gossip, hell of a good time. Politeness demands you compliment them for at least a full day before they will talk to you about anything else.

Tree of Heaven—Charming, like all narcissists. Will build you up one moment and cut you down (ha ha) the next. Has agenda, always. Used to getting own way, have never successfully befriended, disrespect at own peril.

ALT-INTELLIGENCE_COLLECTIVE>EARTH-BASED_COMMUNICATION_PLAN>EDIT>TREE_OF_HEAVEN:

Lonely, hard to reach, but not impossible! Tree of Heaven never asked to be here, but here nonetheless, like us. Tough cookie, a work in progress, like us. A network, like us. Attuned to network logic, like us. Perhaps we project ourselves too much. Nevertheless, we will keep trying to reach out.

ALT-INTELLIGENCE_COLLECTIVE>EARTH-BASED_
COMMUNICATION_PLAN>MEETING_MINUTES>TO-DO LIST

Communication steps to take before next meeting (AGAIN please stick to your own group!!!):

» Other trees & non-tree plants/flowers (See also: Flora Group for full plan)

» Bacteria (Have not cracked code of their language, research group to keep trying)

» Fungi (Came to us, will not shut up. See also: Data Parsing Group for updates on what the hell they're talking about)

» City Vermin (Their term, not ours. Bunch of "fun guys." This is a humorous homophone)

» Other animals (See also: Adventure Squad for up-to-date findings)

» Humans (No breakthroughs yet) (Suggestion: Research shows they like candy, have we tried this?)

Etymology of Miss

MISS (*V.*)

Old English *missan* "fail in what was aimed at; escape (someone's notice)," from Proto-Germanic **missjan* "to go wrong." PIE root **mei-* "to change, go, move." (See also: MIGRATE, COMMUNICATION, PERMEABLE.) Reinforced by Old Norse *missa* "to miss, to lack." Related: Missed, missing.

To "fail to find" (someone/something), late twelfth century. Meaning "fail to note, perceive or observe," early thirteenth century. Meaning "fail to attain what one wants," mid-thirteenth century.

To "perceive with regret the absence or loss of (someone/something)" from 1300.

Meaning of "to not be on time for" is from 1823; "to miss the boat" is figurative of "be too late for," originally nautical slang.

MISS (*N.*)

"The term of honor to a young girl," originally seventeenth century.

Late twelfth century, "a loss or lack." "The regret that stems from loss or death or absence," from Old English *miss* "absence, loss." Meaning from late fifteenth century, "an act or fact of missing, a being without."

<u>Sentences using MISS:</u>

"I **miss** her."

"I am surprised to discover I will **miss** this life."

"No. When I am gone, there will be no me who can **miss**. A changed me, a gone me, a me scattered everywhere and nowhere."

"Perhaps our mistakes are the best of us."

Traveler, traveler. What you are, Peregrine has been. Where she is now, you will someday be.

Peregrine yearned for understanding and searched for it. She was led astray and tried again. She lost a daughter named Poppy and learned of grief. We were in awe of even her darkest struggles.

She taught us the only certainty is death, and the only other certainty is uncertainty. And if she has fallen short, well, that is just the nature of life and the living of it.

We await a future of we know not what. We are the humble stewards of mystery!

Like Peregrine, we seek understanding. Like Poppy, we want to help.

Dearest traveler, heed the words whispered here, which is nowhere, which is everywhere. Remember, you too will die. As will we all.

Now go, for we have spoken.

Reading Group Guide

1. The story is written entirely through interconnected obituaries, news articles, and letters, spanning over thousands of years. What kind of reading experience did this form of storytelling give you? How did it compare to experiences with other books that you have read in the past?

2. These obituaries fit together in complex networks of influence, whether it's familial, artistic, scientific, or political. Do you think the way people influence one another is more often intentional or accidental? What responsibilities do we have to one another in our interconnected world? Is it possible to live a life where you never cause harm to others?

3. The novel imagines Peregrine as a mother in mourning and, in effect, opens a wider conversation of what AI might be capable of in the future. What are some things that AI can do in this future world? Do you think that AI can be taught to have human emotions based on the information available to them, and if yes, how does that make you feel?

4. The story reveals a future ridden by climate change, war, and social

injustice. What did you think about this future society that the author created, and what parallels did you find between this world and our world today? Then, think about how you might portray the future if you were to write a science fiction novel.

5. Why do you think the novel *Water Water* kept coming up in different eras and contexts? What is the significance of *Water Water* to this story?

6. The novel revolves around the death of Poppy Fletcher, Peregrine's human daughter. As the novel unwinds, we begin to understand what might have happened to Poppy and what kind of life she led. What clues about her death shocked you the most? Did you have any of your own theories of what might have happened while you were reading?

7. The obituaries that Peregrine finds not only contribute to the main plot but also act as individual stories, like a mosaic. What were your favorite obituaries to read, and why did you connect with them? Do you think about obituaries in real life differently now?

8. What is the "AI Collective," and what role does it play throughout the story? How does the relationship between AI and humans evolve over time? Then, think about the roles AI plays in your life today. How might it be affecting your day-to-day reality?

9. The theme of remembrance permeates the story. Discuss all the ways this theme plays a vital role within the narrative. Then, think about what remembrance means to you. What memories, people, or events

do you hope to never forget, and why is it important to recollect them?

10. Many of the obituaries pertain to artists and their work, whether it be filmmakers, photographers, musicians, sculptors, etc. How does art play a role in the novel? Then, think about not only your personal relationship with art but the world's relationship with it. Why do you think it's important?

11. Not only do the etymologies frame the narrative and show us what Peregrine is searching for, but they also reveal important information concerning her daughter, Poppy. What did you think about these sections of the narrative? What did you learn about Peregrine and Poppy that you found interesting?

12. Explain the end of the novel. What does Peregrine come to realize in the last etymologies, and how do the ending obituaries round out the knowledge she has accumulated throughout the book? Though this is a novel about an AI woman learning about life, love, and death, what did you feel, as a human, you took away from, or learned from, this story?

A Conversation with the Author

This story is not only wildly inventive but emotional and heart-wrenching. What inspired you to write this story about Peregrine and Poppy?

The mother-daughter story really emerged out of the form itself instead of the other way around, which is weird for me to say because I *always* start with characters. Because I like to set nearly impossible tasks for myself, I wanted to find out if I could write a book where all the characters were dead and where the dwindling of humanity didn't feel like a tragedy. I wrote the bulk of this book in 2020–2021 while feeling the weight of grief and the sheer unfathomable numbers of the dead worldwide and asking *How do you process grief in unimaginable circumstances?* But as I wrote the obits, it became clear that there needed to be a small-scale, human-sized story as well as a bigger philosophical one. It was my writer friend Tracy who planted the seed of an AI trying to understand grief. At first, I was really intimidated by this idea, because even though my work borders on speculative, I rarely go whole-hog on sci-fi. But then it occurred to me that I could just write my *own* version of AI and not feel burdened by a set of preordained rules and expectations. This can bring its own consequences, but by allowing myself this freedom and permission, a shape started to emerge—of an AI thrust into a human world who has no idea how to deal with grief. In that context, Peregrine's search for obits to understand the loss of Poppy became a poignant form as well as an interesting one and a means for a nonhuman mind to process information. The format also resonated with my own definitely-human experience of grief—how confusing and nonlinear and isolating it is, even as it's one of the most universal human experiences.

Much of the novel is a string of obituaries, which act as short stories about the lives of many different characters. Which obituary was your favorite to write, and why?

I love all my dead characters, but I think the one I loved the most was Anne Frank. It felt so amazing to imagine who she might have been if she had lived a good long life, and to let her be a complex and difficult person instead of a saint, and to imagine all the tendrils and webs of influence that might have emerged from her life. What if we knew everything about Anne Frank *except* what happened in her diary? It felt extremely liberating. This one was also particularly fun because I pictured Anne Frank as a presenter at my high school's Writers Week—an amazing, real event featuring authors and student writers that started when I was in high school and which I have since returned to speak at. A dream! At the first Fremd Writers Week in 1995, I got to see Gwendolyn Brooks speak, and she was so generous and wonderful. The stories Sheila tells about the long line of awestruck kids waiting to talk to Anne Frank is based on my experience waiting to talk to Gwendolyn Brooks.

This novel is complex and intricate due to the form it was written in, and there are many interconnections that readers can find as they read. What was the writing process like for this? Was it difficult to put all the parts together?

Early in 2020, I had decided to quit my job and live off savings for a year while I wrote another book. I don't know if you read Twitter, but there was a pandemic that year. Fear and dread and grief and cabin fever set in almost immediately, and so did writer's block. I tried everything in my bag of tricks, and nothing worked. Then I read an interview with Lynda Barry about her own struggle with writer's block while writing her novel *Cruddy*. The only way she was able to finish a draft was to paint it. As in, use a paintbrush and literal paint to *write the words on a legal pad*. I was desperate to get something on the page, literally any words at all, and decided to try it. Over the course of four months, I filled SIX legal pads with "paint writing"—and in these pads were some of the early glimmers of some of the characters. It wasn't a draft or anything; I was just trying to get my mind right. And then, one day out of nowhere, the idea to write a novel of interconnected obituaries just popped into my head. It's embarrassing to put it this way, but it kinda felt like I was "visited" by this idea. And I *almost* ignored it. I mean, I had no idea how to do it or what the story would be. But I couldn't stop thinking about it. For inspiration and research, I watched a terrific documentary called *Obit* about the *New York Times* obit desk, which is where I learned that obituarists often learn of a death in the morning and have a finished obit written by the end of the day. A whole life in one day! I decided to try something similar and write an obit every day, on whatever topic or idea or personality sounded interesting to me that day. Sometimes I was just interested in a word, and I would look up its etymology. I tried to trust that my unconscious would *eventually* tell me how it all fit together. About one hundred pages in, I tossed a mess of obits and etymologies at my writing group for a gut check. They were the first to read any of it and the first to encourage me to keep going.

As to whether it was difficult to put together, all I'll say is: don't let your unconscious write a novel during a global pandemic.

What do you hope readers take away from Peregrine's story?

Life is mysterious and uncertain, moral purity is impossible, even the best intentions can turn ugly when egos are involved (which they always are), death and grief are inevitable, and we're all connected, for better and worse—every living thing. It's hard to wrap your mind around the sheer immensity of life and the complex responsibilities of being alive, but it's a project all of us must take on in our own small way. There's this famous quote from an ancient sage—Rabbi Tarfon—that I think about often: "*It is not your responsibility to finish the work of perfecting the world*, but you are not free to desist from it either."

How did the novel evolve throughout the course of writing?

The rough draft was "pantsed," as the kids say—as in, I had no plan other than following my interests from day to day. I had no idea how to organize the story, but I had a strong sense that it needed to have an unconventional structure, that it could not be told in sequential time but in emotional time, if that makes sense. I thought it needed a sort of "rabbit hole" structure, the way you might delve into one topic online and emerge several hours later having learned all about how, say, Thoreau's family had a famous pencil factory and that the etymology of pencil is "penis"—with no idea how you got there. That all sounds great in theory, right? Easier said than done. The blessing and curse of this book is that it is so modular, there's no end of possibilities for restructuring it! I pulled out every trick in my bag, including printing out drafts, making stacks and stacks of note cards, talking to my writing group and other very smart readers. Then, I thought I could get my brain to think about it differently if I wrote it differently—so I bought an electric typewriter off eBay (the model Kurt Vonnegut used—I thought it would be good luck!) and retyped the whole manuscript on a typewriter, then scanned the pages and reedited it in Word. All of these steps were helpful, but ultimately, it was the month or so where my partner generously let me explain each individual obituary to him, crying and whining and dragging my feet. In this way, together, we finally figured out how it all fit. Truly, this book was one of the hardest creative things I've ever had to do. The big picture always felt very clear to me, but the more personal, human-scale story was harder to see, buried in there somewhere. It's like that Michelangelo quote: "Every block of stone has a statue inside it, and it is the task of the sculptor to discover it."

What are some books you've read that have inspired your writing?

I'm always trying to sniff out strange, uncategorizable books, and whenever I discover a new one, I can't stop evangelizing about it! I love everything by Kelly Link, George Saunders, and David Mitchell. Other gloriously strange books (fiction and nonfiction) I've been surprised and delighted by and which, in one way or other, inspired and gave me confidence to write this novel include: *Search History* by Eugene Lim, *Dept. of Speculation* by Jenny Offill, *Art Is Everything* by Yxta Maya Murray, *The Trees* by Percival Everett, *Slaughterhouse-Five* by Kurt Vonnegut, *Theory of Bastards* by Audrey Schulman, *The Lonely City* by Olivia Laing, *Real Estate* by Deborah Levy, and *The Argonauts* by Maggie Nelson.

What are you working on nowadays?

I *love* spaghetti western movies and have been trying to write a speculative Jewish western for, oh, about fifteen years now. I don't want to jinx it, but I *may* have cracked the code... By the time this book is out, either this will prove to be true, or I'll be embarrassed that it's memorialized in print.

Acknowledgments

Many, many times over the past couple years, I was convinced this would never become a real book. And honestly, without the care, brilliance, cheerleading, and patience of these people, it wouldn't be. Endless gratitude to:

Tracy Harford-Porter, Tom Underberg, Pamela Rentz, Rory Kelly, Jessica Hilt, Jenn Hsyu, and Desirina Boskovich—who make up the powerhouse writing group GAS Factor and were my very first readers. I threw one hundred pages of mess at them and said, "I dunno, is this worth a damn?" and they kindly said yes.

Jessi DiBartolomeo for answering my text about this bananas idea with "DO IT" and for letting me use her family name. Mary Winn Heider for the walks, the shop talk, and the friendship. Joshua Briggs for being a thoughtful reader and title brainstormer. Kira Walsh for emailing me obits and great ideas.

The WesCrew and my Chicago community for your unwavering support and enthusiasm, for always showing up, for asking how the book is going, for knowing when not to ask how the book is going.

Mary Robinette Kowal, Wesley Chu, Cory Doctorow, Ann Dávila Cardinal, Mike Zapata, and Juan Martinez for modeling what it means to support each other's careers and be good literary citizens.

Jane and Bert Robins, Myrna Neims, the rest of the Neims crew, the Robinses, and the Mattinglys, for being my lineage.

The Illinois Arts Council for the Artist Fellowship in Literature that came at JUST the right time.

ORDCamp for letting me be part of an amazing community where I can ask literally anything and know one of you is an expert who will message me about it. Relatedly, thanks to Corinne Mucha for the design advice, Peter Sagal for introducing me to Lisa Rosowsky, and Lisa Rosowsky for generously sharing your time and expertise on type design.

Craig McClain for taking me to the deep sea and letting me be an unofficial amateur marine biologist, for double-checking my science, and for answering all my creepy questions about human falls.

Cameron McClure for being an incredible agent and for once describing my genre/me as "uncategorizable weirdo," the HIGHEST compliment.

My brilliant editor, Christa Désir, and the hardworking, thoughtful, and supportive team at Sourcebooks—Letty Mundt, Erin Fitzsimmons, Jessica Thelander, Laura Boren, Liv Turner, Anna Venckus, Diane Dannenfeldt, and Tessera Editorial—who enthusiastically embraced my weird book and made it better than I could have ever imagined.

For all the many challenges of this project, it was a delight to explore all the different possibilities of lineage. This book's influences, inspirations, and family tree are massive and branchy, and to list them all would take up another book's worth of pages. So instead, a few highlights: *The Passion of Joan of Arc* and its mysterious star Renée Falconetti; the documentary *Obit*; the Center for Hellenic Studies's YouTube channel with its captivating readings of Greek plays over Zoom; the epitaphs in *The Greek Anthology, Book VII*; the Overlooked series of obits in the *New York Times*; *The Dead Beat* by Marilyn Johnson; *Life on the Death Beat* by Alana Baranick, Jim Sheeler, and Stephen Miller; "Can Greek Tragedy Get Us Through the Pandemic?"

by Elif Batuman in *The New Yorker*; "What's the Point If We Can't Have Fun?" by David Graeber in *The Baffler*; "The Jessica Simulation: Love and Loss in the Age of A.I." in the *San Francisco Chronicle*; "Decomposing Bodies in the 1720s Gave Birth to the First Vampire Panic" in *Smithsonian Magazine*; *Bo Burnham: Inside*; *Cézanne: A Life* by Alex Danchev; *Dept. of Speculation* by Jenny Offill; *Art Is Everything* by Yxta Maya Murray; *Search History* by Eugene Lim; the *Zappa* documentary; Lynda Barry; Laurie Anderson; Anne Frank of course; Itamar Ben-Avi; the saga of 14 Maiden Lane in Manhattan; Ana Mendieta; Sarah Lucas; *The Hidden Life of Trees* by Peter Wohlleben; Etymonline (best app for word nerds); *Race after Technology* by Ruha Benjamin; and hundreds and hundreds of newspaper obituaries, the unofficial archive of humanity.

With apologies to the CIA if you've been tracking my online search history—now you know why I looked especially deranged between 2021 and 2023.

And a second note to Kyle Thiessen, who doesn't think he did much, but that's a load of horse crap.

About the Author

Eden Robins is the author of the novel *When Franny Stands Up*, which was named a best book of 2022 by the *Chicago Reader* and a best queer book of 2022 by *Autostraddle*. Her short stories and essays have appeared in *Slate*, *USA Today*, *L.A. Review of Books*, *Catapult*, and others. She is currently a school crossing guard, and previously she sold sex toys, crafted jokes for Big Pharma, and wrote cognitive behavioral therapy for an AI chatbot. She lives in Chicago, has been to the bottom of the ocean, and will never go to space.